NO PLACE FOR MEMORIES

SHERRY LEWIS

BERKLEY PRIME CRIME, NEW YORK

NO PLACE FOR MEMORIES

A Berkley Prime Crime Book / published by arrangement with the author

PRINTING HISTORY
Berkley Prime Crime edition / February 1999

All rights reserved.
Copyright © 1999 by Sherry Lewis.
This book may not be reproduced in whole or in part,
by mimeograph or any other means, without permission.
For information address: The Berkley Publishing Group,
a member of Penguin Putnam Inc.,
375 Hudson Street, New York, New York 10014.

The Penguin Putnam Inc. World Wide Web site address is
http://www.penguinputnam.com

ISBN: 0-425-16736-4

Berkley Prime Crime Books are published
by The Berkley Publishing Group,
a member of Penguin Putnam Inc.,
375 Hudson Street, New York, New York 10014.
The name BERKLEY PRIME CRIME and the BERKLEY PRIME CRIME
design are trademarks belonging to Berkley Publishing Corporation.

PRINTED IN THE UNITED STATES OF AMERICA

10 9 8 7 6 5 4 3 2 1

one

Fred Vickery knew he'd made a mistake. A big one. But he didn't know how to correct it now. He leaned against the refreshment table in the high-school gymnasium, tolerating a headache and watching the crowd in front of him. Every few minutes, a muggy breeze blew in through the open doors that led to the school's rear parking lot, but it didn't relieve the heat inside. And the laughter, conversation, and big-band music blaring from a portable stereo only made the pounding in his head worse.

He served himself a glass of punch from the refreshment table and nodded to a woman who stepped up to the other end of the table. Something about her seemed vaguely familiar, but like most members of his high-school class, the fifty-five years since they'd graduated had aged her so much he couldn't immediately identify her.

She smiled as she picked up a cookie from a tray and inclined her head toward him. "Hello, Fred."

He returned the smile hesitantly and studied her pale blue eyes and ski-jump nose for a few seconds before he recognized her. "Thea? Thea Griffin?"

She laughed and held out her arms. Fred hugged her quickly, and for a moment the years melted away and he caught a glimpse of the young woman she'd been—tall and willowy and beautiful with long blond hair and a sunny disposition that had once captured his heart. "It's been a few years, hasn't it?" she said softly into his ear.

"Too many." He released her and took a step backward. "I haven't seen you since . . ."

"Since our twenty-fifth reunion," she finished for him. "I know. Stewart and I moved to Mobile, Alabama, and it never seemed to work out for us to come back after that."

"But you're here tonight."

"I am. Yes."

"Are you staying for the whole weekend?"

"I'll be here for the banquet tomorrow night, but I'm leaving early Sunday morning." She nibbled the cookie and glanced at him from beneath lowered lashes. "I still feel funny traveling alone. Stewart passed away two years ago."

Once, long before Phoebe, that look had made Fred's heart race. Now it did nothing except bring memories of trips to the movie house and school dances rushing back. "I'm sorry to hear that." He meant it. He'd met her husband years ago, and he'd been pleased to know she'd been happy.

"Thank you." She glanced at her hands, then slanted an uneasy smile at him. "Coralee told me about Phoebe. I know how hard losing her must be for you."

"It is," he admitted. But he didn't say anything else. He didn't want to launch into a long conversation about their missing spouses. "Are you enjoying yourself?"

"Yes. Are you?"

Fred shrugged. "Not really."

Thea laughed. "What a surprise. You never were much for parties, were you?"

"Not really," he said again. "But I'm stuck here. Millie and Al decided to come to the reunion this year, and for some reason, I let them talk me into giving them a ride tonight." He glanced round the room and added, "You remember my sister, Millie, don't you?"

Thea nodded. "Of course I do. She's only a year younger than we are." She craned her neck to look over the crowd. "Where is she?"

Fred waved his hand toward the opposite side of the room. "Over there somewhere. I don't know. She married Al Jarvis, you know."

"I know." Thea's lips curved into a smile. "Do you like him better now than you did when we were kids?"

"No. He still talks constantly and still says absolutely nothing."

Thea nodded and pulled her bottom lip between her teeth as if she wanted to smile but didn't think she should. "It seems odd to have a fifty-fifth reunion."

"It *is* odd," Fred groused. "And it's Percy Neuswander's fault. He's the genius who decided we all have one foot in the grave and can't afford to wait for one of these get-togethers, so now we have one every year."

"Do you come to every one?"

Fred sobered. "No. Phoebe and I did until they diagnosed the cancer. I haven't been to one in five years. I guess I just didn't feel right coming alone."

Thea nodded sadly. "I know what you mean. So, what made you decide to come this year?"

"For some fool reason I can't remember now, I let Millie convince me to come. They're living down in Breckenridge now, and I think she just wanted an excuse to spend the weekend with me. Besides, Al's eyes aren't what they used to be, and if I drive them around, it makes it easier for her to keep him from getting behind the wheel." He made a face he knew would make her smile. "But it was a big mistake. Al spent the entire drive jabbering about some nonsense, and until fifteen minutes ago he followed me around like we were glued together."

She didn't disappoint him. Her smile came back. "How'd you get away?"

Fred nodded toward the bleachers, where Oliver Wellington, tedious as ever, had cornered Al. "I never thought I'd say this, but thank the good Lord for Oliver. Now, if I can just keep Al away from me for the rest of the evening . . ."

From somewhere on the other side of the cavernous room, he heard Millie laugh. He glanced up and saw her standing beside Jeremiah Hunt, smiling as if Jeremiah had said something terribly witty. Fred couldn't imagine that.

Jeremiah hadn't said a witty thing in his life that Fred knew about.

Thea followed his gaze. "Is that Jeremiah?"

"It is."

"And that's Millie with him. I'd recognize her anywhere. She looks just like your mother."

"She does, doesn't she?" Fred studied her for a moment and let his smile grow. Millie did look like their mother— short and almost wafer-thin, with dark hair that grayed slowly. In fact, at nearly seventy-two, she looked no more than sixty.

Thea took another delicate bite of her cookie and nodded toward a small knot of people a few feet away. "It's amazing to me. Even after all this time, everybody looks exactly the same."

Fred darted a glance at her, convinced she must be joking. She looked absolutely serious. He let his gaze trail over the crowd once more.

Coralee DiMeo, who'd been a perky blonde with shapely legs in high school, stood clutching a cane a few feet away. Her hair, now an anemic shade of yellow gray, formed a halo around her head. But she still looked strong and healthy, like the dancer she'd once been.

Her husband, Burl, a tall man with a thick head of silver hair and only a tiny paunch, laughed at something, then broke off with a hacking cough. He jerked a handkerchief from his pocket, wiped his mouth, and looked around to see if anyone had noticed.

As if Thea could read his mind, she laughed again. "Well, maybe not *exactly* the same. But close enough for me to recognize them after all these years."

He supposed she was right. If he looked hard enough, ignored the canes and walkers and wheelchairs, the wrinkles and bags and extra pounds, he could see shadows of his former classmates.

Thea took a step closer and nodded toward a reed-thin woman in a flowery dress a few feet away. "You know who I *didn't* recognize? Iris Macafee." She waved her hand in front of her and amended, "I guess she's Iris Cavalier now, isn't she? It's hard to imagine her married to anyone but LeGrande. But they've been divorced at least twenty years now, haven't they?"

Fred nodded and took another sip of his punch. He supposed it had been about that long. He didn't know. Phoebe had been the one who paid attention to that sort of thing. And Fred had never liked Iris or LeGrande enough to care. In fact, he and LeGrande had never been able to occupy the same room for five minutes without getting into an argument. Thankfully, LeGrande had never decided to attend one of their reunions—the only intelligent thing he'd ever done, if you asked Fred.

Thea ran one small hand over her shoulder and sighed softly. "You heard what happened, didn't you? He walked out on her for another woman after thirty years together."

She sounded shocked, but Fred didn't know why she should be. LeGrande had never had any scruples. He muttered something noncommittal under his breath and took another long drink of punch.

Thea went on as if he hadn't made a sound. "I hear she met her second husband a couple of years after that—just after his wife died. Is he the tall men with the silver hair standing next to her?"

"That's him. Yale Cavalier."

"Is he nice?"

Fred pursed his mouth and gave that some thought. "I suppose so. She seems happy."

"And I hear LeGrande's remarried," Thea went on. "His wife's name is Stormy."

"Stormy?" Fred couldn't help but smile. He lowered his empty cup to the table. "Sounds like you've kept up on all the gossip, even if you haven't been around."

"I talked to Ardella," Thea said. Her grin held a hint of mischief.

Fred's smile grew a bit. "Well, that explains everything."

Ardella Neuswander took pride in knowing everything about everyone. Claimed she had to keep up, since her husband Percy had been their class president, which put them both in charge of planning their reunions. The years had been kind to Ardella. Her skin still had a healthy glow, she still walked tall, and her eyes still held that spark of curiosity that had been her trademark.

They hadn't been as kind to Percy. He'd easily been the best athlete in their class and one of the best-looking young men around. Now wrinkles sagged on his face, one layer over another, making him look more like a hound dog than the young man he'd once been. And these days he got around with the help of a wheelchair.

"Ardella tells me the divorce really upset Iris's children. They had three, you know. Two boys and a girl."

"I didn't know," Fred admitted. Or if anyone had told him, he'd forgotten.

Thea let her gaze drift around the room for another few seconds and finally settled on the DiMeos. "I suppose you heard about Coralee and Burl's son. . . ."

"Killed in Vietnam?" Fred nodded. "I did hear about that. Tragic."

"Their only child, too. I think Burl took it harder than Coralee did, but Ardella says neither of them has ever really gotten over it." Thea tapped one thin finger against her chin and nodded toward the bleachers, where Al had been cornered by Oliver Wellington. Blast. Al had escaped and Jeremiah Hunt had taken his place. Oliver still stood at least a foot shorter than Jeremiah, but what he lacked in height he now made up for in width.

"You know about Oliver Wellington, I suppose," Thea said.

"What about him?"

"I understand he's doing quite well financially. He and LeGrande are probably the most successful members of our class."

If you measured success by dollars, Fred supposed that might be true.

"Oh, and Jeremiah Hunt . . . Now, what did Ardella tell me about him?" Thea thought for a moment, then waved one hand in front of her face. "I can't remember. He's had some sort of trouble."

"We've all had our share," Fred pointed out.

Thea fingered the top button of her blouse. Her lips curved, but the smile didn't make it all the way to her eyes. "We certainly have." Then, as if she'd forgotten the entire conversation: "What have you been doing with yourself since Phoebe passed on?"

Fred shrugged. "This and that."

Thea sidled a step closer. "Ardella tells me you've been involved in a murder or two somehow."

Fred didn't like the way that sounded. "I haven't been involved in any murders," he clarified. "But I have helped the sheriff solve a couple."

Thea widened her eyes and studied him. "I can imagine you doing something like that. It must have been exciting."

Fred shrugged modestly, but before he could say anything more, something behind him caught her attention. Her smile evaporated, and an expression he couldn't read flickered through her eyes.

Curious, he turned to see what had brought about such a sudden change. A man, obviously old enough to be a member of their class, stood just inside the doorway beside a woman of about fifty. She looked young enough to be his daughter, but the way she held his arm and brushed against him as they walked through the door convinced Fred she wasn't his child.

Thea put a hand on his arm and whispered, "Do you know who that is?"

Of course Fred knew. He'd recognize LeGrande Macafee anywhere, even after all these years. He still had the boxy build he'd had in his youth. Still used enough pomade on his hair to make it shine in the light. Still had the thick, dark eyebrows that slanted at such an odd angle over his eyes and gave him a slightly devilish appearance.

Fred nodded slowly and tried to keep his distaste from showing. But if he'd known LeGrande planned to be here, he never would have come.

Thea kept her gaze riveted on LeGrande. "That must be his new wife. She *is* young, isn't she?" She didn't even pause to take a breath. "I can't believe he's here. I wonder why Ardella didn't say something?"

"She probably didn't know," Fred mumbled. "If she *had* known, she'd have warned us."

LeGrande had been a bully as a boy and an arrogant ass as a young man. He'd caused more problems than the rest of their graduating class put together. He'd broken more hearts, instigated more arguments, and hurt more feelings than any one person had a right to. Even Phoebe, who'd liked almost everyone without exception, hadn't cared for him.

Apparently, time hadn't changed him a bit. He still walked into a room as if he owned it. He still preened, as if everyone present should count themselves lucky he'd decided to join them.

Fred didn't count himself lucky. Just when he'd started to enjoy himself for the first time all evening, LeGrande had to show up and spoil everything. Typical.

Resentments Fred thought he'd forgotten boiled to the surface. Animosity he'd thought long dead sprang to life. He told himself to ignore LeGrande, but he couldn't seem to tear his gaze away.

LeGrande's beady eyes darted from one of their former classmates to another, never really lighting on anyone. Oliver Wellington finally shut up and turned a hostile glare in LeGrande's direction. Coralee DiMeo stiffened and gripped Burl's arm with her free hand, hard enough to make him wince. Jeremiah Hunt's face lost its color for a few seconds, then turned a brilliant shade of red.

But all their reactions paled in comparison to Iris Cavalier's when she saw her ex-husband walking into the room with his young wife. She froze in place and raw hatred contorted her features. Unless Fred missed his guess, they could expect trouble.

Millie tore herself away from her group and hurried across the gymnasium toward the refreshment table. She came to a breathless stop at Fred's side and whispered, "Don't start anything."

Fred scowled down at her. "What makes you think I'm going to start anything? I'm just standing here."

"You're getting red in the face."

"It's warm in here."

Millie rolled her eyes, let out a heavy sigh, and looked at Thea as if she wanted someone to agree with her. "Don't make trouble, that's all I ask."

"I don't make trouble," Fred assured her, "but I don't run away if it finds me."

Millie slanted forward to catch Thea's gaze. "Did you hear that? Fred says he doesn't make trouble." She leaned back to face him again. "Which one of you two started that big fight outside the church?"

Fred glared at her. "For Pete's sake, Millie. That was over fifty years ago."

That didn't seem to make much of an impression. She propped her hands on her hips and tilted her chin so she could stare into his eyes. "Which one of you started it?"

"He did."

Behind him, Thea laughed softly. "*He* did?"

"Yes." Fred drew himself up to his full height and divided an indignant glare between them. "He was bothering Phoebe."

Millie rolled her eyes in exasperation. "He was trying to *talk* to her."

"Well, *she* didn't want to talk to *him*," Fred reminded her. "It was obvious to everyone but him."

"Maybe she *didn't* want to," Millie conceded, "but she could have handled it herself. You didn't need to hit him."

"She was my wife. I had every right to defend her. But there's no sense rehashing something that happened more than fifty years ago."

"Exactly." Millie nodded, as if Fred had proved her point for her. When she got like this, only a fool would argue with her.

Fred might be many things, but he wasn't a fool. He

shrugged in frustration and started to turn away, only to find himself face-to-face with Al.

A groan of dismay escaped his lips before he could stop it. Millie scowled at him, but Al didn't seem to notice. He put both hands on Fred's shoulders and leaned in close. "This doesn't have to be a problem, does it?"

The slim grasp Fred had maintained on his temper slipped. "There's no problem. *None*. I don't know why all of you are acting as if there should be."

Al kept talking, as if Fred hadn't spoken. "Because it all happened a long time ago."

That was the first sensible thing Al had said in years. "Yes, it did," Fred agreed. "And as far as I'm concerned, it's forgotten."

Thea and Millie exchanged glances. Al's eyes narrowed in disbelief.

Fred ignored them all.

Millie firmed her grip on his arm. "Well, good. If you mean that, let's say hello."

"I suppose we should," Thea said, and started slowly across the gymnasium.

Fred had no intention of following her. He yanked his arm out of Millie's grasp and took a step backward. "Look, Millie, I don't plan to start trouble, but I won't pretend I'm glad to see him. If you want to say hello, go right ahead. I'll stay here."

"It all happened over fifty years ago," Al mumbled, more to himself than anyone else. "That's a long time. *Long* time. No sense dredging up everything now, is there?"

Millie sighed again and glared up at Fred. "You're as stubborn and bullheaded as Daddy ever was. Why on earth do you have to behave like this?"

"Like *what*?" Fred demanded. "I'm not doing a blasted thing."

"You're being rude."

"I'm not being rude," Fred assured her. "I'm being honest. I don't like the man. Never have. And I don't see any reason to pretend that I do."

"Doesn't have to like him," Al mumbled, shaking his head at Millie. "When you come right down to it, it's probably best this way."

Millie's scowl deepened. "Fine," she snapped, but she didn't sound as if she meant it.

Fred didn't let that bother him. She'd get over it.

Millie took one step away, then turned back and shook a finger in his face. "Don't leave, or I'll come after you."

Fred forced a reassuring smile, but he didn't say a word. No sense making a promise he might not keep. For years, he'd let LeGrande goad him into arguments he'd have been smarter to avoid. He'd reacted first and thought later. No matter what it took, he wouldn't let LeGrande get under his skin again.

But his headache intensified and moved down into his neck, and he couldn't ignore the growing certainty that LeGrande showing up after all these years meant nothing but trouble.

two

Fred kept one wary eye on LeGrande as Millie and Al crossed the gymnasium to greet him. A trickle of perspiration ran from his temple down the side of his cheek. He dashed it away with the back of his hand and ran a finger between his neck and shirt collar, hoping to make it easier to catch a breath. Nothing helped. The music on the stereo changed and the frantic beat of "In the Mood" beat in time with the pounding in his head.

LeGrande caught sight of Millie and Al and pulled back in exaggerated surprise. "Millie? Al? I didn't know you two would be here." He grabbed Al's hand and pumped it, gripping his arm just above the elbow with his free hand.

Fred expected Al to smile and chatter the way he always did. Instead, he jerked his hand away and distaste distorted his features for a second.

Strange. Fred didn't remember Al disliking LeGrande that much. His unexpected reaction made Fred feel a little better. Al might sometimes seem half a sandwich short of a picnic, but he was loyal. Fred couldn't deny that.

An expression Fred couldn't identify flashed across LeGrande's broad face, but it disappeared again so quickly he wondered if he'd only imagined it. Unfortunately, LeGrande chose that moment to sweep the crowd again with his beady eyes.

This time his gaze landed squarely on Fred, and a

predatory gleam filled his eyes. "Fred? Fred Vickery? Good Lord, you've gotten old."

Fred didn't even try to sound friendly. "LeGrande. You haven't changed a bit."

Al sidled a little closer to LeGrande. Even from a distance Fred could see his lips moving as he kept up his running monologue.

LeGrande threw back his head and laughed. "I'm still tall, dark, and handsome, eh?" He patted his swollen stomach and grinned at several nearby people.

Those weren't the words Fred would have chosen to describe him, but he didn't say so. He just wanted to get the moment over with so he could ignore LeGrande for the rest of the weekend.

Apparently, LeGrande didn't feel the same way. His smile stiffened almost imperceptibly, and he took a step closer. "You know, I never could understand why that beautiful wife of yours chose you over me."

Amazing. He still had an ego as big as all of Colorado. Still thought every woman in their class found him irresistible.

Fred lifted his shoulders in a casual shrug and tried to keep his tone light. "She was just smart, I guess."

LeGrande's eyes narrowed and his smile froze. "Well, where is she?" he demanded, darting his gaze around the crowd again. "We'll ask *her* if she's figured out what a mistake she made."

Someone behind Fred pulled in a sharp breath. LeGrande's wife scowled up at him. Millie put one hand on LeGrande's arm and spoke too softly for Fred to hear. It didn't matter. He knew what she said, and he thanked her silently for saving him from having to answer.

LeGrande's expression sobered and he stared at Fred in disbelief. "She's gone?"

Fred nodded. Even that tiny movement sent his headache into overdrive, but he did his best not to show it. "Has been for nearly four years now."

LeGrande dragged his gaze around the room again, as if

he expected someone to contradict Fred. No one did. "But she *can't* be gone," he insisted. "I need to talk to her. She's one of the reasons I came tonight."

Maybe Fred should have kept his mouth shut, but LeGrande's overinflated sense of his own importance had always grated on his nerves. "Well, *that* certainly makes a difference. If Phoebe had only known, I'm sure she would have held on a few more years."

Someone standing near LeGrande snorted a laugh. A couple of others shifted uncomfortably. LeGrande's eyebrows knit together in the center and winged upward on either end. "There's no need to be sarcastic."

There wasn't any need to be stupid either, but LeGrande hadn't ever let that stop him.

And tonight was no exception. He took a couple of steps closer and tried to look sincere. "I've always wondered why you disliked me so much. I mean, it's not as if I've ever done anything to you."

Apparently, he wasn't only stupid, he was also absent-minded. But this time Fred didn't let himself respond. Every time he spoke he only encouraged LeGrande.

Like an actor playing to an audience, LeGrande turned a pleading glance toward those standing nearest him. "It's taken me years to figure it out, and I've realized there's only one possible explanation."

Fred could have offered him half a dozen, but he didn't. He waited, exhibiting remarkable patience, for LeGrande to finish his performance.

LeGrande took another step closer. He didn't seem to notice that his wife released his arm and stayed behind. "I came here to set the record straight, once and for all."

"Is that right?" A flicker of apprehension wormed its way up Fred's spine, but he pushed it away and firmed his resolve. He'd let whatever LeGrande said go in one ear and out the other. "Well, go ahead. Set the record straight, then."

Al trailed LeGrande, shaking his head wildly and muttering, "Not a good idea."

Fred ignored him.

So did LeGrande. He jutted out his chins and took a deep breath before he spoke again. "I probably should have said something years ago."

"Well, you've got your audience now," Fred pointed out. "Quit being so blasted melodramatic and get it over with."

LeGrande let out a pitiful sigh. "I'm not being melodramatic. This is difficult to say." He made another play for sympathy with a hang-dog expression.

"Not a good idea," Al muttered again. "No sense dragging things up from the past."

LeGrande's pitiful expression hardened for an instant. He flicked a scathing glance at Al. "I'll thank you to stay out of this. This is between Fred and me."

Obviously. That's why he'd chosen to discuss it tonight, in front of all their classmates. Fred had shown remarkable restraint to this point, but he could feel his patience slipping. "Whatever it is, say it," he snapped. "I haven't got all night."

LeGrande heaved another pathetic sigh. "I know how much you loved Phoebe—"

Again, the tingle of apprehension assaulted him. Again, he ignored it. "What does she have to do with this?"

LeGrande went on as if Fred hadn't interrupted. "I know you'd like to believe what she told you, but she lied to you."

Fred might have been able to control his temper if the dirtbag had said something about him, but he wouldn't tolerate him talking about Phoebe that way. He squared his shoulders and met LeGrande's gaze steadily. "This may come as a shock to you LeGrande, but Phoebe didn't waste her time talking about you."

"She never . . . ?" LeGrande's eyes rounded, then narrowed again almost immediately. "I don't believe you."

Al stepped in a little closer. "Now is not the best time to talk about this. I think you should wait."

Fred knew he meant well, but he didn't want or need Al's interference. He kept his gaze riveted on LeGrande. "You can believe me or not, that's up to you."

LeGrande hoisted himself another step closer. "I *don't*

believe you. I think that's why you hate me so much. I think she told you what happened between us, but I think she made up a story to make herself sound innocent so you wouldn't blame her."

His implication couldn't have been more clear if he'd spelled it out for the whole damned crowd. Anger, bitter as bile, rose in Fred's throat. "That's a damned lie, and you know it."

"See?" LeGrande held out his hands to the people nearest them. "Do you see what I mean?"

Al muttered something, but rage pounded so insistently in Fred's ears he couldn't understand a word. He clenched his fists and put his face so close to LeGrande's he could see the veins in his nose. "You want to know why I hate you, you son of a bitch? Because you're a liar. Always have been. You'll say anything to make yourself seem important, and you don't care who you hurt."

Someone behind him muttered agreement. Someone else laughed nervously.

Color flooded LeGrande's ugly face. "I'm *not* lying. You just don't want to hear the truth." He shoved a finger into Fred's face. "You've always been that way, Fred. You hear what you want to hear. You believe what you want to believe."

Fred pushed the finger away. He kept his voice low. "*If* my wife had ever said anything about you, it would have been the absolute truth. Phoebe didn't lie."

LeGrande held up both hands in a gesture of innocence. "Look, I just want to set the record straight, that's all."

If he didn't shut his big mouth, Fred would set the record straight in his own way. But before he could say or do anything, someone stepped between him and LeGrande. He didn't recognize Jeremiah Hunt until he started talking.

"I always knew you were a lowlife, LeGrande. But I never thought you'd stoop to something like this. Talking about a dead woman that way. Hell, she's not even here to defend herself."

LeGrande didn't even blink. "Defend herself? Why

would she need to do that? Seems to me she had all of you snowed with her innocent act."

That did it. Fred didn't even bother to think. He shoved Jeremiah out of his way and put his fist squarely in LeGrande's big, ugly face. The blow didn't give him the satisfaction he longed for. Instead, it loosened something inside him and made him want to hit the scumbag again. But all hell broke loose and kept him from giving in to the urge.

As if in slow motion, LeGrande staggered backward—out of Fred's reach—and brought one hand up to touch his nose. "Dammit, Fred. What in the hell is wrong with you?"

The new Mrs. Macafee raced to his side and alternated between comforting her husband and shouting at Fred. Jeremiah tipped back his head and laughed aloud. Percy Neuswander held both hands in the air and tried to restore order from his wheelchair. Coralee DiMeo sagged against Burl's side as if she couldn't bear the sight of two men fighting. Oliver Wellington's pudgy face flamed and his mouth moved, but Fred couldn't hear a word he said. Thea Griffin stood a little to one side, eyes wide with horror.

Dimly, Fred became aware of Millie pushing through the crowd toward him. She didn't look happy.

Iris Cavalier watched from the sidelines. Her eyes glittered with satisfaction and her lips curved in an unpleasant smile. Apparently, she didn't mind Fred belting her ex-husband. Yale didn't look upset, either. In fact, he looked immensely gratified.

LeGrande must have decided he'd received enough sympathy. He shoved his wife away and probably would have hit Fred back if Al hadn't pushed between them and gripped him by the shoulders. "Let it go, LeGrande."

LeGrande shook him off and tried to dodge around him.

To Fred's surprise, Al blocked him again. "I said, let it go." His voice sounded strangely ominous. Not like Al at all.

"Get the hell out of my way," LeGrande demanded.

Al stood his ground. "Drop it," he warned.

Fred expected LeGrande to laugh and shove him away.

After all, Al had never been the type to stand up for himself—much less for anyone else. Fred couldn't imagine what he thought he'd accomplish by starting now. Not only did LeGrande have more experience when it came to fighting—he'd actually been in a few—but he outweighed Al by at least fifty pounds. Probably more.

Some of Fred's anger faded and exasperation took its place. He appreciated Al standing up for him, but if the fool didn't back down, he'd get seriously hurt.

Fred couldn't let that happen. Millie would never forgive him. He pulled in a steadying breath, but before he could move, LeGrande muttered something, spun on his heel, and marched away. His wife fell into step beside him and struggled to match his stride.

Fred's mouth fell open. Literally. He slanted a shocked glance at Al and another at LeGrande's retreating back. At least half the people in the room looked equally stunned.

Jeremiah Hunt laughed again and pounded Al on the back. Coralee DiMeo managed to pull herself away from Burl's protective embrace and steady herself with her cane. But Burl didn't seem to realize the danger had passed. He kept his gaze locked on LeGrande, his jaw clenched, and his stance rigid.

Al turned to face Fred, and his expression slowly returned to normal. Fred snagged his arm and pulled him away from the others just as Millie finally made it through the crowd and drew even with them.

She grabbed Fred by both arms and pulled him around to face her. "You hit him."

"I had to."

"You *had* to?" She laughed angrily. "For heaven's sake, Fred. You don't expect me to believe that, do you?"

Fred didn't need this from her. Not now. He put everything he had into a disapproving scowl. "You heard what he said."

"Yes I did, but you didn't need to hit him." She gestured toward the rest of their classmates, who were obviously still in an uproar. "Look what you started."

"What did you expect me to do? Stand by twiddling my thumbs while he talked about my wife that way?"

"Of course not—"

"Is that what you'd expect Al to do if LeGrande had said those things about you?"

"Well, no. But . . ." She had the sense to look sheepish.

"All right, then," he snapped, and swept one arm toward their chattering classmates. "Don't blame me for this. Why don't you lay the blame where it really belongs for once—with the son of a bitch who started it."

Millie flushed an unbecoming shade of red. "Really, Fred. Your language."

"You'll have to worry about more than my language if he comes anywhere near me the rest of this weekend," Fred assured her. He drew in a steadying breath, tried to get his temper under control again, and turned to face Al. "And you—I appreciate what you did, but you didn't need to step in. I had everything under control."

Al started shaking his head with Fred's first word and kept shaking until he finished. "No, you didn't."

"I don't need you to fight my battles for me. It was between LeGrande and me. You didn't need to step in."

"It wasn't between LeGrande and you," Al argued. "It was between LeGrande and Phoebe."

That caught Fred off guard and short-circuited his anger. "Well, yes," he agreed slowly. "It was. But you didn't need to get involved on my behalf."

Al pulled back a step and stared at him for a long moment. "I didn't do it for you," he said at last. He sounded confused, as if couldn't imagine how Fred could have made such a mistake. "I did it for Phoebe."

Fred rolled his eyes in exasperation. Phoebe'd always had a soft spot for Al—one Fred had never understood until now.

Al wagged a hand in LeGrande's general direction and lowered his voice a notch. "He was lying about her. I couldn't let him do that."

"Yes," Fred said, lowering his voice to match Al's. "But you could have gotten hurt."

"Hurt?"

"He could have hit you."

"Hit me?" Al looked baffled. He slanted a glance across the room, then looked back at Fred and shook his head quickly. "He wouldn't dare."

Fred stared at him. He couldn't seem to do anything else. If that didn't beat all.

Al put an arm around Millie's shoulders and led her away. She went reluctantly, darting concerned glances over her shoulder at Fred the whole way.

Fred watched them go and tried to tell himself it was over. But he didn't believe it. Not by a long shot.

three

Casting one last glance over his shoulder to make sure no one was watching, Fred slipped out of the gymnasium and hurried down the darkened corridor. Nearly an hour had passed since he'd punched LeGrande in the nose, and now it seemed no one at the reunion wanted to talk about anything else.

Well, Fred didn't want to talk about it anymore. He wanted to put LeGrande and his monstrous lies out of his mind. He wanted to get on with the reunion and forget the whole ugly mess had ever happened. Better yet, he wanted to leave. But Millie wanted to stay, and Fred wouldn't feel right leaving them stranded. He could just imagine how Millie would react to that. Since they were houseguests, he'd spend the rest of the weekend hearing about it.

But none of that meant he had to stay inside the gymnasium, smiling as if nothing had happened. No, he'd sit out the rest of the evening alone somewhere—in an empty classroom, maybe. Or, if he couldn't find one open, on a staircase. It didn't matter where he waited, just as long as he didn't have to see LeGrande Macafee again or hear his voice.

Fred's shadow disappeared into the inky darkness, emerging only when he passed beneath one of the emergency lights that burned all night. As the former buildings-and-grounds supervisor for the school district, he'd spent more hours in this building than he could count. Of course he'd had keys for everything then. Now he had to rely on luck to find an open door.

In his day, teachers and custodians had been notorious for leaving doors open despite his frequent warnings. He couldn't imagine they'd changed *that* much over the years.

In the distance, a Benny Goodman tune underscored the chatter of his former classmates. Fred certainly hoped they were enjoying themselves. As for him . . . well, apparently he'd indulged in too many cups of punch. He realized suddenly that *his* first order of business was to find a rest room. After that, he could look for a place to wait.

He made his way down the science corridor to the men's room there and tried the door. It didn't budge. Wonderful. *Now* they listened to him.

Sighing with frustration, he tried to decide where to go next. Unfortunately, he didn't have time for futile searches. He needed the facilities, and he needed them now. Of course, the rest rooms nearest the gymnasium had been left unlocked for the reunion. He could always go back there. And, judging from the urgency of his need, that's exactly what he'd have to do.

He hotfooted it past the home economics and math departments and crossed the foyer lined with trophy cases that separated the gymnasium and music rooms from the rest of the school. But the closer he drew to the music and laughter, the slower his feet moved.

Keeping one eye on the open door to the gym, he crossed to the lavatory and slipped inside without running into anyone. Luck had been with him so far, and it held. The lavatory was blessedly empty. But he still didn't want to take any chances.

He stepped inside one of the stalls and latched the door behind him. That way, even if someone else came in, they wouldn't see him.

He went about his business quickly, but just as he unlocked the stall door again, the outer door whooshed open and someone else came into the room. Fred relatched the door without making a sound and held his breath.

Hushed, angry whispers echoed off the tile floor and walls, which meant at least two people had joined him.

"I can't believe your nerve," a voice whispered harshly. "Where do you get off?"

"I just want to make it up to you." The second voice tried to whisper, but without much success. "To *all* of you."

Fred's heart dropped. He recognized that voice. LeGrande Macafee, of all people.

Stiffening, he pulled back from the stall's door and glanced around quickly. He couldn't escape the stall, but he'd be damned if he'd let LeGrande find him. Quickly, silently, he sat on the porcelain seat and lifted his feet from the floor. His knees protested, but he ignored the pain and propped his feet noiselessly against the stall's door.

"You can't make it up." Not a whisper any longer, but still hushed. "You've lied. Cheated. Stolen. What in the hell's next? Why should I trust you?"

Fred couldn't tell which of his classmates that voice belonged to, but the conversation certainly roused his curiosity. He leaned forward ever so slightly to see through the narrow opening between the door and the wall. But one of the men stood close enough to keep him from seeing anything but the gray fabric of his suit.

"I've changed," LeGrande insisted.

Fred held back a disbelieving snort. *Sure* he had. They'd all seen evidence of that.

"Changed?" The first man let out a harsh laugh. "You'll never change. I'm warning you, don't ever try to pull another stunt like the one you did last night."

So, LeGrande had already been up to his tricks with someone else. Not a bit surprising. But it did Fred's heart good to know someone else saw the truth about LeGrande.

The men shifted position, the gray suit moved out of Fred's line of vision, and an inch or two of LeGrande's companion came into focus. To Fred's surprise, he looked young—no more than fifty or so. Dark hair shot with flecks of gray. Several inches taller than LeGrande. Broad shoulders and burly arms that stretched the fabric of his black

T-shirt to the limit. Leg muscles bulged beneath the denim of his jeans. A hulk of a man.

For some stupid reason, LeGrande tried to touch the younger man. The hulk shoved him away and sent him reeling into the metal towel dispenser. "Don't touch me, you son of a bitch."

Ugly. But, then, LeGrande had always inspired ugliness.

He righted himself and straightened his shoulders. Fred could see enough of his face to know the younger man had made him angry, but his voice came out deceptively calm. "Look, Roger, I only want to make things right."

Roger. The name didn't ring any bells for Fred either, but he didn't know why it should.

Roger snorted a brittle laugh. "Don't bother. It's too late."

"I know you're angry with me," LeGrande said, "but don't you think you're carrying this a bit too far?"

"*Too far?* After everything you've done?"

An irritated sigh echoed off the tile walls as LeGrande took a step forward.

Roger shoved him again. "Get the hell away from me."

LeGrande careened into the sink. Wincing, he clutched his leg with one hand and moved out of Fred's line of vision again. "What in God's name is wrong with you?"

"*You're* what's wrong with me. You come back here and show up on my doorstep. . . ." The young man paced. Fred could tell by the tread of his step. "Well, get this straight, old man. If you want to talk, you do it on *my* terms."

"All right. What are they?" LeGrande's voice sounded reasonable enough. Even a bit subdued. But Fred didn't trust him.

"First, you do *not* come to my house. Ever."

"I—"

"No!" The word exploded from the young man and bounced off the walls for a few seconds. "You stay away from my wife and kids, and tell that whore of yours not to call my house again. This is between you and me."

Without warning, LeGrande swung his arm and back-handed the young man across the mouth. "Don't you dare talk about my wife like that."

Fred expected Roger to hit back, but he somehow managed to control himself. The shadows on the opposite wall grew, then shrank again as the two men jockeyed for position amid the porcelain. "What's the matter?" Roger taunted. "Can't stand the truth? Well, here's some more for you. You want to know what she was doing last night while you were out pulling your shit?"

LeGrande caught hold of Roger's T-shirt and hauled him close.

But the younger man only laughed. "She called me. Asked me to meet her at the Copper Penny."

"That's a lie."

"Is it?" A slow smile spread across the young man's face. "Want to know what she offered me if I'd talk to you?"

LeGrande slapped him again. Fred figured that meant he didn't want to know.

But the young man told him anyway. "She offered to take me to your hotel room and—"

"Shut your damned mouth," LeGrande warned.

Another harsh laugh. "What? You don't believe me?" Roger broke LeGrande's grip on his shirt and took a step backward. "Don't tell me you honestly thought she loved you?"

With a growl, LeGrande butted Roger up against Fred's stall door. "You're lying."

Shock waves of pain zinged up Fred's leg, but he kept his feet planted on the door and swallowed a groan.

"*Am* I?" Roger's voice came out sounding choked. "Why don't you ask her?"

"I don't have to. She wouldn't do that to me."

"Why not? I'll bet you'd do it to *her* in a heartbeat."

The door rattled again. Fred clenched his teeth and prayed the latch wouldn't give way.

"You've heard that old saying, haven't you?" Roger sounded as if he was enjoying himself. "What goes around comes around. Well, you've screwed so many people over, maybe you're just getting some of it back now. Maybe I should have gone back to the hotel with her. Maybe I should have let her screw—"

LeGrande hit him once more, this time hard enough to cut him off mid-sentence and knock him to his knees. "I've changed my mind, you little son of a bitch. Stormy's right. You are a loser. And you can go to hell for all I care."

Roger lurched to his feet and lunged, but LeGrande sidestepped and shoved him away. Before Roger could go after him again, LeGrande wheeled toward the door, jerked it open, and disappeared into the school's corridor.

Roger rocked back on his heels, pressed the back of his hand to his mouth, and swore violently. Raw hatred distorted his features and sent fingers of ice up Fred's spine.

Another stabbing pain shot up his legs. He bit his lip, squeezed his eyes shut, struggled to hold himself still. He willed his heart to stop thumping in his chest and tried to take shallow, silent breaths. More than ever, he didn't want to give himself away.

After what felt like forever, Roger's slow footsteps moved across the tile floor. A second later the door squeaked open and banged shut again.

Fred didn't move immediately. He waited another minute or two for good measure, then slowly lowered his feet to the floor and held on to the door latch while he worked himself upright. But he'd been cramped for so long, his knees didn't want to move.

Slowly, he let himself out of the stall, rinsed his hands and face, and patted them dry with a paper towel. He stared at his reflection in the mirror and wondered about what he'd just heard.

Some part of him enjoyed knowing LeGrande had finally gotten a taste of his own medicine. But he also knew from experience that when tempers ran that hot, sooner or later there'd be trouble. At least, he told himself with a satisfied smile, this time the trouble had nothing to do with him.

He stopped at the doorway and listened for sounds coming from the corridor. Nothing. He was safe. Breathing a sigh of relief, he tugged open the door and started through. But just as he did, someone stepped into his path.

Fred stopped, blinked, and found himself looking straight into LeGrande's surprised eyes. He swore under his breath, firmed his stance, and kept his gaze firmly riveted on LeGrande's.

LeGrande's eyes narrowed into slits and his face flamed. "How did you get in there?"

His obvious uneasiness did Fred's old heart good. "I opened the door and walked in."

LeGrande didn't look amused. "How long have you been in there?"

"That's kind of a personal question—" Fred began.

LeGrande cut him off. "You know what I mean. How much did you hear?"

Fred thought about pretending confusion, but it wouldn't do any good. LeGrande knew he'd overheard that argument. He made a noise in his throat that Legrande could interpret however he chose and tried to push past him into the corridor.

Legrande refused to budge. "You haven't changed a bit, have you? You're still a smart-ass."

Fred would have thanked him for the compliment, but he didn't want to prolong their conversation.

LeGrande rubbed one pudgy hand across his chins and puffed out his chest a bit. "So, are you ready to talk about it?"

"Nope."

LeGrande leaned in closer—close enough to let Fred smell the alcohol on his breath. "Why not? You afraid?" The fumes didn't surprise Fred. LeGrande always had liked to drink, and he'd always gotten pushy when he did.

Fred shook his head. "Nope."

"Well, then . . . ?"

"Well nothing," Fred snapped. "I have nothing to say to you."

LeGrande took a step into the lavatory. "Well, *I've* got something to say to you."

Fred took a step back. "Whatever it is, keep it to yourself."

"I can't do that."

"Sure you can. Just keep your damned mouth shut."

LeGrande tried to snag Fred's arm. "You don't understand. It wasn't my fault."

Fred jerked away. "Nothing's ever your fault," he agreed. "You've always been good at shifting blame to other people."

LeGrande took another step closer, wobbled a bit, and leaned against the tile wall. "You think it was, don't you?"

"Honestly? I don't care."

LeGrande barked a laugh. "Now I *know* you're lying. If anyone cares about what happened that night, you do."

That night? *What* night? Fred put some space between them.

LeGrande closed it again and sent another blast of fumes up Fred's nose. "I don't care what she told you. She led me on."

Led him on? *Phoebe?* Fred would have laughed aloud if the idea hadn't been so disgusting. "You're up in the night. Phoebe didn't even like you."

"Of course she did. We dated for a while before you came along. You know that."

Ridiculous. Phoebe and LeGrande? The thought made Fred's stomach roll.

"What *did* she tell you about that night?" LeGrande demanded.

Fred didn't have the foggiest idea what LeGrande was talking about, but pride wouldn't let him admit that aloud. He lifted his shoulders in an eloquent shrug and worked up a thin smile. "The truth."

"The truth?" LeGrande laughed bitterly and rubbed the back of his neck. "I doubt that."

Fred's temper surged, but he managed to keep a slender hold on it. He wouldn't let LeGrande goad him into an argument. Not again. He repeated what he'd said earlier. "Phoebe never lied."

"Well, she must have lied about this," LeGrande insisted. "Why else have you been so pissed off at me all these years?"

Fred could have given him several dozen reasons, but he didn't. LeGrande would have blamed someone else for every one of them. Squaring his shoulders, he tried once more to work his way around LeGrande's bulk and out of the tile-walled lavatory.

But LeGrande planted his feet and refused to move. "I came here tonight to set the record straight. I don't want to go to my grave with things unresolved." Again that pathetic look darted across his beefy face.

This time a tiny flicker of doubt niggled at the back of Fred's brain. *Had* something happened between LeGrande and Phoebe all those years ago? *Should* he hate LeGrande for it? No. If anything had happened, Phoebe would have told him. They hadn't kept secrets from one another. Ever.

He took advantage of LeGrande's self-pity to slip past him and out the door. "Consider it resolved, then."

Apparently, that didn't satisfy LeGrande. He followed Fred into the hallway and snagged his arm again. "I can't. Not until we've talked. Not until you tell me what Phoebe told you and give me a chance to tell my side of it."

In spite of himself, the doubt came back. He pushed it away again. "There's nothing to resolve."

"But there *is*. I've let this go on too long. I've let *everything* go on too long. But I don't have much time left. I've got cancer, Fred." Desperation filled his eyes. If he'd been anyone else, Fred might have felt sorry for him. "The doctors tell me I've only got a few months left, and I want to clear up all the misunderstandings before I die. Can't you understand that?"

Fred supposed he could in a general way, but he still didn't want to hear LeGrande talk about Phoebe.

"It wasn't the way she made it sound." LeGrande's voice rose a notch. "Not at all. She *wanted* it."

Fred told himself to ignore him and walk away. But he couldn't. Even impending death didn't excuse LeGrande from making up a story like that. "Wanted *what*?" he demanded, though he knew very well what LeGrande meant, and the very idea made him sick to his stomach.

LeGrande lifted both eyebrows in a suggestive waggle. "You know."

"Why in hell's name would Phoebe have wanted something like *that* from *you*?" Fred knew the question came out too loud. His voice echoed in the deserted corridor and probably carried into the party.

"It was after the two of you got together," LeGrande said, "but before you were married." As if that would make Fred feel better.

It didn't.

Fred pulled in a steadying breath. Bad enough that *he* had to listen to such hogwash from LeGrande. He certainly didn't want anyone else to hear.

"I think she was having second thoughts," LeGrande went on. "You always were hot-tempered, and I think you frightened her."

Everything inside Fred turned to ice. Lies. Nothing but lies. Just like always. "You're full of—"

"Hear me out," LeGrande interrupted. "She came to see me one night. I was working at the market then, you know. I came out the back door, and there she was."

Sweat pooled under Fred's arms and trickled down his back. The air around him grew heavy, as if someone had sucked all the oxygen from it. "You're lying," Fred told him. "And I'm through listening."

"I'm not lying. She was a beautiful woman. Hell, *you* know that. Those eyes of hers . . . and her smile." LeGrande shook his head, as if he needed to rid himself of her image. "She was a real looker."

"Don't say another word," Fred warned.

The idiot didn't listen. Or maybe he just didn't understand plain English. "I could tell she'd been crying, so I stopped to talk to her. She was upset, so I took her to my car and we sat there awhile . . . talking."

"Shut your damned mouth before I do something I'll

regret." The words ground out between Fred's teeth and he had to ball his hands into fists to keep from hitting LeGrande again. Dimly, he became aware of footsteps behind him, but he kept his gaze locked on LeGrande's. Something close to fear flashed through the scumbag's beady eyes.

Good. He *should* be afraid.

But he still ignored Fred's warning. "She really got to me, Fred. I have to admit that. You know how she was, so soft and sweet—"

Fred didn't wait for him to finish. Before another ugly lie could fall out of his mouth, Fred hit him for the second time in an hour. Pain tore through his fingers and up his arm.

Blood spurted from LeGrande's lip. "Damn you—"

"Keep your damned mouth shut and stay away from me the rest of this weekend or you'll be sorry." Fred struggled to pull in a ragged breath, but his lungs refused to take in the sultry night air. He tried to still his rampaging heart, but anger set its unsteady rhythm. His hand throbbed, but the pain gave him a strange sense of fulfillment. He'd be smart to put some distance between himself and LeGrande before he hit him again.

He pivoted away and started down the corridor.

But LeGrande's voice followed him. "This is *exactly* like you, Fred. Hit first, ask questions later."

If he didn't shut up, Fred would hit again and skip the questions.

"You're wrong about me," LeGrande shouted. "Wrong. And you're wrong about Phoebe. She wasn't the angel you've made her out to be."

Damn him to hell. Why didn't he shut his big, ugly mouth? Fred refused to look back. Instead, he picked up his pace and kept his eyes riveted on the intersecting corridor at the end of the hall.

But he couldn't walk fast enough to escape LeGrande's voice.

"She asked for it, Fred. She *begged*."

Nonsense. Insane. Unthinkable. Absolute bullshit.

Of course, things like that had gone on fifty years ago. Fred wasn't *that* naive. There'd been enough shotgun weddings and "seven-month babies" to dispel the doubts of any but the most gullible. But premarital relations hadn't been considered acceptable in those days, and Phoebe hadn't been the type of woman to . . . to do something like that.

She'd been shy. Modest. Even with Fred, she'd been hesitant with intimacy in the beginning. It had taken her a long time to truly enjoy that part of their marriage. So the thought that she would have given in if LeGrande made a pass at her was ridiculous, and the idea that she'd been the one to initiate such a thing unthinkable.

LeGrande shouted something else, but Fred's own thoughts blocked the words this time. Seething, Fred kept going until he rounded the corner and knew LeGrande couldn't see him any longer. Then he ducked inside the recessed doorway of a classroom, leaned his forehead against the glass, and tried once more to calm himself.

But instead of settling down, his imagination ran wild, plotting ways to wipe the ugly lies from LeGrande's fat lips.

All Fred could say was that it was a damned good thing the son of a bitch had only a few months to live. Because that was the only thing that kept Fred from going back and killing him where he stood.

four

Sometime later Fred stepped out of the doorway, shook his throbbing hand, and stared at the empty corridor around him. He had no idea how long he'd been standing there. Long enough to imagine ridding the world of LeGrande in several creative ways. Long enough to slip one of the heart pills his daughter, Margaret, insisted he carry with him under his tongue. Long enough for his breathing to steady and his pulse to slow again. It might have been five minutes, or it could have been an hour.

Not that it mattered. He didn't want to see anyone. And he certainly didn't want to go near the gymnasium and risk running into LeGrande again.

Rubbing his forehead, he glanced at his watch. Nearly seven-thirty. Wonderful. The party wouldn't be over for another hour or more. What was he supposed to do now?

More than ever, he wanted to leave. But he still couldn't justify leaving Millie and Al stranded. Unless . . . He smiled slowly and turned an idea over in his mind once more. Unless he could convince them to get a ride home with someone else. Why not? After all, he lived only a few miles away. Surely someone would be willing to drive them that far.

Of course, he'd have to come up with a convincing reason for leaving—one that Millie wouldn't try to argue him out of. One he wouldn't have to spend half the night explaining. Pondering his options, he stepped out of the doorway and walked away from the gymnasium to the far end of the corridor. If he gave himself a few minutes, surely he could come up with an idea.

Maybe he could say he didn't feel well. No, she'd never believe that. And if she did, she'd fuss over him, and she'd tell Margaret, and *she'd* come rushing over and try to baby him. He tossed that idea out immediately. Margaret was a good daughter, but she had an annoying tendency to coddle him.

He couldn't very well claim a family emergency. Millie would see right through him. He could, of course, simply tell the truth. But he knew what Millie would say to that. Frankly, he didn't have the energy to argue with her.

He rounded the corner into the school's main foyer, but when he saw something on the floor in front of the trophy case, he stopped in his tracks. Not some*thing,* he amended silently. Some*one.*

In the murky light and from such a distance, he couldn't tell who lay facedown and unmoving. But before he'd gone even halfway, he recognized LeGrande Macafee's inert body.

Instinct urged him forward. Common sense held him back. All things considered, Fred might be wiser to avoid going near him. But he didn't believe for one minute LeGrande had suddenly decided to take a nap on the cold tile floor.

Maybe he'd had a heart attack. If so, Fred couldn't just leave him lying there, no matter how much he disliked him.

Pulling in a steadying breath, he inched forward and called out softly. "LeGrande? Are you all right?"

No answer.

Fred moved a little closer. "Macafee?"

Nothing. Not even a twitch of his fingers.

Wonderful. Something was horribly wrong. Fred could feel it in his bones. He'd had some experience with unexpected death, and his sixth sense told him LeGrande wouldn't be getting up again. But he couldn't help wondering why *he* had to be the one to find him.

He increased his pace slightly and drew closer still. Immediately, he wished he hadn't. Blood matted LeGrande's hair. His eyes—empty and lifeless—stared at the trophy case on the far wall, and his mouth gaped open.

Fred turned away quickly, but not quickly enough to keep from gagging. Death filled the air. The horror of it wrapped itself around Fred's heart and clawed at his throat. He covered his mouth with one hand and tried to calm his stomach by taking a deep breath, but the sickly-sweet smell nearly suffocated him.

Gulping air through his mouth, he kept his back turned until he regained a bit of control. But the instant he turned for a second look, his stomach lurched again.

The strains of "Don't Get Around Much Anymore" echoed through the corridors from the gymnasium. Laughter and muted conversation ebbed and flowed like the tide. But Fred just stood there, staring at LeGrande. After what felt like an eternity, he made himself move again. Slowly. Even then, his knees threatened to buckle and land him on the floor beside his old nemesis.

Fred supposed he should at least check the man's pulse. There was a chance LeGrande might still be alive. Carefully, he crouched at LeGrande's side and felt his wrist. His skin still felt warm but Fred couldn't pick up a heartbeat. He lowered LeGrande's wrist to the floor again and straightened.

Somewhere in the back of his mind, he knew he was letting too much time pass. He needed to do something, but if the others found out about this, there'd be mass hysteria. He could either let LeGrande lie here and run the risk of someone else stumbling across him, or he could stay and keep watch. But if he did that, and if LeGrande *was* still alive, his inaction might cost the man his life.

That realization galvanized him to action. He couldn't just stand here like an idiot. He had to get to a telephone and call for help. After he'd done that, he could come back and keep watch until help arrived.

Giving the body a wide berth, he started toward the

opposite end of the foyer. Last time he'd been in the school, there'd been a pay phone just around that corner. He just hoped nobody had removed it and that it still worked.

To his dismay, the sound of rapidly approaching footsteps echoed in the distance. Fred listened closely and willed whoever it was to turn a corner and go somewhere else. As if in answer to a prayer, the footsteps slowed.

Instead of turning, they started moving again—straight toward him. Determined to keep whoever it was from stumbling across the grisly scene he'd just left, Fred picked up his pace again.

Before he'd gone even ten feet, a new thought hit him. Maybe he didn't want to meet whoever was in the hallway. Maybe LeGrande's attacker had come back for some reason.

Fred decided not to take any chances. He glanced around quickly, looking for a place to slip out of sight. But the broad foyer with its glittering glass trophy cases didn't provide a single decent hiding place.

Wonderful.

Pulling in a deep breath, he started forward again and started around the corner just as the other set of footsteps reached it. Steeling himself for a fight, Fred held out both hands and caught the other person by the shoulders.

To his surprise, he realized the shoulders belonged to a woman. She let out a frightened shriek and stepped back into the soft glow of an emergency light. Fred took in her wide, frightened eyes and the halo of dark hair around her face. The faint scent of cigarette smoke mingled with her perfume and the smell of wind in her hair.

His heart dropped, but he forced himself to speak. "Mrs. Macafee?"

Stormy nodded, then squinted to see him better. When she realized who he was, she pulled back and frowned. "Oh. It's *you.*"

She tried to step around him, but he caught her shoulders again and held her in place. He couldn't risk her finding LeGrande.

Her frown deepened into an expression of distaste. "What do you think you're doing? Get your hands off me."

Maybe he should have let go, but he didn't. He wouldn't wish a shock like the one he'd just had on anyone, especially the man's wife. "I'm sorry, but—"

Stormy didn't wait for him to finish. Twisting slightly, she used both arms to knock his hands from her shoulders. The look she gave him could have frozen hell over. "I said, get your hands off me."

"Mrs. Macafee. Stop. Please."

She wheeled around to face him. "Why? I need to find my husband."

"I'm afraid there's been some trouble and I need your help." He dug into his pocket and held out a quarter. "I need you to call our sheriff. His name is Enos Asay, and I want you to tell him I said to come over here right away. And tell him to get Doc over here, too."

She narrowed her eyes a little further and held out a hesitant hand for the quarter. "What kind of trouble? Is someone ill?"

Fred could say yes, but he didn't want to actually *lie* to her. "Someone's been hurt."

"Who?" She made a move to leave. "Maybe I can help."

Fred caught her arm again. "Don't. Please."

Confusion filled her eyes for about a second. Realization gradually replaced it. "Is it LeGrande?"

Fully expecting her to make a break for it when he answered, Fred tightened his grip on her arm and nodded slowly. "I'm afraid so. I don't know how badly he's hurt. So, please, call the sheriff and get help."

She shoved him away with more strength than he'd expected from someone so small and raced around the corner before he could stop her.

Trying to ignore the ache in his knees, he ran after her. But every time his feet hit the floor, pain jolted up his legs. He cursed his old body silently. There was a time when he could have run circles around her. Now he had to practically kill himself just to keep up.

She caught sight of LeGrande before he could reach her and let out a scream that must have echoed through the entire school. "Oh, God. LeGrande! *LeGrande?* Are you all right?" Her voice grew louder with each word, and Fred abandoned all hope of keeping the others from finding out.

She made it almost to her husband's side before Fred caught up with her. Desperate to keep her from disturbing the evidence, he snagged her arm and jerked her back a step. "Don't touch anything. We need to get the sheriff over here."

But she'd already gone beyond listening. She pummeled him with her fists, kicked and twisted and fought, and all the while huge heartbreaking tears coursed down her cheeks.

In spite of the blows she landed and the bruises Fred could feel forming, he managed to hold on. He understood the horror and could almost feel her pain. He pulled her gently toward him and tried to comfort her, if only for a moment.

But she didn't want comfort. "Damn you," she shouted and tried to shove him away again. "Let *go* of me."

He couldn't do that. He didn't want her to look at LeGrande too closely. He didn't want to leave her with that image of her husband. "Don't look at him." He kept his voice gentle. Soothing. But he didn't know if she could hear him over the sounds of her own wretched crying.

He raised his voice a notch and tried again, struggling to keep her face turned away from her husband's inert body. "Mrs. Macafee. Stormy. Please, don't look at him."

Strangely, that seemed to reach her somehow. She collapsed against him as violently as she'd fought only a moment before.

Fred stumbled a little, but managed to hold them both upright. "Come with me to call the sheriff."

"I can't. Legrande—"

"The best thing we can do for him right now is to get help." He brushed a lock of hair away from her forehead and looked into her eyes. The anguish there touched him deeply, but he managed to keep his voice steady. "Do you under-stand? We need to call for help."

She nodded slowly. "Yes."

"Good." He wrapped one aching arm around her shoulder and steered her back in the direction they'd come. And he kept up a steady stream of conversation, hoping it would help ground her. "The sheriff is a friend of mine," he said gently. "Actually, he's more like a son to me than a friend. He only lives a few minutes away. And the doctor . . . Well, I've known Doc Huggins for years, too. He's a good man."

She nodded again and shuddered when the remnants of a sob tore through her.

"Is there someone you'd like me to call?" he asked. "Someone who could sit with you until the sheriff can tell us what's going on?"

"I don't know anyone here." Her voice came out soft, nothing more than a whisper.

No, of course she didn't. "My sister's here," he suggested. "I could ask her to stay with you. You may have met her earlier when you and—" He broke off and adjusted to avoid hurting her any more. "When you first got here. I'm sure she'd be glad to do whatever she could."

Stormy shook her head quickly, but didn't answer. In the silence that fell between them, he heard the telltale sounds of people moving about in the hallways.

Voices echoed in the deserted corridors. "Where did it come from?" . . . "Do you see anyone?" . . . "I swear it came from this direction." They sounded close but with the echo Fred couldn't tell where they were.

"We'll have company in a minute," he warned. "Are you going to be okay?"

Stormy nodded, but the effort drained her.

When they reached the pay phone at last, Fred made sure she could stand on her own, dropped a quarter into the coin slot, and dialed Enos's home number quickly.

The phone rang once. Twice. On the third ring, Enos's wife answered. Fred could hear the television playing at what must have been full volume in the background. He held back a sigh of exasperation and raised his voice. "Jessica? It's Fred. Put Enos on the line, would you? It's important."

"Fred?" She didn't sound pleased to hear his voice. No surprise there. She never did. "He's busy. What do you want?"

Fred bit back his irritation. "I need to talk to him."

"Well, he can't come to the phone right now. You'll have to call back later."

"No!" The word exploded from his mouth, echoed off the walls, and stilled the voices of the others. Great. He'd lead them straight to LeGrande this way. Closing his eyes for a second to still his mounting anxiety, he tried again, softer this time. "It's important, Jess. There's trouble. I need him to come to the high school immediately."

"What kind of trouble?"

Lord Almighty, she was an aggravating woman. "For hell's sake," he yelled "would you just put him on the damned phone?" He knew immediately that he'd made a mistake by raising his voice. Jessica sucked in a disapproving breath, and the sound of rapidly approaching footsteps filled the air.

"Who was that?" someone shouted.

"Fred?" Another voice bounced off the walls nearby. "Is that you? What's wrong?"

To his surprise, Stormy pulled herself together, pushed away from the wall, and ran toward the voices. "Somebody help me," she shouted. "Please."

Fred took a step after her, then realized he still had the receiver in his hand. Jessica's voice blared through it into his ear. "What's going on there?"

"Nothing," Fred said. "Everything." While Stormy bolted down the hallway, still shouting for help, he glanced over his shoulder at the corner that protected LeGrande from view. "Tell Enos to get here immediately. *Immediately,* Jessica. I don't care what he's doing. There's been a murder."

Without waiting for her response, he slammed down the receiver and hurried after Stormy. She started around the far corner, stopped suddenly, and reached toward someone Fred couldn't see. Fred picked up his pace and put a few more lockers and another classroom behind him while she cried and waved her arms around, pointing first at him, then in the direction of the foyer.

Jeremiah Hunt's lean profile appeared, then Oliver Wellington's stubby one. Burl and Coralee. Millie. Al. Fred caught a glimpse of Percy Neuswander's wheelchair and what must have been Ardella's shadow against the far wall. Iris Cavalier stood a little to one side, clutching Yale's arm and listening with obvious distaste to the woman who'd taken her place at LeGrande's side.

Fire shot through Fred's knees. In fact, every inch of his body ached. But he kept going.

Thankfully, Stormy looked back and saw him coming. She stopped talking and buried her head in the shoulder of the person standing closest to her—Thea Griffin. Well, good. Thea could comfort her while Fred explained what happened.

Perspiration dampened his shirt, and the stagnant air made it difficult to breathe. He drew up to the crowd and gave himself a second to catch his breath before he explained.

Percy Neuswander didn't wait. He took charge as he always had. "What in the hell is going on here?"

Fred gulped air and gestured for Percy to give him a second.

But before he could speak, Stormy pushed away from Thea and pointed a trembling finger at him. "Somebody stop that man," she shouted. "He killed my husband."

five

Stormy's accusation caught Fred completely off guard. While the whole blasted lot of his former classmates started babbling, his breath stopped coming. A moment later it started up again—painfully.

"My husband is dead," Stormy sobbed, "over there . . . in the foyer. And *he* killed him."

Percy wheeled himself around and started down the hall. Jeremiah hurried after him. Oliver snagged Fred's arms and tried to pin them behind his back.

But Fred had had enough. He jerked away from Oliver and roared, "Stop!" He used his best voice—the one that had always frozen his kids in their tracks. It had the same effect now.

Percy screeched to a halt. Jeremiah spun around, open-mouthed, to stare at him.

"LeGrande is either badly hurt or dead," he admitted. "But I didn't do it."

The babble started up again—some of it disbelieving, some of it reassuring. He held up both hands and raised his voice again. "Be quiet. All of you. I've already called the sheriff. He's on his way. For now, unless one of you is a doctor who can help LeGrande if he's still alive, we all stay right here."

Percy scowled deeply. He never had liked having his authority threatened. "I'm going to check on him."

Fred took another couple of steps away from Oliver and

firmed up his stance. "No, you're not. We're not going to disturb anything until the sheriff gets here."

Respect tinged a few faces. Fear a few others. Suspicion lit the rest.

Fred tried not to notice it. "Percy, Jeremiah, why don't you stand guard at either end of the foyer. But don't go near him." For want of a better person, he nodded toward Al. "You wait at the front door to let Enos in when he gets here."

Percy and Jeremiah hesitated, but Al started away without argument. At least *someone* paid attention to him.

"We need to make sure nobody disturbs anything around the body," Fred insisted. "If you don't want to do it, I will."

That galvanized Percy to action. He nodded once at Jeremiah and started giving directions as if Fred needed an interpreter. "You take the north end, Jeremiah. I'll take the south. Don't let anybody in until the sheriff gets here. Oliver, you stay here and keep everything under control. And Fred—" He broke off and sent Fred a warning with his eyes. "Don't move until we figure out what's going on."

Fred knew how bullheaded Percy would get if he challenged him, but he refused to let the man treat him like a criminal. "Meanwhile," he pointed out rationally, "whoever did this to LeGrande is getting away."

Percy's eyes narrowed. "So you want us to let you chase after him? Not a chance. If you *did* kill LeGrande, I'm not giving you a chance to run off."

Fred's knees throbbed so painfully he didn't think he could run anywhere. "For the record, and for the last time, I didn't kill LeGrande. I found him. I called the sheriff, for hell's sake."

Someone in the back of the crowd called out, "You fought with him earlier. We all heard you threaten him."

"I won't deny that," Fred said. "But that doesn't mean I killed him. You heard what he said—he came here tonight to set things straight. And I'll bet a month's retirement check I'm not the only one of us he wanted to set them straight with."

Millie, bless her heart, planted herself beside him and scowled at the whole group. "He's right. Half the class had trouble with LeGrande of one sort or another." She sent Stormy an apologetic smile, but she didn't let up. "What about you, Iris? And Coralee? You dated him for a while, didn't you?"

Coralee gripped her cane so tightly her knuckles turned white. "That was over a long time ago. A *long* time ago. And there were no hard feelings between us—ever."

Burl flushed a dangerous shade of red. Fred could see that even in the dim lighting. "My wife had nothing to do with this." The words came out low and tightly controlled. Almost ominous.

"I didn't say she did," Millie assured him. "I'm only trying to point out—"

"You're trying to throw us offtrack." Oliver puffed his chest in an effort to look intimidating.

It didn't work. Millie pulled herself together and went after him. "For heaven's sake, Oliver. Use your head. Fred wouldn't be stupid enough to kill LeGrande—*especially* after he had an argument with him in front of all of us."

Faint praise, but Fred would take whatever he could get.

Someone agreed with her. A few others looked a little less ready to lynch him. One or two started speculating about the others.

Fred held up both hands, trying to get their attention. "Listen to me for a minute," he demanded. "Whoever did this isn't necessarily one of us." That brought the house down, and it took several minutes to get everyone quieted enough for him to continue. "There was someone else here tonight. A young man—probably in his early fifties. Did anyone see him?"

Another murmur arose from the crowd and everyone spent a few minutes consulting with the people closest to them. But nobody volunteered anything.

"He and LeGrande had an argument in the men's room," Fred prompted.

Nothing.

"LeGrande called him by name if that helps." *Something* certainly had to.

"This is ridiculous," Yale Cavalier snapped. "Why are we even listening to him? There wasn't any young man here. He's making it up. Everyone knows how much Fred hated LeGrande."

The accusation wore on Fred's already frazzled nerves, and his temper finally snapped. But before he could say a word, the sound of quick, heavy footsteps coming down the hallway reached him.

Fred would recognize them anywhere, and he didn't think he'd ever been so glad to hear them. A moment later Enos strode into view, his sandy eyebrows knit in consternation, his face set in the rigid lines that showed he meant business. Deputy Grady Hatch walked beside him, towering over him by a good six inches. The expression on his thin face matched Enos's. All business.

Good. They could use someone with a clear head.

Fred stepped forward to meet them, but Enos waved him back. He pulled his battered black cowboy hat from his head and stepped in front of the group. "Apparently, you've all heard what happened. I'd like all of you to go back into the gymnasium with my deputy and wait there. We'll want to talk to each of you for a few minutes before we let you go home."

"Is he dead?" Oliver demanded.

Enos looked a little surprised by the question. "Yes, I'm afraid he is."

Stormy let out another scream and sagged against Thea. But this time Fred couldn't work up nearly as much sympathy for her.

Enos slanted a curious glance at her.

"The dead man's wife," Fred whispered.

Enos's face softened slightly. He motioned for Grady to help her. "Mrs. Macafee. I'm sorry. If you'll go with Deputy Hatch, he'll see that you have a place to lie down."

She shook her head almost wildly. "I don't want to lie down. I want my husband's murderer arrested."

A cold knot of apprehension filled Fred's stomach, but he pushed it away. Surely she didn't still think he'd done it. Not after everything he and Millie had said.

Enos put a gentle hand on her shoulder. "I understand, ma'am. And we'll do everything we can to find the person who did this."

Just as she had with Fred earlier, she shoved Enos's hand away. "You don't have to *find* anyone, Sheriff. He's standing right here."

Enos looked confused. He cocked an eyebrow at her. "Ma'am?"

"That man right there," she shouted, pointing at Fred again. "Fred Vickery killed my husband."

Fred followed Enos into the principal's office, waited until Enos shut the door behind them, and let out a long sigh of relief.

Enos dropped his set of master keys onto the desk and raised his sandy eyebrows. "Sounds like it's been one hell of a night."

"It has," Fred agreed. He nodded toward one of the chairs in front of the desk. "Mind if I sit down"

"Go ahead." Enos perched on one corner of the desk and waited until Fred had made himself reasonably comfortable. "Now, do you want to tell me what the hell is going on here?"

"I think I know who killed him."

Enos let out a heavy sigh and rubbed his face with one big open palm. "Why doesn't that surprise me?"

Fred didn't bother responding to that. He didn't have the time or the energy to banter with Enos tonight. "I overheard LeGrande arguing with a young man maybe an hour before he was killed."

Enos flicked a surprised glance at him. "A young man?"

"About your age," Fred clarified. "LeGrande called him Roger. I don't know his last name, but I can give you a description."

Enos lowered his hat to the desk and studied Fred for a

moment. "I suppose you just happened to be standing there—"

"Sitting."

Enos scowled. "All right. Sitting. And I suppose you weren't *trying* to overhear their argument."

Fred didn't need Enos's sarcasm, and Enos didn't have time to dish it out—not if he was going to catch Roger before he disappeared. "No," he snapped, "I wasn't trying to overhear their argument. I just happened to be sitting inside a stall in the men's room—"

Enos interrupted him with a laugh. "Good billy hell, Fred. You don't stop at *anything*, do you?"

Fred scowled at him. He'd had a long, hard night already, and he didn't find Enos's comments even slightly amusing. "Do you want to hear what I have to say, or are you going to make jokes?"

Enos sobered instantly and held up both hands in surrender. "Of course I want to hear what you have to say."

That made Fred feel a little better, but not much. "I was already in the men's room when they came in," he said, just to clear up any misunderstanding Enos might still have. "Naturally, I hesitated to let them know I was there—"

"Naturally."

"They were obviously upset, and I didn't want to get in the middle of anything."

"You heard what they were arguing about?"

"I didn't hear how it started," he admitted. "But this Roger whoever shoved LeGrande around a bit and said some pretty harsh things about his wife."

Enos leaned forward and rested his elbows on his knees. "He hit LeGrande?"

"He shoved him a couple of times. Sent him into the sink or the wall. But LeGrande *did* hit him."

Concern tugged at the corners of Enos's mouth. "Did they see you?"

"No."

"Are you sure?"

"I'm positive," Fred assured him. "I was inside the stall."

"That doesn't mean anything. They might have noticed your feet."

"They didn't."

"How do you know?"

"Because." Fred flushed slightly. "Because I didn't have my feet on the floor."

Enos's lips twitched, as if Fred had said something amusing. "I see. Where were they?"

"On the door."

Enos chuckled and rubbed his forehead with the fingers of one hand. "I'm getting mental images I'm not sure I want."

"For Pete's sake," Fred snapped. "I propped them on the door because I didn't want LeGrande to see me."

Enos stopped grinning and slanted a glance at him. "Why not?"

Fred drew in a steadying breath and shoved his hands into his pockets. "Are you going to ask any questions about the murder, or are you more fascinated by my feet?"

"Humor me," Enos said. "Why didn't you want him to see you?"

Fred didn't want to tell him, but he'd find out soon enough. The building was full of people who'd love to fill him in. "He said some things about Phoebe when he first got here. All a pack of lies. But, then, that's nothing new for LeGrande."

Enos's expression sobered. "What did he say?"

"It's not important," Fred said quickly, and immediately regretted it. Not only did he sound as if he had something to hide, but everyone at the reunion had overheard their first argument. He worked up a thin smile. "He claimed she'd—" He broke off, unable to get the words out. He pulled in a steadying breath and tried again. "He insinuated that they'd had a romantic relationship."

Enos's eyes clouded. "Phoebe? I don't believe it."

"Neither do I. But that just shows you what kind of man LeGrande Macafee was. I lost my temper and punched him."

Enos ground to a halt and rubbed his face again. "Tell me you didn't say what I thought you said."

"You'd have done the same thing," Fred insisted. "Any man would have."

Enos shook his head sadly. "That's why you didn't want him to see you inside the stall."

"That's why," Fred admitted. He told Enos everything else he could remember, gave Enos a description of Roger, and leaned back in his chair.

Enos scribbled something in a small notebook, then dragged his palm across his face again. "All right. But I have one last question. Where does your second argument with LeGrande fit into this picture?"

Fred's stomach lurched. How had Enos heard about that? Nobody had seen them. Nobody had overheard them. At least, no one Fred knew about. He pulled in a steadying breath and let it out again slowly. No sense denying it, he supposed. "They'd both left the lavatory, and I was getting ready to leave. But LeGrande came back for some reason, and that's when I bumped into him."

"So you argued with him *after* this Roger person did. And you hit him again. Why?"

"He'd been drinking, and he always got obnoxious when he drank."

"So, you hit him because he'd had a drink or two?"

Fred glared at him. "Why are you grilling me? I didn't kill the son of a bitch. You should be out looking for this Roger character."

Enos scowled at him. "Don't start with me, Fred. I know how to do my job. I'll find him and I'll talk to him."

"Talk?" Fred couldn't believe his ears. "I've practically handed you the solution to the case on a silver platter—"

"You may have," Enos admitted, "but before I go charging off after him, I need to ask you a few more questions. Like why is Mrs. Macafee so convinced you killed her husband?"

"Hell if I know," Fred snapped. "I was on my way to call you when I ran in to her. I tried to calm her down and keep her away from the body. I didn't think she needed to see him like that."

"That's all?" Enos looked faintly suspicious. He tucked his pencil behind his ear and readjusted himself on the desk. "Did anyone else see this Roger around?"

"No one admits it if they did."

"But you don't believe them?"

"It stands to reason," Fred said. "If someone overheard me arguing with LeGrande the second time, they *must* have seen Roger, too. A few good questions . . ."

Enos narrowed his eyes and wagged a finger near his face. "Let's get one thing straight, my friend. I'll ask the questions in this case. You're not doing a damned thing."

His reaction irritated Fred. "Did I say—"

Enos held up both hands to block his words. "You don't have to say. I know what you're thinking. You always convince yourself you need to ask a couple of innocent questions, and before I know it, you're up to your neck in trouble."

"Believe me—" Fred began again.

But Enos wouldn't let him even finish one sentence. "Listen to me, Fred. This is important." He leaned closer and held Fred's gaze with his own. "You're already up to your neck in this one. You can't step out of line even once."

Fred didn't like the sound of that. "You don't honestly believe I killed him."

"Of course, I don't. But you're lucky. If I didn't know you so well, I'd probably already have you down at the station."

"Ridiculous."

"You had two fights with a man who was murdered less than an hour later," Enos reminded him. "*And* someone found you hurrying away from the scene of the crime."

"I didn't kill him. If I did, wouldn't I have blood all over me?"

"Not necessarily. Doc says his skull was crushed, but there's no evidence of splattering." Enos pushed to his feet, worked his hat into place over his thinning hair, and tried to smile. But his efforts fell flat. He looked miserable. "Just go home and stay out of trouble so we can convince the prosecuting attorney that you're innocent."

Fred stomach's knotted. He told himself he had nothing to worry about. After all, they played out the same scenario every time trouble hit Cutler. Fred offered helpful suggestions. Enos ignored them. But in the end Fred was always right. And Enos always came around—eventually.

As if Enos could read his mind, he fixed him with another meaningful glance. "I'm warning you right now, Fred. Everybody's going to be pushing me for a solution on this one. We've got an old man murdered in cold blood. Cases like this one work up a lot of public sympathy. Everybody's going to want the murderer caught—and soon."

"Then go catch him."

"I intend to. But you know how things work. I can't give you preferential treatment, no matter how much I might be tempted to. I know you're innocent, and you know you're innocent. But you sure as hell look guilty. And if I so much as blink wrong, they'll have my butt in a sling."

Fred knew that. He understood it. But he didn't like hearing it one bit. He knew Enos could put personal feelings aside when his job demanded it. He'd seen him do it before. He just never thought *he'd* be on this side of the line.

Enos crossed to the door, pulled it open, and waited for Fred to stand. "Go home," he said again. "Spend time with Maggie and your grandkids. Work in your yard. Watch television. Walk around the lake all day if you have to, but keep your nose out of the investigation."

Fred nodded. He couldn't do anything else. He stepped through the door and listened to it click shut behind him.

He walked away slowly, dimly aware that Millie and Al waited for him a few feet away. But he couldn't shake the anger that built slowly within him. Just as he'd always done, LeGrande Macafee had landed Fred in a pile of trouble. And this time Fred would have to be very careful how he got himself out.

six

In the relative cool of early morning, Fred walked slowly along the path that followed the shore of Spirit Lake. A slight breeze fanned the spruce and aspen trees around him and rustled the leaves of the undergrowth lining the trail. The sun hadn't yet climbed over the mountains behind him, but the sky had grown light enough to expose the uneven ground.

Usually Fred loved mornings like this one. Walking around the lake started his day off right, cleared away the cobwebs in his mind, and got his blood pumping. Today, with every muscle in his body aching and his mind reeling, he felt as if Mother Nature had decided to play a cruel joke on him by letting the sun shine in spite of last night's turmoil.

He hadn't slept a wink all night. He'd escaped into his bedroom the instant he got home, but only because he wanted to avoid discussing the murder with Millie and Al. Millie had ranted about it all the way home, and her anger had fed his own. But he knew getting angry was the worst thing he could do under the circumstances.

And Al . . . Al had babbled endlessly about Phoebe and LeGrande, as if he'd taken that ridiculous, ugly story seriously. But Fred hadn't wanted to hear anything Al had to say. Not one stupid word.

So he'd tossed and turned, almost drifting off several times but waking up in a sweat as LeGrande Macafee moved in and out of his dreams. Phoebe had been part of the nightmares, too. He'd sensed her there, even though he couldn't see her. Once, she'd started to materialize for him. But she'd turned into Stormy Macafee, pointing an accusing finger and shouting that she'd seen Fred commit the murder.

He hadn't wanted to close his eyes after that. But his thoughts had tormented him even though he'd stayed awake. So, the minute the sky started to lighten, he'd climbed out of bed, thrown on his clothes, and left the house.

Somewhere nearby, a chimpmunk set up an angry squawk and sent startled birds winging their way into the morning sky. A boat on the lake putted slowly across the water, no doubt carrying someone toward a favorite fishing hole—someone who hadn't been accused of killing an old nemesis. Someone whose childhood friends hadn't turned on him. Someone whose thoughts weren't tormented by the idea of LeGrande Macafee manhandling his wife.

Sighing heavily, Fred pushed past an overgrown choke-cherry bush. Instead of continuing along the path, he stopped and gazed at the water lapping gently against the shore.

He couldn't believe what a turn his life had taken. One minute, everything had been normal. The next, he'd been defending his wife's honor. And before he knew what happened, he'd been sitting in the hot seat, trying to clear his good name.

A bitter laugh left his throat as he stepped off the path and settled himself on a boulder near the water's edge. The boat's engine stilled, and nature's silence engulfed him again. He turned his face toward the sky and watched the rising sun paint the clouds overhead pink, lavender, and pale orange. Beautiful. Just the way he liked it.

Within the hour the temperature would begin to rise again and the day would grow uncomfortably hot. Within weeks the glory of summer would fade and autumn would tint the leaves of the forest. Within months snow would blanket everything in sight. The seasons passed too quickly these days. Life passed too quickly.

How many more summers would Fred spend along the shores of the lake? How many more walks would he take before time passed its relentless hand across his path?

Making an effort to put such morbid thoughts out of his mind, he reached for a pebble and sent it skipping across the lake. One, two, three skips, then the stone sank to the bottom. Letting out another deep sigh, Fred looked for another stone. This one only skipped twice before it sank. He couldn't even skip rocks anymore.

"I've always wanted to know how to do that."

The voice startled him. He dropped the pebble he'd been about to throw and shifted on the rock toward the sound. To his surprise, Millie stood on the path directly behind him. Weariness had etched wrinkles into her face he hadn't noticed before, and dark circles gave her eyes a haunted look.

Fred figured he probably looked very much the same. Old. Tired. Defeated. "What are you doing?" he demanded. "Following me?"

"Yes." For an instant, he caught a glimpse of the young girl she'd once been—the one who'd tagged behind him like a shadow. The one who'd been convinced he'd do something exciting and that she'd miss out on it if she let him get too far away. In the next breath the girl disappeared again. "We need to talk."

"There's nothing to talk about," he muttered.

She ignored him, took an unsteady step from the path, and used her arms to steady herself as she closed the distance between them. But she didn't speak again until she'd joined him on the boulder, close enough to brush against him when she moved. "What really happened between you and LeGrande last night?"

The question irritated him. "Why? Are you trying to figure out whether or not I killed him?"

"No." Millie touched a tentative hand to his knee. "I

know you didn't kill him, Fred. But I also know how upset you were by what he said."

Fred didn't want to talk about that.

"So . . . ?" she prodded. "What did he say to you in the hallway? Why did you hit him a second time?"

If he could tell anyone, he could tell Millie. She and Phoebe had been close friends from girlhood. She wouldn't believe LeGrande's claims. But he couldn't make himself repeat the ugly story aloud. Doing so might make it real.

He glanced away and fixed his gaze on the lake. "It's not important."

"Nonsense." Millie clicked her tongue and sighed. "I know you too well to believe that. He must have said *something*."

Fred didn't confirm or deny that. Instead, he sent another pebble skittering across the water's surface.

Thankfully, Millie stayed silent for a few seconds. She drew her knees up to her chest and wrapped her arms around them. But just as Fred started to believe she'd let the subject drop, she spoke again. "It was about Phoebe, wasn't it?"

Fred's heartbeat slowed and dread filled him. But he still couldn't make himself admit it.

"I knew it." Millie practically crowed in triumph, but she sobered again instantly. "What did he tell you?"

Fred tried to think of some way to protect the truth without actually lying. But his mind remained a stubborn blank.

"It had to be something about them. About when they were dating."

Fred reared back as if she'd hit him. "Dating? They never dated."

Millie's smile faded and her eyes clouded. "You didn't know?"

"Know what?"

"That they dated for a while?"

"It's not true," he insisted. "If LaGrande told you that, he was lying."

Millie shifted on the boulder so she could face him. "LeGrande didn't tell me," she said softly. "Phoebe did."

Fred's heart stopped beating altogether. Or maybe he only thought it did because his stomach lurched into his chest and flopped around. He forced himself to speak around the lump that followed it into his throat. "What?"

"They didn't go out for very long," Millie assured him quickly. "And it was over long before you even knew she was alive."

Nonsense. Fred had always known Phoebe was alive. She and Millie had been friends, for heaven's sake.

"In fact," Millie went on, oblivious to the damage her words were doing, "they were dating about the same time you and Thea went together."

The sun suddenly seemed too warm. The boulder beneath him too hard. The loamy soil of the lake shore too pungent. He thought he might be sick to his stomach, but he forced himself to remind her of something she'd apparently forgotten. "That's ridiculous. Phoebe didn't even like Le-Grande."

"No, she didn't . . . after they broke up."

It wasn't true. It couldn't be. Surely, in the forty-seven years they'd been married, Phoebe would have said something. "If that were true," he challenged, "why didn't I know about it?"

"Because it didn't matter at the time. If you'll remember, you only had eyes for Thea."

He shook his head. "No. Phoebe would have told me about it. Later. We didn't keep secrets from each other."

Millie reached a hand toward him, but Fred pulled back quickly. He didn't want her to pat him like a child. She dropped her hand onto her lap and knit her fingers together. "She didn't lie to you, Fred. She just didn't tell you one little thing about herself. She knew how you were. She knew how hot your temper was. You and LeGrande didn't like each other anyway, so what good would it have done to tell you?"

Nonsense. Fred didn't want to listen to anything more. He pushed to his feet, but his knees had grown stiff and he straightened slowly. "You don't know what you're talking about."

Millie scrambled to her feet faster than Fred had and glared back, just like she'd always done when they were younger. "Yes, I do," she insisted. "I know a lot more about it than you do."

That didn't mean a whole lot. She had to know only one thing to know more than he did. But Fred didn't admit that aloud. Nor did he ask if Phoebe had ever had second thoughts about dating him, though the question raised itself in his mind. Instead, he snorted a response and started back toward the trail.

"Why do you have to be stubborn?" Millie shouted after him.

Fred didn't answer. He just kept walking, determined to ignore her and trying desperately to push his own doubts away.

He wanted to believe that Millie's memory was playing tricks on her, but he couldn't delude himself that far. He might protest aloud, but he couldn't ignore the truth. Still, that didn't mean he had to talk about it.

"Dammit, Fred. Quit running away."

Fred didn't think he'd ever heard Millie swear before. Not once in seventy-two years. In spite of his resolve to get away, he stopped and turned to face her. "I'm not running away."

"Yes, you are. I know how upset you must have been by what LeGrande said last night—"

She didn't know. She couldn't even begin to imagine.

"—but you have to remember, no matter *what* he said to you later, no matter what you're not telling me, Phoebe loved you."

Tears stung his eyes. He averted his gaze and blinked rapidly, hoping to get rid of them before Millie noticed.

"You had nearly fifty years together," she reminded him gently. "Don't let LeGrande destroy even one minute of that time for you." She put a hand on his chin and pulled his face around so she could look at him. "If you do, he will have won."

Her understanding nearly did him in. He struggled to hold back his emotions, but it was a losing battle, and he knew it. He hated knowing how much LeGrande's cruel words had disturbed him, how close he'd come to believing them, even if he claimed not to. He hated realizing he'd let LeGrande raise doubts in his mind about the woman he'd loved with all his heart.

Thankfully, Millie decided to let up on him. "So, are you going to finish your walk, or are you coming back home with me?"

He shook his head, cleared his throat, and managed to sound fairly normal when he answered. "I'm not ready to go home yet. I think I'll stay out here awhile longer."

She patted his arm once more, and started away. "Don't stay too long. I'll have breakfast ready when you get back."

He watched her until she disappeared around a bend in the trail, then stuffed his hands into his pockets and turned his face to the sky again. Surprisingly, he felt a little better—about Phoebe, anyway. Now, if he could put his other problem to rest.

As he'd done repeatedly during the night, he told himself not to worry. Enos would find LeGrande's killer. Fred just hoped he'd do it soon.

He started walking again and sent something scurrying through the bushes a few feet to his left. He pulled in a deep breath of fresh mountain air and tried to still his rampaging thoughts. But images of LeGrande lying on the cold floor and of the wound that had caused his death flashed through his mind with every step.

Again, he tried to force the images away. Only frustration would come from thinking about it and he couldn't do anything but wait.

Fred hated waiting. He'd never been good at relying on someone else to solve his problems, and doing so now wouldn't be easy. But this time he had no choice.

As the sun climbed higher in the morning sky, he rounded

a few more curves and passed the place where the path fell away sharply to the lake. Usually, he walked all the way to the far edge of Doc Huggins's land before doubling back and heading home. But that meant he had to cross Summer Dey's property—something he didn't want to do today. He didn't want to chance running into her.

Not that Summer was a bad sort. She meant well, Fred supposed. But she drove him to distraction with her talk of auras and past lives and claims of psychic ability. Nothing she said ever made a lick of sense to Fred. It was all just a bunch of hogwash. But that didn't stop her from saying it. And Fred was in no mood to hear it today. He'd turn around and head home well before he reached her property line.

Feeling a bit more in control, he rounded another bend in the path. But when he saw a black-clad figure on the trail ahead of him, he stopped cold.

Summer Dey. Good hell.

She smiled when she saw him, but her expression held no surprise. In fact, she looked as if she'd been expecting him.

Of course she had. Fred had walked this trail at the same time every morning for twenty years or more. If anyone ever wanted to find him, they knew where to look. But Summer always acted as if she'd accomplished something spectacular by anticipating his arrival.

Today was no exception. She swept both arms out and let the breeze catch the gauzy material of the day's costume. Black, of course. She always wore black. Said she had to keep her spirits down to create the hideous paintings she called art. Today her outfit consisted of tiny black shorts, thick black boots, and a filmy blouse with long, sweeping sleeves.

"Fred. I knew you'd come."

Amazing. He wished *he'd* had a psychic flash to warn him she'd waylay him so far from her own property.

She brushed a lock of her straight blond hair over her shoulder and took a step toward him. "You're in trouble again."

"Did you figure that out by reading my mind, or was it the

look on my face?" He didn't even try to keep the sarcasm from his voice.

As usual, Summer didn't notice it. Or she pretended not to. She smiled gently. "My spirit guides told me during the night."

"Well, they certainly keep up with the news and the gossip."

Her smile faded. "The trouble isn't with you, but it's all around you. There's darkness. Clouds. Lies and hidden truths and misunderstandings."

She might not have known LeGrande, but she certainly had him pegged.

"You must unravel the secrets." Her voice dropped to a stage whisper. "You'll find the truth, but it will be a difficult path."

He shook his head. "Not this time. I'm staying out of it."

"Oh, but you can't." She sounded urgent. "There are souls waiting to help you."

"They'll have to wait a long time. I'm not getting involved."

She slanted a curious glance at him. "Why do you resist the truth? Is it so difficult for you to believe there are spirits around us who want to help? Or are you uncomfortable because you *know* they're here?"

She'd left out a third possibility—that the whole thing was utter nonsense. But Fred didn't mention it. He didn't want to encourage her.

She held out one hand and showed him two small stones resting on her palm. "These are for you."

He cocked an eyebrow at her.

"Gemstones," she said, as if that explained everything.

"Very nice." He didn't know what else to say.

She pushed her hand toward him again, silently urging the rocks at him. "They contain healing properties," she said when he made no move to take them. "Powers directly from the earth."

Fred held back a groan of dismay and stuffed both hands into his pockets. Of all the silly notions . . .

"Unikite for balancing the emotional body," she said, rubbing her thumb over a splotchy green-and-brown stone. She smiled again and moved her thumb to the pale pink stone lying beside it. "And the rose quartz will restore harmony to your mind and help you find peace in your relationships."

Fred shook his head and took a step backward. "That's nice," he muttered, "but I'm not interested."

Summer let out a long-suffering sigh, but she didn't put the rocks away. "You need them."

If he wanted to carry pebbles around with him, he could find a million of them along the shores of the lake. "Look, Summer," he began with as much patience as he could muster.

But she didn't let him finish. "You're troubled. You need to restore harmony and balance to your relationship with Phoebe."

How in the hell had she heard about *that*? Gossip always raced through Cutler with mind-boggling speed, but this time they'd outdone themselves. "My relationship with Phoebe is just fine," he insisted.

She shook her head gently and tilted it to one side. Her eyes glazed over and she swept her arms in front of her, closing her hand over the stones so she wouldn't drop them. "She's unsettled," she said at last. "She knows you're worried."

Fred had tolerated a lot from Summer over the years, but he wouldn't permit her to degrade Phoebe's memory. "Put your damned rocks away." His voice came out sharp. Harsh. He didn't care.

Summer's eyes widened in surprise and a flush spread across her pale, freckled face.

A flash of guilt unsettled him, but he forced it away. "I don't want your rocks. I don't want to hear your supernatural gibberish. And I won't allow you to use my wife to amuse yourself."

She looked horrified. "But I—"

"Enough," he shouted, pivoting away from her. Big

mistake. Pain shot through his knees and he nearly lost his balance.

Summer ran toward him and put one arm around him to steady him.

He jerked away from her touch. "I don't need you to hold me up. I'm not *that* old."

Blessedly, she dropped her arms to her side. But, to his surprise, a delighted smile curved her lips. "Oh, I *do* like you, Fred. Even if you are an old grouch."

In all the years he'd known her, he'd never heard her say anything so . . . *normal*. In spite of his annoyance, an answering smile tugged at his mouth. He refused to give in to it and tried instead of look stern and disapproving. "If you like me so much, why do you keep pestering me?"

She laughed aloud. A normal woman's laugh. "*Because* I like you." Her smile faded slowly and her eyes darkened to a deep shade of blue that matched the summer sky. "You remind me of my father."

Before he could react, she took his hand and pressed the stones into it. He thought he caught a glimmer of moisture in her eyes, but he couldn't be sure. She ducked off the trail and ran into the forest with her sleeves trailing behind her.

Fred told himself to say something—*anything*—but he honestly didn't know what to say. He'd asked himself a thousand times why Summer wouldn't leave him alone, but he'd never in his wildest dreams imagined she felt like that.

He stared down at the stones she'd left in his hand. A moment ago he would have tossed them into the bushes. Now he slipped them into his pocket and turned toward home. He'd been right about her all along. She wasn't a bad sort, and she really did mean well. She just had an odd way of going about it.

seven

Sighing with contentment, Fred helped himself to another slice of bacon and heaped a second spoonful of
scrambled eggs on his plate. At least one good thing had
come out of this mess. Millie, bless her, had fixed him
breakfast—a *real* breakfast. The kind their mother used to
make. Eggs and bacon and fried potatoes, with toast and
orange juice thrown in for good measure. And coffee. Real
coffee, not that decaffeinated swill Doc Huggins expected
Fred to drink.

Fred didn't get meals like this every day. Ever since that
one tiny episode with his heart—nothing more than a blip,
really—Doc Huggins had watched his diet like a hawk.
Worse, he'd enlisted Margaret's help to keep Fred away
from cholesterol, sodium and caffeine. Nothing but a bunch
of hogwash if you asked Fred. But nobody asked him.

On the other side of the table, Al fussed with a single
piece of toast and a minuscule dab of potatoes. But Millie
ate everything with enthusiasm. A woman after Fred's own
heart.

Thankfully, neither of them had said a word about the
murder since Fred came back inside. And Fred wanted to
keep it that way. There wasn't a blasted thing he could do
about it, and he didn't intend to spend all morning talking
about it.

As if he could read Fred's mind, Al pushed away his plate
and hooked his thumbs in the waistband of his pants. "I

don't suppose we'll be having the banquet tonight, what with everything that's happened."

Millie paused with her coffee cup halfway to her lips. "No, I don't suppose we will." She sipped carefully and lowered the cup to the table again. "I could call Ardella to find out."

Now *there* was an idea. Call Ardella and let her pump them for information. Or . . . Fred bit back a smile. Or they could find out what she knew. Unless Ardella had changed overnight, she'd be more than willing to talk.

He lifted one shoulder in a casual shrug. "You could, I suppose."

"She'll want to gossip," Al warned.

Millie sent him a satisfied smile and pushed away from the table. "Of course she will. Why else do you think I'm calling?"

Fred shouldn't have been surprised, he supposed. Millie always had been sharp.

Not Al, though. He scowled in confusion. "You *want* to talk to her about Fred?"

"No." Millie sounded exasperated, and with good reason. "And I'm not going to. I want to hear what she has to say about the other people who were there."

Al leaned back in his seat and scratched his head. "Maybe she won't tell you."

Poor dumb Al. Fred took a bracing sip of coffee and tried to explain. "Have you ever known Ardella to keep her mouth shut if she knew something about someone?"

"Nooo," Al admitted slowly. "But you're the one Mrs. Macafee accused of murdering LeGrande."

"But I didn't do it. Someone else did." He turned his attention to Millie. "I'd like to know if anyone else saw the young man who fought with LeGrande in the men's room. Roger Whoever."

Nodding, Millie ran one finger down the list of numbers Fred had pinned to the bulletin board beside the phone. "I'll do my best. Anything else?"

"It would be nice to know who else had trouble with

LeGrande—especially if it happened more recently than fifty years ago."

She sent him a sideways glance. "Besides Iris?"

"Besides Iris." He sipped again and leaned back in his seat. "Of course, it might be nice to know more about LeGrande and Iris's divorce. And about his marriage to the new Mrs. Macafee. Something's not right there."

Al looked from Fred to Millie and back again. "What about Jeremiah?"

Fred lowered his cup to the table. "What about him?"

"I don't know," Al said with a shrug. "But they did work together for a while."

Fred flicked a surprised glance at Millie. She looked as startled as he felt. He turned a smile back toward Al. "How did you know that?"

"He told me. Last night. You know, Fred, if you'd just talk to people—"

Fred didn't want or need Al's commentary on his social skills. He pushed his cup a little farther away and rested his elbows on the table. "What else did Jeremiah say?"

"Not much," Al admitted. "Just that he worked for LeGrande. But he didn't seem really happy to see LeGrande walk in, if you know what I mean." He leaned back in his seat and laced his hands over his stomach.

Millie nodded eagerly. "He called LeGrande a lowlife last night—remember?"

"I remember," Fred said. "I didn't think anything of it at the time. I just assumed Jeremiah remembered LeGrande from school. He *was* a lowlife."

Scowling in thought, Millie moved away from the telephone and back toward the table. "Do you think there's something else going on?"

Fred slanted a glance at Al. "Did he say why he quit?"

"Just that he finally got fed up."

"Fed up with what?" Fred prodded.

Al's brows knit in the center of his forehead. "I don't know. He didn't say."

"Did he say how long ago he quit?"

Al shook his head slowly, trying to remember. "I don't think so."

"If anyone knows," Millie said firmly, "Ardella will. I'm calling her."

Fred caught her hand and stopped her halfway back to the phone. "Just keep the conversation casual. I don't want anyone to think I'm behind this."

"For heaven's sake, Fred. How stupid do you think I am?"

"I don't think you're stupid, but I've got to be careful. I can't afford to have Enos think I'm asking any questions."

She waved his concern away with her free hand. "Don't worry. Ardella won't suspect a thing."

Fred wished he could believe that, but he couldn't rid himself of the nagging worry. He let go of Millie's hand and nodded her toward the telephone. But before she could lift the receiver from the hook, a car door slammed in the driveway outside and running footsteps started toward the back door.

"It's Margaret," he whispered. "Sit down. I don't want her to know anything about this."

Without a word, Millie hurried back to the table once more and slipped into her seat.

"She'll have to know," Al argued.

"Not if I can help it," Fred vowed. "Promise me, Al. Not a word about LeGrande or the murder while she's here."

Al didn't look convinced. "Don't know how you're going to keep it from her," he muttered. "The whole town'll be talking about it."

"Maybe so," Fred snapped as the footsteps reached the back deck. Honestly, the man tried his patience almost beyond endurance. "But it's still early. She probably hasn't heard about it yet. And if we're lucky, the whole mess will be cleared up before she does. But whatever happens," he warned, "I don't want her to know what LeGrande said about her mother. She doesn't need to know."

Millie put a hand on one of Al's and tipped her head to look into his eyes. "We won't say a word, will we, Al?"

Before Al could respond, Margaret reached the door. She threw it open and stepped into the kitchen. Fred thought she looked younger every time he saw her. The separation from her no-good husband had been good for her.

This morning, she looked no more than forty in her cutoff jeans, tennis shoes without socks, and denim shirt. Her skin looked fresh, her eyes bright—maybe too bright, Fred realized with dismay.

She didn't even bother to say hello, but launched into an attack before she even closed the door behind her. "What in the hell is going on, Dad?"

Al flicked an I-told-you-so look in Fred's direction. Millie bit her bottom lip.

Fred tried to look innocently confused. After all, she could be talking about anything from the ice cream he'd bought at Lacey's General Store two days earlier, to the pot of coffee he'd ordered at the Bluebird Café yesterday morning, to murder. "Is something wrong?"

Her eyes narrowed dangerously. "Don't try to act like you don't know what I'm talking about."

"I *don't* know until you tell me." Fred thought he sounded reasonable.

Apparently, Margaret didn't. Even from a distance, he could see that peculiar golden light in her dark eyes that had always signaled a fine temper in her mother. "Why did the sheriff's department wake me up this morning asking questions about you?"

Well, that certainly ruled out the first two possibilities. Fred didn't even try to hide his irritation. "The sheriff's department? What did they want?"

"To talk about the Broncos," she snapped. "What do you think they wanted?"

Margaret didn't use sarcasm often, and the fact that she did now warned Fred to tread carefully.

Millie's face creased with disapproval. Al's puckered with concentration. Thankfully, he kept his big mouth shut.

Margaret pulled in a steadying breath and planted herself in front of Fred, as if she expected him to make a break for it. "They asked all sorts of questions about this LeGrande Macafee person. They wanted to know if I've ever heard you talk about him before, or if I knew why you fought with him last night, or if I saw you last night." Her scowl deepened. "You didn't have anything to do with this mess, did you?"

He didn't like the question, not one little bit. "You shouldn't even have to ask something like that."

At least she had the decency to look embarrassed. "Then what in the hell is going on?"

Al opened his mouth as if he intended to say something, darted a glance at Fred, and snapped it shut again. Wise decision.

"I don't know what's going on," Fred admitted. "I wish I did."

Margaret scowled at him. "You don't know *anything* about the murder?"

Fred cocked an ankle across one knee and waved one hand in dismissal. "I knew the guy, of course. We went to school together. But that was over fifty years ago. I haven't seen him since we graduated."

Margaret looked first at Millie, then at Al, as if she expected them to contradict him. When they didn't, she turned her scowl back on Fred. "Then why are they asking all those questions?"

"Why are you asking me?" Fred did his best to sound outraged instead of concerned. "How am I supposed to know what Enos has on his mind?"

Margaret's gaze shifted. "It wasn't Enos," she admitted. "It was Ivan Neeley."

"Ivan?" Fred snorted a laugh. "That figures. He always gets too big for his britches. Just ignore him."

"*Ignore* him?" Margaret paced to the sink, repositioned the soap tray on the drainboard, and stashed the dish soap beneath the sink. "How can I ignore him when he wakes me up at six-thirty in the morning to ask questions about my father's connection to a murder?"

"See?" Al demanded with a self-satisfied nod. "I told you this would happen."

Fred sent him a reminder scowl. "Does Enos know Ivan's been bothering you?"

Margaret flicked him an uneasy glance and a slow flush crept into her cheeks. As it usually did, the mention of Enos's name wiped another ten years from her face. "I don't know. I haven't talked to him."

No, of course she hadn't. Once, years ago, Fred had expected the two of them to marry—until Webb swept Margaret off her feet and Enos responded by marrying Jessica Rich six months later. Both knew almost immediately they'd made a mistake, but until Margaret finally kicked Webb out a few months back, they'd suffered in silence. Their feelings for each other had never died. You only had to be in a room with one when the other's name came up to know that. But they'd managed to all but avoid each other for thirty years.

"Well, I'm sure he doesn't know," Fred assured her. "He'd never allow it."

The flush in her cheeks deepened, but she sidestepped the issue. "All I know is, Ivan made it sound as if they suspect you of murder. They don't, do they?"

Fred didn't want to admit the truth. He didn't want Margaret any more upset than she was already. "They're questioning everybody with any connection to LeGrande."

Margaret didn't look particularly reassured. "Did you really have an argument with the guy who was murdered?" When he didn't immediately answer, her frown deepened. "Did you *hit* him?"

"Twice," Al said with a sharp nod.

Millie smacked him on the arm with the palm of her hand. "You don't need to tell her that."

Margaret's eyes rounded. "*Twice?* Dad—" She jerked open the refrigerator door, then immediately slammed it shut again and rubbed her forehead. "Why?"

"Your father didn't kill him," Millie assured her.

Margaret lowered her hand and glared at all three of them. "Then why does Ivan think he did?"

Al, damn him, decided to help out again. "Because LeGrande's wife accused Fred of killing him." And if that wasn't bad enough, he added, "In front of everyone."

Margaret sagged against the refrigerator. "Oh, my God."

"I didn't kill him," Fred insisted just in case she hadn't heard Millie. "And I don't want your kids to know anything about this. They've had enough to deal with lately. They don't need to think their Grandpa's in trouble."

"You're right," Margaret said, shaking her head slowly as if she couldn't take it all in. "I don't want them to know about it, either." She paused, frowned, and shook one finger in his face. "You're not getting involved this time."

"I have no intention of getting involved."

"Then you don't have any big ideas about who did it? You don't have any questions you want answered? You don't have any one of a dozen excuses for getting in the middle of the investigation?"

For Pete's sake. She made it sound as if Fred had a habit of making up excuses. "I'm not getting involved," he said again, "even though I think I know who did it."

He expected her to look surprised. Or maybe a bit ashamed. Instead, she rolled her eyes in annoyance and pushed away from the refrigerator. "Not again. I suppose you think Enos and the guys can't possibly crack the case without your help."

"If they're all behaving the way Ivan did this morning," Fred snapped, "they probably can't. But I'm not a fool, Margaret, no matter what you think. I'm not going anywhere near this one."

"Why should I believe you? You've said the same thing before."

"You shouldn't use that tone," Millie warned. "He's still your father." But she used such a gentle voice, Fred didn't think Margaret could possibly take offense.

He underestimated her.

Margaret waved a hand toward him, nearly knocking over a chair in her agitation. "You don't know what he's like, Aunt Millie. You really don't." She shook her head hard enough to make hair fall into her face and brushed it away again. "Before you know what's happening, he'll be right in the middle of everything, sneaking around, putting himself in danger—"

"He can't do that this time," Al mumbled. "Nobody will talk to him."

Margaret laughed. "That won't stop him."

Fred could feel the slender hold he had on his temper slipping. He hated listening to them talk about him as if he wasn't in the room. "I don't need to get involved. I've already given Enos my statement. The rest is up to him."

"Why does Mrs. Macafee think you did it?" Margaret dropped into the chair nearest his. "Why did you hit him? What could he possibly have said that upset you that much?"

Fred had no intention of answering that, and if Millie and Al knew what was good for them, they wouldn't, either. "It's not important."

"Not important?" Margaret's voice rose in disbelief. "You hit a man who was murdered."

"I hit him before he was murdered," Fred pointed out.

Margaret scowled at him. "You're not funny."

"I wasn't trying to be."

She let out a heavy sigh and sent a pleading glance to Millie. When Millie stayed silent, she tried Al. "Do *you* know why Dad fought with this guy?"

Fred's heart sank like a stone. Al wouldn't lie for him. Al didn't know how to lie. He'd take one look at Margaret's big brown eyes and crack.

While Fred held his breath, Al trailed his gaze slowly along the table, up the wall, and across the ceiling. Half a dozen times Fred opened his mouth to supply an answer, then shut it again. If he spoke up too quickly, Margaret would know he had something to hide. Somewhere outside a bird cawed. The temperature inside the room climbed by at least ten degrees.

Slowly, Al looked into Margaret's eyes and surprised Fred for the second time in two days. "It wasn't important." Al's lips had trouble getting around the lie, but he did it. He flicked a glance at Fred and added, "Just an old competition from high school, only this time your dad won."

Fred let out the breath he'd been holding. Millie patted Al's arm and smiled into his eyes.

Margaret's eyes darted around the room, from one of them to the next without lighting anywhere. "What are the three of you hiding?"

"Hiding?" Millie managed to sound perplexed.

Al turned his attention to the cold breakfast on his plate. Fred shook his head as if the question confused him. "Sweetheart, I—"

"You're keeping something from me. I can feel it. Aunt Millie?"

Something flickered in Millie's eyes. Guilt, maybe. She stood and came around the table. "Margaret, dear, you're overreacting. Your father has had a rough night, and I think it would be better if he avoids stress this morning."

Margaret looked as if she might argue for a moment, but Millie had struck a nerve. Fred could count on his daughter's concern over his health. Millie obviously knew that, too.

Margaret's dark eyes clouded but some of the agitation left her. She tucked a lock of hair behind one ear and touched Fred's hand with a gentle one of her own. "You're right. I'm sorry, Dad. It's just that I worry about you, and it's not like you to get into fights with people."

To hear everyone else talk, it was exactly like him. But Fred didn't correct her. He wasn't that angry young man anymore, and Margaret didn't need to hear stories about that time in his life. Thankfully, Millie and Al kept quiet, too.

Margaret leaned a little closer and that strange golden glint came back. "But I'm warning you, Dad. If you are hiding something from me, I'll find out. I always do."

That's what frightened Fred the most—that LeGrande's ugly lies would make their way to Margaret's ears. Margaret had idolized her mother, and Fred wouldn't let anyone or anything destroy the image or the memories she carried with her. No matter what it took.

eight

Panting from exertion, Fred crossed the intersection of Main Street and Aspen. High overhead, the sun beat down relentlessly, drying his mouth and wetting his shirt with perspiration. Even the birds and chipmunks had stopped chattering and gone in search of shade.

But not Fred. Fred had groceries to buy and a life to get back to. After hours of getting a busy signal, Millie had finally gotten through to Ardella Neuswander. After all that, they'd learned nothing. Nothing except that the rest of the reunion had been canceled, half of their graduating class had already left town, and the verdict was still out on Fred.

Thankfully, Millie and Al had gone home. Al willingly. Millie reluctantly. She didn't want to leave Fred alone.

Fred wanted to be alone. Much as he loved Millie, much as he appreciated her concern, he looked forward to a little peace and quiet and a chance to gather his thoughts.

Across the street, the door to Silver City Bank opened and Iris Cavalier stepped outside. She adjusted her purse on her arm, darted a quick glance over her shoulder, and started away. Fred tried to ignore her, but something about the way she moved kept his attention riveted. She looked almost secretive, as if she didn't want anyone to see her.

Giving in to instinct, he stepped into the recessed doorway of the Book Exchange and watched her follow the boardwalk to the other end of the block. Instead of walking toward one of the cars parked nearby, she glanced around and made her way across the intersection to his side of the street.

Fred stepped out of the doorway and started after her, not certain even as he did it what prompted him to follow her. She didn't walk fast, so he had no trouble keeping up and even closing some of the distance between them. To his surprise, she paused on the next block outside the tiny shingled building that housed High Mountain Realtors.

Odd. First the bank, now a realtor, on the day after her ex-husband's murder. There might not be anything to it, of course. Fred didn't expect her to mourn the death of a man who'd walked out on her for another woman. Still, it did seem strange that she had business in Cutler when she hadn't lived here for fifty years.

Letting curiosity get the best of him, he increased his pace and worked up an expression of friendly curiosity. When he drew near enough, he called to her. "Iris?"

After last night he didn't know how she'd react to seeing him, so he prepared himself for anything.

To his relief, she smiled when she saw him. "Fred? Fancy meeting you here."

He smiled at the joke and stuffed his hands into his pockets. "I just saw you standing here and thought I'd say hello. Am I keeping you from something important?"

She shook her head quickly. A little too quickly, in Fred's opinion. "No. I'm just window-shopping." She worked up another smile and glanced at the glassed-in photos of available properties—a few nearby summer cabins, several unimproved lots, and a condominium unit in Winter Park. "Just dreaming a little, I guess."

"Are you thinking of moving back here?"

Another shake of her head, this one more determined than the last. "No." She tried to soften her expression. "I wouldn't mind coming back now that Yale's retired, but he doesn't want to live here. He wants to stay close to his children."

Fred could understand that. He loved having Margaret

and her family nearby, and often wished his three boys lived closer. "What about your children? Do you live near them?"

Her lips curved in a wistful smile. "No. One of my boys lives in Winter Park. The other one and my daughter are out of state."

"Well, maybe one of these days Yale will change his mind."

Her eyes hardened again. "I doubt it. Yale doesn't change his mind." She must have realized how harsh and angry she sounded, because she managed an uneasy laugh. "Listen to me. I sound like I'm complaining, don't I?"

She did, but Fred didn't think he should say so aloud. Instead, he asked, "Are you staying with your son while you're here?"

The hard edge returned. "No. He and Yale don't get along. We're staying with my sister and her husband. But I'm meeting my son for lunch in a few minutes."

Apparently, her children were a bad topic all the way around. One Fred thought he'd be wise to avoid from here on out. "How long are you planning to stay?"

She frowned at that. "We *were* planning to stay just until tomorrow. Now I don't know. LeGrande's funeral will be on Thursday. That is, it will be if the autopsy's finished by then."

That surprised Fred. "The funeral will be *here*?"

"Apparently so." Iris sighed softly and brushed a limp curl away from her forehead. "I understand that's what LeGrande wanted."

"I'm surprised," he admitted. "After all, he left here so long ago—"

"Yes, I know." Iris's lips curved into that wistful smile once more. "But he always wanted to come back eventually. We used to talk about retiring here." The smile disappeared again. "I suppose *she* doesn't want to live here any more than Yale does."

Fred didn't have to ask who Iris meant. Nor did he admit aloud how glad he was Stormy had kept LeGrande away.

Irish let a few seconds of silence pass before she spoke again. "So, are you going to the funeral?"

The question caught him off guard. "I don't know," he admitted. "I didn't even know about it until now."

"I suppose there will be some who think you should stay away," Iris said thoughtfully. "But for the record, *I* don't believe you killed him."

"For the record," he said with a tight smile, "I didn't."

Iris dabbed at the fine sheen of perspiration on her upper lip and pushed the curl away from her eyes again. "Of course you didn't. *She's* as big a liar as LeGrande ever was. What bothers me is, nobody's bothered to ask *her* what she was doing there."

Fred slanted a surprised glance at her. "You mean Stormy? She said she was looking for LeGrande."

Irish laughed bitterly. "I don't believe that for a second."

"What do you think she was doing there?"

Iris's eyes narrowed into slits. "Running away, what else?"

"You think she killed LeGrande?"

"Of course she did. And when she saw you there, she took advantage of the opportunity to blame you."

The suggestion had a certain appeal, but Fred wasn't sure he believed it. "Why would she kill him?"

Iris looked at him as if she'd never seen anyone quite so slow on the uptake. "Because of me."

"You?" The word escaped before Fred had a chance to stop it, and he could tell from the look on Iris's face he hadn't made her happy. "I'm sorry. It's just that you surprised me. Why would she kill him because of you?"

Iris smiled softly. "Because he wanted to see me while he was here, and I have a good idea what he wanted. I think he was *finally* going to do right by me."

"So she killed him to stop him?" Sounded a bit farfetched to Fred.

"You have no idea how much that woman loves money and things. She's nothing but a gold digger, and she'd do anything to keep LeGrande's money to herself. She even turned him against his own children. Those kids haven't seen a penny of his money since the day he walked out on me. He's been living high on the hog in that big house of his, driving his Mercedes, taking his little cruises to the Caribbean. But when our oldest grandson needed surgery, LeGrande didn't part with one red cent to help out. Gary ended up having to file bankruptcy because of all the medical bills."

The confession left Fred uneasy. He'd never believed in discussing family problems with outsiders, and he wondered how Iris's son would feel, knowing his mother had shared such an intimate secret with a stranger.

Iris went on, almost without taking a breath. "And when Diana's husband left her with four kids to raise, do you think LeGrande did anything to help?"

Fred figured he knew the answer to that, but he didn't say a word. Iris didn't expect an answer, anyway.

"He left *me* to pick up the pieces alone, as if the kids didn't even exist anymore." She met his gaze slowly. Anger and resentment had replaced the softer emotions he'd seen there before. "And it's *her* fault. *She's* had a fine life for the past twenty years. An easy life, while the rest of us have struggled just to make ends meet. If LeGrande suddenly wanted to do right by us, she'd find some way to stop him. Believe me."

Fred wasn't sure what to think. It was possible, he supposed. Maybe Stormy *had* killed him, run away to hide the murder weapon, and then come back. But he couldn't forget the other possibility that seemed far more realistic in his mind—Roger What's-his-name, who must live fairly close if he took advantage of LeGrande's visit to do away with him. "Do you know if LeGrande ever did business with anyone up here?"

"I don't know who he did business with," she admitted. "Once he left me, I didn't know anything about what he did."

From what she'd said earlier, it sounded as if she knew plenty. But Fred didn't correct her. "When you talked to him, did he tell you who else he planned to see while he was here?"

"I didn't talk to him," she said.

"Then how did you know he wanted to see you?"

Iris drew herself up sharply and brushed back the curl once more. "I just knew."

"But he didn't call you?"

"No." Her lips tightened enough to accentuate the lines around her mouth.

"He didn't write to you?"

Her shoulders stiffened and her gaze faltered. "No."

Fred didn't believe her. Something didn't feel right, but he had no idea what felt wrong, or why she didn't want to tell him. He didn't even know what to ask next.

Before he could decide, she focused on something behind him and relief flashed across her face. "Here's my son now. It's been good talking to you, Fred."

Without waiting for a response, she started toward the far end of the boardwalk. Confused, Fred watched her step down to the street and walk toward a maroon Chevy Spectrum that pulled to the side of the road. Just as he started to turn away, the driver's door opened and a dark-haired man climbed out to meet her. Fred couldn't see his face, but he had the same surly build LeGrande had as a younger man, the same broad shoulders, the same swagger in his step.

Some sixth sense kept Fred from turning away. And when the man turned to the side and revealed his face for the first time, Fred understood why.

Roger. After last night, Fred would have known him anywhere. And he would have known him as LeGrande's son last night if he'd gotten a good look at his face. He had LeGrande's cocky smile and devilish eyebrows.

The young man met Iris near the front of the car, wrapped an arm around her shoulders, and led her toward the door. He smiled at something she said, then glanced up without warning and focused on Fred.

Fred took an instinctive step backward, then remembered that Roger had no idea he'd been hiding in the lavatory stall.

Roger nodded at him, a polite greeting, nothing sinister.

Fred sketched a nod in return and tried to still his rampaging heart while he looked into the face of the murderer. He needed every ounce of self-control he could muster not to give himself away.

Iris waved and slid into her seat. With one last glance in Fred's direction, Roger rounded the back of the car, opened his own door, slipped behind the wheel. A moment later the Spectrum jerked back onto the street and disappeared around a corner. Only then did Fred allow himself to let out the breath he'd been holding.

Without wasting a second, he turned around in his tracks and hotfooted it back across town toward the sheriff's office. The argument he'd overheard made sense to him now. Even Roger's comments about Stormy fell into place. LeGrande had tried to make up with his son, but Roger had spurned him. And when LeGrande changed his mind about leaving Roger money, Roger had killed him.

Simple. It made perfect sense. And, after a hellish night and day, Fred's luck had finally changed.

Sweating heavily and more than a little out of breath, Fred burst through the door to Enos's office and slammed it behind him. The aroma of stale coffee filled the air. A fan on the floor beside the desk rattled as it made a vain attempt to create a breeze.

Enos sat behind his battered wooden desk studying an open file. He glanced up when the door opened and started to smile, but when he saw the look on Fred's face, his expression froze. Standing quickly, he started around the desk. "Fred? Are you all right?"

Fred waved away his concern and tried to pull in a steadying breath. "I'm fine," he gasped. "Fine."

"You don't look fine. Should I call Doc?"

"No." Fred dropped into one of the old wooden chairs in front of the desk. "I'm all right."

Enos stopped moving toward him, but he still looked worried. "Then, what in the hell . . . ?"

Fred swallowed and tried to put a little moisture back into his dry throat so he could speak. It didn't work. He tried again to get his breathing under control, but he'd walked too far and too fast in the heat. He held up a hand to signal for a moment, and went on as soon as he could take a deep breath. "I found him."

Enos perched against the edge of his desk. "Found who?"

"Roger."

Disapproval darkened Enos's features. He leaned close enough for Fred to see the beads of sweat on his nose. "I thought I told you to stay out of this investigation."

"You did," Fred agreed. "And I stayed out. I wasn't trying to find him."

Enos laughed without humor. "Yeah, yea, I know. What's your excuse this time?" He held up one hand to stop Fred from answering. "No, let me guess. You couldn't have been in the men's room—you did that already."

"Very funny," Fred snapped. He felt a bit stronger now. "I found him while I was talking to Iris Cavalier outside the realtor's office—"

Enos didn't even let him finish. "Dammit, Fred. Don't you listen to a word I say?"

"I listen to every word you say," Fred groused. "I wish you'd return the favor."

Enos held up both hands in a gesture of surrender. "All right. Fine. But first, tell me why you were talking to Iris Cavalier when I specifically asked you not to talk to anyone about the murder."

"I ran into her," Fred explained.

Enos snorted a laugh. "I'll bet."

"I ran into her," Fred insisted. "What did you expect me to do, cross the street to avoid her?"

Enos narrowed his gaze. "As a matter of fact, yes."

"Don't be ridiculous. You don't really expect me not to speak to another living soul until you have this case sewn up?"

"If possible."

"Well, it's not possible," Fred snapped. "And I don't think you're funny."

"I'm not trying to be."

Fred took a deep breath and tried once more to calm himself. No good would come from arguing with Enos when he was in this mood. He propped his hands on his thighs and started over. "Are you going to let me tell you this, or not?"

"Fine," Enos said grudgingly. "Tell me."

"I was on my way to the Bluebird when I saw Iris coming out of the bank. I stayed on my own side of the street, but then she crossed and stopped in front of the real-estate office. Naturally, I had to say hello."

"Naturally."

Fred glared at him. "I'm *not* going to make myself look guilty by avoiding people."

Some of Enos's hostility faded. He sent Fred a grudging nod. "I can understand that, I guess."

Not exactly an apology, but better than nothing. "I didn't bring up the murder," he said. "But she did."

"And, of course, you didn't want to be rude."

Fred's temper started to simmer. He tried not to let it show. "Did you know she thinks Stormy Macafee killed her husband?"

He expected Enos to look surprised. Instead, he nodded slowly. "I knew that."

"Good." Fred ran the back of his hand across his forehead to remove the perspiration he could feel there and took another deep breath. Thankfully, his heart had finally stopped hammering in his chest. "She told me LeGrande wanted to see her while he was here. Did you know *that*?"

Enos nodded again. "Yes, I did."

"But he didn't call her or write to her. Did she tell you that?"

"Yes."

"Don't you think that's odd?" Fred demanded. "Why did she think LeGrande wanted to see her?"

"Woman's intuition."

Fred stared at him for a second. "What?"

"Woman's intuition. That's what she told me."

"You're not going to tell me you believe that."

Enos shook his head again. "Of course not. Did she tell you anything different?"

"No," Fred admitted.

Enos locked his fingers together. He didn't look happy. "What does all this have to do with Roger?"

Fred smiled. He couldn't help himself. "Roger is Iris and LeGrande's son."

Enos didn't even blink. He didn't look a bit surprised. He just nodded slowly. "I know."

"You know?" Fred bolted out of his chair and glared down at him. "You *know*?"

"I realized who he was this morning when I talked to Stormy. She gave me the names of LeGrande's children."

"And you didn't tell me?"

"Why should I?"

"Because—" Fred began, but he broke off when he couldn't think of a reason Enos wouldn't shoot down. "Because."

Enos laughed without humor and shifted his weight. "That's what I thought." He let out a frustrated sigh. "Look, Fred, I did what I said I'd do. I found your mysterious Roger. Hell, I even paid him a visit."

Fred dropped into his chair again. "You did?"

Enos nodded. "Yep. We had a nice, long chat."

"Then why is he driving around Cutler instead of sitting inside a jail cell?"

"For the same reason you are." Enos rubbed the back of his neck. "Because the only evidence I have against him is circumstantial."

"You have a witness," Fred argued.

"I have a witness who overheard an argument, *not* a witness to murder. Hell, if that's all I needed to put somebody behind bars, you'd have been there last night."

He had a point, but Fred didn't want to admit it. "What

did Roger say when you asked about his fight with LeGrande?"

Enos stopped rubbing and dropped his hand to the desk. "Well, now, that's the interesting part. He says he didn't have an argument with his father last night."

"He lied. Did you tell him you had a witness who saw him?"

Enos nodded. "Yes, but he didn't change his story. He claims he was home all night."

nine

Fred could only stare at Enos for several long seconds while his words sank in. "He's lying," he managed at last. "I saw him there."

"I believe you," Enos said. "The trouble is, his wife backs up his story. She says he was at home with her all night."

"She's lying, too," Fred insisted.

Enos's expression softened. "I know she is, but I can't prove it—yet."

Fred sat back in his seat. "Well, that proves he's guilty."

"It doesn't *prove* anything," Enos said. "Not by a long shot. She could be lying for any number of reasons. People lie when there's a murder involved, even if they're not guilty. You know that as well as I do."

Fred knew he was right, but he also knew what he'd seen and heard in the lavatory the previous night. His elation faded and discouragement replaced it. "So, what's next?"

Enos rubbed his neck a little harder, and lifted one shoulder in a casual shrug. "We're still looking for the murder weapon. A blunt instrument, that's all we know. A blunt instrument with a distinctive pattern we haven't been able to match yet. If we can find it, hopefully we'll be able to lift a print or there'll be something else that will help us figure out who used it."

Not much in that to give a man hope. "And in the meantime? Are you talking to the others who were there, or am I the only one you're worried about?"

Enos frowned at him. "You're not helping your case any by being sarcastic, you know."

"I'm not helping my case any by sitting in my rocking chair, either," Fred reminded him.

Enos rubbed his face with his hand and wagged his head slowly. "There's nothing else you *can* do. Let me and the boys handle this, Fred. Don't push your luck."

"You and the boys?" Fred let out an acid laugh. "Did you know Ivan's been questioning Margaret?"

That took some of the wind out of Enos's sails. "Maggie? Why?"

The shock on Enos's face made Fred feel a little better, but not much. "You tell me."

Enos's shoulders slumped. "He's determined to solve this case," he said softly. "He's decided to run for sheriff in November."

"Ivan?" Fred laughed outright at that.

Enos didn't even crack a smile. "He's convinced that if he solves the case, he'll make a name for himself and he'll be able to pull in a hefty share of votes."

"He could make a fool of himself by going after the wrong person."

Enos sent him a halfhearted smile. "You're right about that."

"Of course I am."

"But that still doesn't mean I'm going to let you get involved."

"I'm not asking," Fred assured him. If he decided to break Roger's alibi, he wouldn't be foolish enough to ask permission. He studied Enos's face again, surprised by the worry lines he saw there. "You're not worried about the election?"

Enos stood and stepped behind his desk again. "Worried? No. But I am having second thoughts about running again, myself."

Fred sat back in his chair—hard. "What do you mean 'second thoughts'? Are you crazy?"

Enos paced to the filing cabinet against the far wall. "I'm

not sure I can do it anymore, Fred." He glanced over his shoulder. "Jessica's taken a turn for the worse. The cancer's spreading."

A chill of foreboding raced up Fred's spine. "How long have you known?"

"Just a couple of weeks." Enos rubbed the back of his neck and look away again. "She's going to need me."

Fred couldn't argue with that. After all, he'd had his own painful experience with cancer. He'd watched Phoebe suffer and eventually die from it. He knew how much Jessica would need Enos by her side.

But he couldn't imagine anyone else in Enos's place. Or maybe he didn't *want* to imagine anyone else there— especially Ivan. He tried for several long, achingly silent moments to think of something to say, but his mind remained a stubborn blank.

Slowly, he pushed to his feet and crossed the room toward his friend. Only the sound of his feet dragging across the floor and the fan's pointless rattling broke the stillness. He put a comforting hand on Enos's shoulder. "I'm sorry. I know how you feel."

Enos nodded without looking at him. "I know you do." He sent a thin smile over his shoulder. "You know, I married her for all the wrong reasons. Our life together hasn't been easy."

Fred knew.

Enos turned a miserable glance in his direction. "I don't think I've ever been truly in love with her, but I do *love* her."

Fred increased the pressure on his arm slightly. "I know you do, son."

Enos started to say something else, but the words caught in his throat. He shook his head again and leaned his forehead on his hands on top of the filing cabinet. Fred didn't move. He didn't speak. He just stood there for what felt like forever, offering silent comfort and aching with his friend.

Memories he'd rather forget rolled through him. He tried to clear the lump that filled his throat, but it wouldn't budge.

Instead, it seemed to grow larger with every heartbeat. "If there's anything I can do to help—" His voice came out choked with emotion and the offer sounded weak and useless. There was nothing Fred could do. Nothing anyone could do.

Enos slanted another glance at him. Pain lined his face and added at least ten years to his age. "Just be a friend."

Fred nodded weakly. "I can do that." To his dismay, the telephone on Enos's desk interrupted him before he could say anything else.

Enos's shoulder stiffened beneath Fred's hand.

"Let it ring," Fred suggested.

"No." Enos made a visible effort to pull himself together. "I'm in the middle of a murder investigation, remember? Working keeps me busy. I need something to keep my mind occupied. Besides, it might be Jess."

Enos never had been one to shirk his duty. And Fred couldn't imagine what he'd do if he gave up his career to spend endless empty hours watching his wife die. There'd be nothing to stand between him and the memories of every harsh word he'd ever said, every angry look, every sigh of frustration. Fred knew that from his own painful experience.

He watched Enos cross to his desk and answer the phone. He stood there for another minute, but the set of Enos's shoulders told him they wouldn't pick up where they'd left off, even if he waited.

Sighing softly, he walked to the door and let himself out. But the minute he knew Enos couldn't see him any longer, he leaned against the boardwalk's railing and closed his eyes.

He wouldn't wish the pain of watching a spouse die on anyone, especially not on someone he cared so deeply about. Selfishly, he hated the idea of having someone as foolish as Ivan Neeley in Enos's place. But there wasn't a thing he could do about it—not a blasted thing.

He opened his eyes again and watched people moving about on Main Street as if the world hadn't shifted off balance. He heard someone laugh, as if they hadn't a care in the world. And he wondered what else could possibly go wrong.

With his thoughts racing, Fred strode along the Main Street boardwalk past the Kwik Kleen. The sun beat down on his shoulders and little puffs of dust rose from the boards under his feet with every step. He abandoned his original plan to buy groceries. Right now he needed to collect his thoughts. And he could think of only one place to go for that—the Bluebird Café.

Concerned for Enos and Jessica and worried about himself, he crossed Aspen Street and climbed the steps to the boardwalk on the other side. He's always found comfort inside the Bluebird. It had been his home away from home for many years—since long before Lizzie Hatch took over running it. If he could find peace and quiet anywhere, he'd find it there, especially at this time of day, when the breakfast crowd had already cleared out and lunch was still at least an hour away.

Lost in thought, he didn't notice the door to Lacey's General Store opening until Burl DiMeo stepped directly into his path. Fred ground to a halt and held back the exclamation that rose automatically to his lips.

Burl took a step backward and let out an uncomfortable laugh. "Well. Good morning. You're just the man I'm looking for."

Fred couldn't imagine why, and in his current mood, he didn't want to know. "Morning."

"You headin' inside?"

"No." Fred took a step away from the door. He could think of a thousand people he'd rather see right now than Janice Lacey. She made it her business to know everything that went on in three counties and to share what she knew with everyone she met. Fred had no intention of discussing anything with her. He backed another step away and checked to make sure she couldn't see him through the windows. "I'm on my way to the Bluebird for lunch."

Burl let out a wistful sigh. "They serve great food.

Coralee and I eat there every time we come back." He shook his head sadly and glanced back at Fred. "The visits get fewer and farther apart, though. We only live over in Glenwood Springs, but it gets harder every year to make the drive. We're not as young as we used to be."

"None of us are." Fred moved another step away from the windows for good measure. "Why did you want to see me?"

Burl adjusted the bag of groceries in his arms and squinted into the sun. "It's about Coralee. I'm worried about her."

Concern took the place of Fred's slight irritation. "Is she ill?"

"No. No. Not physically. She uses the cane, but just to steady herself a bit. It's just that she hasn't been the same since Kenneth—" He broke off and shook his head sadly. "Well, you know."

Fred did. Everyone knew how deeply losing their only child in Vietnam had affected both of them.

"And now, this." Burl sent another sideways glance in Fred's direction. "She didn't sleep well at all last night."

"I doubt any of us did."

"Maybe not," Burl said with a shrug. "But the rest of you will get over it."

"And you don't think Coralee will?"

Burl let out a sharp laugh. One note without humor. "Coralee doesn't *get* over things, Fred." He glanced away again, then seemed to think twice about what he'd said. "'Course, I guess I don't either. So maybe I shouldn't throw stones."

Fred had no idea how to respond to either statement. He stuffed his hands in his pockets and rocked back on his heels. "I suppose that's a good rule for all of us to follow."

Burl nodded, but he seemed so distracted, Fred wondered if he'd even heard what he said. He shifted the groceries again and let his gaze drift away. "I hear you're friendly with the sheriff here."

The abrupt change of subject caught Fred off guard. He stopped rocking. "I am."

"The lady inside the store told me," Burl said quickly, as if Fred couldn't have guessed on his own. "What's her name? Janice?"

Fred nodded. He wondered what else Janice had told him and what she'd pried out of Burl, but he didn't ask. Sometimes it was better not to know.

Burl met Fred's gaze again, but Fred could tell he had to force himself to do it. "I don't suppose you could do me a favor?"

A favor? Doubtful, especially if it involved Enos. But Fred didn't want to admit that aloud. "What do you need?"

"It's Coralee. Like I said, she's taking LeGrande's death hard. Real hard."

Fred tried not to look overly interested, but the admission certainly caught his attention. "I didn't realize they were so close."

"They weren't close," Burl snapped. "They weren't close at all. But she almost ran into the murderer, and it's left her a little shaky."

That caught Fred's attention. "Did she see who did it?"

Burl shook his head quickly. "No. But she wasn't feeling well, so she went to the ladies' room. She was gone awhile, so I went looking for her."

"What time was that?"

"About seven-thirty. Right before we heard Stormy screaming." Burl's scowl deepened. "This whole thing has upset her horribly."

"It's upset all of us," Fred reminded him. "And until it's revolved, it will keep on upsetting everybody."

"Yes, I know." Burl looked away again and let his gaze linger on the windows of stores across the street. "The thing is, Fred, she doesn't want to talk about it."

"None of us do."

"Yes, but . . ." Burl flushed, shifted his weight, and rubbed the back of his neck.

"I understand Coralee's upset, but this isn't easy on any of us. We're all old. We're all tired. We all have health problems—"

"It's not the same," Burl argued.

"We're all getting older," Fred said again. He sent Burl a sideways glance and added, "Even LeGrande. He had cancer, you know."

Burl pulled back sharply. "I didn't know."

Fred nodded. "He told me he only had a few more months to live. I guess facing his mortality made him think twice about some of the things he'd done."

"Yeah?" Burl rubbed the back of his neck, but he kept his gaze averted. "Well, he *should* have thought twice."

"I didn't realize you knew him."

"I didn't," Burl admitted. "I didn't need to. I heard about him."

In spite of himself, Fred chuckled.

Burl turned an annoyed glance at him. "It's not funny, Fred. Coralee's . . ." He paused, searching, Fred supposed, for the right word. "She's delicate. Has been ever since Kenny's death."

Delicate. The word surprised Fred. He'd never thought of Coralee as particularly delicate before. But, then, he remembered her as the young girl who'd liked to dance, not the woman whose only child had been taken away from her.

The color in Burl's cheeks deepened. "I know this whole thing has upset her, but she won't talk to me about it. Says she wants to forget it ever happened." He shifted his groceries again. "She doesn't take death well. Tries to pretend it doesn't happen. She hasn't even been to a funeral since Kenny's. Losing our boy just about did us both in."

Fred grunted his response to that. He'd been caught in these conversations with Burl before, and the man's emotions always left Fred slightly uneasy. Helpless might be a better word. He couldn't imagine trying to survive the death of a child. He didn't *want* to imagine.

"Kenny was a good kid, you know." Burl's voice softened and he blinked rapidly.

To Fred's dismay, the man's eyes filled with tears. Hell.

"He was in the top ten of his graduating class. He'd started college and had plans to go on to medical school. He had his whole life ahead of him." Burl made a vain attempt to wipe away a few of the tears and met Fred's gaze again, silently demanding some reaction.

Fred put one tentative hand on his slumped shoulder.

Pain distorted Burl's features and his blinking escalated. "He was my boy. My only child."

Fred thought about pulling his hand away, then decided to leave it there. "I know."

Burl sniffed loudly. "You're lucky. You have three sons, don't you?"

"And a daughter," Fred admitted.

"You still have them all." It sounded almost like an accusation.

"Yes," Fred said softly. "Yes, they're all still alive. But I lost my wife, so I do understand some of what you're feeling."

Burl shook his head. "It's not the same. Not the same at all. Kenny was supposed to bury *me*, not the other way around. He was supposed to live, to marry the girl he fell in love with, and give Coralee and me grandchildren. He was supposed to look after his mother if I went first. Now—" He broke off and wiped his eyes with the back of his hand.

Fred made a noise in his throat and hoped it sounded comforting.

"She married somebody else, you know. That girl. Lisa. Didn't even wait two years." Burl sounded bitter, as if Lisa had betrayed Kenny by getting on with her life.

And Fred supposed, in some way, Burl believed she had. The whole idea disconcerted Fred. He understood grieving only too well, but it didn't seem right to let time stop the way Burl and Coralee had.

He didn't say any of that to Burl. Instead, he patted the man's shoulder a couple of times. "Well, she was young. And unfortunately, life goes on."

To Fred's relief, Burl managed to get control of himself again. "I'm sorry. You don't want to hear all that. I guess this murder thing has brought it all back again."

Death had a way of doing that, Fred thought. Of bringing

back memories, of raising emotions a person would rather ignore, of disturbing the walls around a person's heart.

Burl pulled in a deep, steadying breath and let it out in a whoosh. "Anyway, you understand why I don't want anyone bothering Coralee. I don't know what it will do to her, and I can't lose her, too, Fred. I *can't*."

"I understand," Fred assured him. "But Enos isn't going to welcome any interference from me. In fact, after what Stormy said, anything I say would probably make him more determined to question Coralee, not less."

Burl looked as if he might cry again.

Fred held back a groan of dismay and wished he could think of something to say that would stop him.

Before he could come up with even one idea, the front door to Lacey's swung open and Janice Lacey stepped out into the sunshine. A dark green chef's apron stretched across her substantial middle. Her tight gray curls glinted blue in the sunlight. She'd wedged a pencil behind one ear, and she carried a broom in one hand, as if she'd come outside to clean the boardwalk.

Fred knew better. He had no doubt she'd decided the boardwalk needed cleaning only after she saw Fred standing on it.

He had to hand it to her—she did a good job of looking surprised to see him. She gasped and put one hand on her generous bosom. But her eyes betrayed her. She'd calculated every step. And Fred knew exactly what she was after. But he'd be dipped if he'd give it to her. This time Fred would keep the upper hand, come hell or high water.

ten

Fred turned away from Janice and kept his attention riveted on Burl. He could hear her sweeping, moving closer, listening carefully. He could almost see her nose twitching with the thrill of the hunt.

"Just think about it," Burl said softly. "Please. If there's anything you can do to help—"

Fred nodded, but he knew it was an empty promise. He couldn't worry about Coralee. He had enough on his plate. Janice moved still closer, and when Burl wheeled away and started toward his car, she swept her way to Fred's side and let out a sympathetic sigh.

Fred wished he could ignore her completely, but he knew how her mind worked. She would read all sorts of things into his attempt to get away and speculate about them at length to everyone who set foot in the store.

He turned slowly to face her and tried to look friendly. "Hello, Janice."

He must have looked downright congenial. She closed the remaining distance between them and put on her expression of deep concern. "I'm so glad to see you. You can't imagine how worried I've been."

Curious might be a more accurate word. Fred kept his face impassive. He didn't want to encourage her. "There's nothing to worry about."

She patted the back of her blue-gray curls and looked

steadily at him. "I just heard about what happened at your reunion last night. Burl was telling me about it."

Wonderful.

"I *must* say I don't know when I've ever heard of anything so horrible." She took a swipe at a leaf with her broom. It dropped to the boardwalk again a few inches away.

"Yes. Well, it was a rough night."

Big mistake. A gleam appeared in Janice's eyes. "Especially for you."

"It's been difficult for everyone who was there."

"Well, yes. Of course. But not everyone was accused of murder, were they?"

"No." Unfortunately. Fred tried not to let his mounting frustration show. "Look, Janice, I hadn't even seen Le-Grande for more than fifty years. None of us had."

Janice took another swipe with her broom. "Oh, that's not true, is it? *Some* of you must have kept in touch with him over the years. Someone told him about the reunion."

"Well, it certainly wasn't me," Fred assured her. "Ardella and Percy Neuswander are in charge of the reunions, and LeGrande's ex-wife was a member of our class. One of them must have told him."

"Well, yes." Janice sent him a sidelong glance. "But surely they're not the only ones who've talked to him." Something glinted in her eye. Fred had seen that look before. She knew something. He could feel it in his bones. Unfortunately, she'd expect something in return. He'd been the object of her fishing expeditions too often not to recognize the bait.

He offered another suggestion. "Jeremiah Hunt used to work for him, but if anyone else kept in touch with LeGrande, I don't know who it would be."

"Well, of course, *I* don't know anything." Janice pulled a handkerchief from one apron pocket and gently dabbed her forehead. "Most of your class moved away when I was so young—"

She hadn't been *that* young, but Fred didn't argue.

"—but I do remember a few of the people I've seen this week. Iris came in just this morning. I recognized her, of course. I always thought she was so pretty."

Iris had been pretty, but Fred didn't think now was the time to discuss it. Instead, he tried to steer Janice back on track. "Have you actually talked to someone else who kept in touch with LeGrande over the years?"

She gave her apron a twitch and shook her head. "No. Of course, there was that one tiny argument I overheard the day of the reunion."

Fred's heart skipped a beat, but he tried to look only casually interested. Janice didn't like telling him anything he actually wanted to know. "Well," he said carefully. "LeGrande had a lot of enemies."

She patted her hair again and let out a sigh. "I suppose you're right. And I'm sure I shouldn't say anything. After all, I don't *know* that it had anything to do with what happened later."

"Well, then, it probably didn't."

She sent him a hesitant glance. "But I *do* have to admit, they certainly sounded upset with each other."

Fred decided to take a chance with a more direct question. At this rate, they'd dance around the subject all day. "It wasn't a younger man, was it? About fifty or so . . . ?"

"No. Of course not."

Fred tried not to look disappointed. He tried again. "I don't suppose you recognized the other person?"

To his surprise, she looked annoyed. "Of course I recognized him. Honestly. I've known Al for years."

Fred rocked back on his heels and stared at her. "Al Jarvis? My brother-in-law?" Surely she didn't mean *his* Al.

She sniffed as if he'd asked something stupid. "Yes, of course."

"Are you sure?"

"Positive. Like I said, I've known Al forever."

Fred tried for several seconds to make sense of what she'd said. But she'd raised more questions than she'd answered. "What were they arguing about?"

"I wouldn't call it an argument, exactly. They sounded upset—at least, *LeGrande* sounded upset. I couldn't hear much of what Al said."

He tried to hold on to his patience. He honestly did. But no one exasperated him quite the way Janice did. "For hell's sake," he snapped. "Would you quit dragging this out? Just tell me what you heard."

He pulled the ragged edges of his patience together and held on while she slowly looked him up and down. He bit back the words that rose to his lips and waited. After what felt like forever, she sniffed again and shook her head. "Well," she said at last. "If you *must* know, they were talking about Phoebe."

Fred's mouth dried and his mind raced, trying to convince himself that he hadn't heard her right. Fear that Janice had overheard LeGrande's ugly story rose like bile in his throat. If she knew, everyone would know—if they didn't already. And nothing Fred could say would convince her to keep that ugly rumor to herself. Anger with Al for not telling him about the encounter pumped through his veins with every heartbeat.

Janice smiled gently and put a hand on his arm. "I didn't want to tell you like that—straight out."

Of course she had. She'd probably gotten a kick out of watching his reaction. Fred pulled away.

Janice, damn her, grabbed his hand and held on, tilting her head this way and that until he finally, reluctantly, met her gaze. "I'm serious, Fred. You know how much I care about you. We've been friends too long. I wouldn't hurt you for anything in the world."

Friends? Fred nearly snorted a laugh, but the sincerity in her eyes caught him short and stopped him.

"I didn't hear everything, of course. They were standing near the end of the aisle, and I was dusting cans of soup—"

No doubt trying to get close enough to overhear without giving herself away.

"But I did hear LeGrande tell Al that he was wrong, and Al told LeGrande to keep his mouth shut." She glanced away and drew a deep breath before she went on. "Al said that Phoebe had sworn him to secrecy over fifty years ago, and he wasn't going to let LeGrande make him break that promise now. And if she'd wanted you to know about it, she would have told you."

Fred's stomach lurched. His hand trembled. He couldn't seem to control it. His fingers grew icy, then numb. Phoebe had kept a secret from him, but she'd told *Al*? An over-whelming sense of betrayal rocked him, but he didn't want Janice to see it. "What else?"

"Nothing. Coralee DiMeo came in, and when LeGrande saw her in the produce aisle he seemed to forget all about Al. But she wouldn't even talk to him. The minute she saw him, she dropped her apples into the orange bin and left. She certainly has changed a lot, don't you think?"

Fred nodded, but he couldn't make himself answer. He didn't care about Burl and Coralee. He didn't care about anything.

Janice patted his hand. "I want you to know, Fred, I haven't said a word about what I heard to anyone. Not a single soul." She glanced over her shoulder and let out an annoyed sigh. "Darn it. I've got customers waiting. I'm going to have to get back inside. But I won't say a word to anyone. You can count on me."

With one last, thin smile, she released Fred's hand and hurried toward the glass door. Still reeling, still numb, Fred watched her disappear. Count on her, she'd said. Fred's stomach pitched and rolled. Count on Janice. Count on the biggest mouth within two hundred miles to keep itself shut.

He rubbed his eyes with one hand and fought to pull air into his lungs. But he didn't let himself move until the trembling in his legs lessened.

All he could say was, it was a good thing Millie and Al had decided to go home that morning. A damned good thing Al wasn't sitting in his kitchen at that moment, eating his food, drinking his coffee, planting his lying butt in one of Fred's chairs.

It had been a long time—if ever—since he'd been this

hurt and angry. Even LeGrande hadn't upset him as much as learning that Phoebe had kept something secret from him all the years they were together but she'd told Al. *Al,* of all people. Stupid, bumbling Al.

He clenched his fists at his side so tightly his nails bit into his palms. He welcomed the blistering heat on his shoulders, the sweat pouring down his back, the mind-numbing anger that kept him from feeling the ache in his heart. But he wondered how long it would take him to get over this—or if he ever would.

Still seething, Fred pushed open the door to the Bluebird Café. The tantalizing aroma of fresh coffee rushed out to meet him, but he didn't find his usual pleasure in it. He pulled in a steadying breath. In. Out. Slowly.

First, he'd spend a few minutes pulling himself together and getting his anger under control. Then he'd figure out his next step. He took another breath, this one deep and satisfying. If anything would help, being here at the Bluebird would.

Someone in the kitchen dropped something metal, Elvis on the jukebox came to life with the first slow notes of "Love Me Tender," and Grandpa Jones looked up at Fred from his usual place at the lunch counter.

Fred couldn't remember a time he'd come into the Bluebird and found Grandpa's perch empty, and seeing him there today made him feel almost normal again—as normal as he *could* feel, considering.

Fred nodded a greeting. Grandpa nodded back, but something in his expression seemed different this morning. Cranky. Or maybe worried. Fred tried not to let it bother him. At Grandpa's age—Fred figured he must be in his mid-eighties by now—he deserved to feel out of sorts. And Fred didn't need one more thing to worry about.

He moved quickly into the dining area and slid into his favorite corner booth beneath the *Kissin' Cousins* poster. Years ago, when Fred and Phoebe were young and, in retrospect, carefree, the walls had been covered in ivy-twined wallpaper. If he closed his eyes, he could see the place as it had been then. He could see Phoebe sitting across the booth from him—the booth that had always been theirs.

He didn't close his eyes. He didn't want to see a secret in Phoebe's dark eyes. Didn't want to imagine her sharing it with Al. Instead, he let his gaze travel slowly around the dining area and tried to think of something else. *Anything* else.

When Lizzie Hatch bought the place, she'd changed everything. She'd ripped down that faded old wallpaper and put up wood paneling. She'd covered the walls with Elvis memorabilia—a picture of the King painted on black velvet, movie posters, even a clock with swinging legs to mark the time. Some people had complained about the changes. Claimed it didn't seem like a family restaurant any longer.

Fred had to admit the memorial to Elvis gave the place a different feel than it once had, but he didn't agree that Lizzie had ruined the place. What did a few pictures matter? Or stuffing the jukebox with recordings of the King's songs? Lizzie still served the kind of food that stuck to a man's ribs, still made a good cup of coffee, and Fred didn't have to pay an arm and a leg for a meal. That's all he cared about.

Sighing softly, he settled back in his seat and waited for Lizzie to notice him. Coffee, that's what he needed. A soothing cup of coffee and some time alone. It shouldn't take Lizzie long to see him. After all, he and Grandpa were her only customers.

But instead of relaxing, his mind started to race again. No matter how hard he tried, he couldn't block the echo of Janice's voice from his memory. First, LeGrande's hideous story. Now this. Surely, it wasn't true. Surely, Phoebe hadn't changed her mind about him and searched out LeGrande. It couldn't be true. Fred didn't think he could survive that.

Before he could even turn over his coffee mug, the door opened again and Doc Huggins stepped inside. Fred groaned aloud. He didn't want to deal with Doc. Not today. He shifted in his seat and focused on a car moving slowly along Main Street.

From the corner of his eye, he watched Doc spend a minute talking to Grandpa, then glance around and notice him sitting there. Hell.

Fred tried to ignore him.

Doc pretended not to notice. He clomped across the floor and slid onto the seat across from Fred with a old man's groan. "Morning."

Fred flicked a glance at him. Doc actually checked in a few years younger than Fred, but he acted older. Much older. Fred muttered a greeting in return and turned his gaze away again.

Doc sighed heavily, turned over his coffee cup, and settled it on its chipped saucer. "I'm glad I caught up with you. I've been wanting to see how you're doing."

"Caught up with me?" Fred laughed bitterly. "I haven't been hard to find. I've been sitting in my damned rocking chair all day." His voice came out harsh. Angry.

Doc's expression sobered. "Just where you should be. I want you to stop by for a checkup, Fred. This whole thing *has* to be taking its toll on you."

Fred glared at him. "What whole thing?"

Doc waved a vague hand in front of him. "You know . . . the murder." He dropped his hand into his lap and glanced around as if he wanted to make sure no one could hear him. "You know I don't think you're guilty."

"I'm not," Fred snapped. But if he'd known that night what he knew now, he just might have been.

Doc watched like a hawk while Fred tried to pull himself together. "You know, Fred," he said at last. "You stuck by me when I was in trouble. The least I can do is return the favor."

Fred started to say he didn't need any favors, but stopped himself. That would have been a lie. He needed all the favors he could get. He made a noise in his throat that Doc could interpret any way he wanted.

A hint of wariness crept into Doc's expression. "Are you all right?"

"I'm fine," Fred snapped. "I just want to be left alone."

Anyone but Doc would have taken the hint. But Doc never had been good at understanding subtlety. He shifted around on the bench for a second. "I heard—" He cut himself off and glanced around to make sure no one could hear him. "I heard what happened that night. I know what LeGrande said about Phoebe."

Almost without thinking, Fred pushed to his feet. "Maybe you didn't hear me, Doc. I want to be alone." He would have walked away, but Doc snagged his arm and held on.

"Sit down." Fred tried to jerk his arm away, but Doc didn't let go. "Sit down, Fred."

Fred glared at him. "Let go of me." Dimly, from the corner of his eye, he became aware of Lizzie standing in the kitchen doorway. Grandpa spun around on his stool to watch. He widened the glare to include all of them. "What in the hell's the matter with people in this town? Can't a man get a little peace and quiet when he wants it?"

Lizzie turned away. Grandpa went back to his plate of french fries. But Doc didn't look even slightly affected, and he didn't loosen his grip. "I know how you must be feeling—"

That was probably the stupidest thing Fred had ever heard him say—and he'd heard Doc say some mighty stupid things over the years. But he pretended not to understand what Doc meant by it. "Good," he snapped. "Then you know I want you to let go of my damned arm."

Apparently, Doc didn't know anything of the kind. If anything, he tightened his grip a bit more. "You don't honestly believe what he said, do you?"

Fred didn't answer. He had no answer to give. He didn't know what he believed.

Doc interpreted his silence as a yes. He shook his head sadly. "You know, I remember way back in the olden days when we were all young and you and Phoebe were first married. I remember how insecure you were about her. You were absolutely convinced you didn't deserve her, remember?"

Of course he remembered. How could he forget? Phoebe had been everything a man could ever want in a woman, but Fred had wanted to be so much more than he was. For her. But he didn't want to discuss the past. He was in no mood for a trip down memory lane.

If Doc noticed, he didn't let on. "And I remember what she was like before you got married. I saw that shy young girl blossom into a hell of a woman. And do you know why?"

Fred couldn't even begin to imagine. He gave an almost imperceptible shake of his head.

"Because she loved you, though only God knows why." He sent Fred a thin smile and loosened the death grip he had on his arm. "And because she knew you loved her."

"I did love her," Fred admitted, then amended quickly. "I *do* love her."

Doc wagged his hand between them. "Hell, I know that. Everybody knows that. You were the most stable couple I ever knew—once you got over being so damned insecure. In fact, I've never told anyone this before, but I used to wish Velma and I could have the kind of marriage the two of you had."

That surprised Fred. He sent Doc a sideways glance. "You did. You *do*."

Doc shook his head quickly. "No. No, we don't. Don't get me wrong—we have a good marriage. A really good marriage. And I love her. But it's not the same." He sighed softly and turned his gaze toward the poster on the wall. "Velma and I have built a good life together, but you and Phoebe . . . Well, you two were the only people I ever knew who belonged together absolutely."

Fred had always believed that, too. Now he wondered.

Doc palmed the gray fringe of hair that rimmed his head. "Don't let some blowhard like LeGrande Macafee get to you."

Easier said than done, but Fred didn't argue. Doc had no

idea what Fred had been through, and Fred was in no mood to set him straight. He lowered himself to the edge of his seat again. Not because he wanted to talk to Doc again—he didn't. But because he still wanted his coffee, and he *had* been here first.

Doc seemed to think he'd said something to soften Fred. He rested both arms on the table and smiled.

Fred didn't smile back. Instead, he asked, "Are you finished?"

Doc's smile evaporated and a ridge formed between his eyes. "No, I'm not. I know this is tough on you, Fred. The whole thing, from having to see LeGrande again and hear what he said, to finding his body, to being accused of his murder. But you're about the most stubborn damn fool I've ever met."

"Take a look in the mirror," Fred muttered.

Doc's scowl darkened. "No, *you* take a look in the mirror. You're not acting like yourself. I've never seen you like this."

Maybe because Fred had never *felt* like this before. Hurt. Angry. Betrayed. Lied to, and by the person who'd mattered to him most. But he didn't share any of that with Doc.

Doc leaned a bit closer. "You know what, Fred? I'm disappointed in you. Why don't you stop feeling sorry for yourself?"

"Oh, well, I'm sorry," Fred snarled. "It's selfish of me, I suppose, to let a little thing like this bother me."

The wrinkles on Doc's face deepened. "It's *stupid*," he snapped. "That's what it is. Everybody who ever knew LeGrande Macafee knows what a liar he was. And if you don't know better than to believe one word he said, you're nothing but a fool. And if you don't know the kind of woman Phoebe was by now, you were right all those years ago. You *didn't* deserve her."

Fred clenched his fists under the table to keep from belting Doc right in his big mouth. He tightened his jaw to keep from saying anything that might keep this conversation going.

Doc finally seemed to understand. He pushed to his feet, but instead of getting the hell away from Fred, he propped his hands on his hips and glared down at him. "Enos would have my hide if he knew I'd said something like this to you, but it's time for you to stop moping around and feeling picked on."

"I'm not feeling picked on," Fred argued. But it was a lie, and they both knew it.

"When I was in trouble," Doc went on, "you got out there and did everything you could to prove me innocent." He waved his hand in the air again. "You poked and prodded and dug around until you found out what really happened. You didn't let anyone talk bad about me. I know. People have told me what you did."

Fred slanted a glance at him. "That's because you weren't guilty."

"Yeah?" Doc snorted. "Well, neither are you."

With that parting shot, he pivoted and stormed away. His footsteps echoed on the linoleum. Agitation radiated from every jerky step and movement of his arms.

More than a little flabbergasted, Fred watched him for a second. The damned old fool didn't understand. He couldn't. Still, Fred had to admit, he had a point—a weak one, but a point of sorts.

This certainly wasn't the first time there'd been trouble in Cutler. Not even the first time there'd been a murder. Every time Enos warned Fred away. But Fred had always done what he knew to be right—until now.

Now, when he needed to rely upon himself most, he chose to rely on everyone else. Now, when he had more at stake than he'd ever had in his life, he decided to sit in his rocking chair and hope somebody would do something—anything.

He sent one more glance at Doc and grudgingly admitted the old coot was right. He thought about going after him, then decided against it. He knew Doc too well. If Fred admitted he'd been wrong, even once, Doc would never let him forget it.

Leaning back in his seat, he gave in to a bitter smile. He knew exactly what Margaret would say if he started digging into the murder. He knew what Enos would say. But he didn't care. Anything would be better than sitting around home and thinking.

eleven

Fred paused in front of the newly opened Gypsy Dypsy Ice Cream Parlor to wipe his brow. He hesitated for a moment and thought about going inside. Fred loved ice cream, and he usually didn't pass up an opportunity to treat himself. But though his temper had cooled a bit in the nearly two days since his conversations with Enos, Janice, and Doc, everything else, including his appetite, had suffered.

Digging his hands into his pockets, he glanced inside the wide picture window at the people standing in line. For the most part, signs and the sun's glare blocked his view, but he could see Pete Scott's new young wife behind the counter and Faith Arnesson holding a double-dip cone.

If he went inside, Margaret would find out about it. Doc had the whole blasted town brainwashed into reporting his diet violations. But he didn't worry about that. Let Margaret say whatever she wanted, Fred didn't care.

Nor did he care that he'd somehow managed to misplace his heart pills sometime during the past few days. He must have taken them out of his pocket and put them somewhere. Now he couldn't remember where.

The sensible thing to do would be to ask Doc for a refill. But Fred didn't want to see Doc, and he certainly didn't want to give the old fool a chance to shoot off his big mouth to Margaret. Fred didn't need the blasted pills, anyway. And he'd find them eventually.

Faith Arnesson stepped out of the door, nodded a greet-

ing, and hurried away. Pete Scott's new young wife handed
a cone to Sterling Jeppson. The line inched forward.

Fred made up his mind. Life was too short to pass up an
opportunity for ice cream in August. He stepped through the
door and took up the empty space Faith had left. Squinting
at the long blackboard that took up a wall behind the
counter, he tried to read the flavors, but his eyes couldn't
make out the words.

Disgusting to get so old.

As he glanced away, he noticed a familiar dark head near
the front of the line and smiled slowly. His granddaughter,
Sarah. If anyone could make him feel better, one of his
grandkids could.

He'd missed Sarah since she went away to college, and he
hadn't seen nearly enough of her since she came home for
the summer. He knew she'd been having a difficult time
adjusting to her parents' separation and that Margaret was
having trouble adjusting to having an adult daughter.

At twenty-one, Sarah had moved into an adult role—at
least she thought of herself as an adult. From Fred's vantage
point, twenty-one seemed like little more than a child. As a
grandparent, he'd been shifted to the role of observer, where
he had even less influence than he'd had as a parent. But this
would be the perfect chance to visit with Sarah for a few
minutes, and see for himself how she was getting along.

He worked his way past a couple of people who didn't
look thrilled by the idea of letting him pass. He ignored
them and kept his eye on Sarah. But when he saw her lean
against a gangly young man with scraggly white-blond hair
on top of dark brown roots, he stopped in his tracks.

The young man looked down at Sarah and put an arm
around her in a gesture so intimate it caught Fred off guard.
She beamed up at him with a look of adoration and traced
one finger along a scruffy brown mustache that bled down
the sides of his mouth into an equally scruffy goatee.

Fred told himself he didn't mind Sarah having a boy-
friend, he just wished she'd found one who looked a little

less . . . less . . . Well, he couldn't think of the word, but less of whatever it was.

Fred knew Sarah would think him old-fashioned, but the wrinkled shirt, the baggy shorts hanging from the kid's scrawny body, the uncombed hair and unshaven face made him look like a loser. And he *wasn't* the type for Sarah.

Just then someone else pushed into the store, shoving Fred into the backs of the young couple standing in front of him. The entire crowd shifted, and Sarah tore her gaze away from her companion for the first time to scowl at the person behind her.

When she spied Fred, a bright smile spread across her face. "Grandpa. Hi."

The warmth of her greeting made him feel a little better. He smiled and sketched a wave.

Her friend turned to follow Sarah's gaze and gave Fred a slow once-over. His cheeks formed deep hollows in his narrow face, and he looked, in general, as if he could benefit from a good meal.

Sarah said something to the people behind her, then motioned Fred forward. "Come up here with us."

Fred didn't even hesitate. Not only did he hate waiting in line, but he wanted a better look at the scarecrow with his granddaughter. He pushed his way through the crowd, muttering an apology when he felt someone's toes beneath his foot, and came to a stop just behind Sarah and her friend.

She gripped the young man's bony arm and pulled him forward as Fred approached. "Grandpa, this is Dane." She said the name as if she thought Fred had heard of him.

Fred hadn't. He would have remembered. Especially if anyone had warned him about the thin gold chain that dangled from a loop high on one pierced ear, the four other earrings split evenly between both lobes, or the tiny gold ball that decorated one side of his nose.

Good Lord.

Fred tried to work up a smile and forced himself to extend a hand to shake. Instead of shaking, Earring Boy wrapped his hand around the fleshy part of Fred's thumb, slid his hand along the length of his palm, and snagged his fingertips with his own. "Whoa. So you're Sarah's grandpa. She's told me about you, man."

"And you're Dane." For Sarah's sake, Fred tried to sound as if he'd heard of him.

Dane grinned down at Sarah, and for an instant the smile transformed his face. If he let his hair go back to its original color and lost the jewelry, he might not be a bad-looking kid.

Sarah sent Fred a conspiratorial grin. "So, Grandpa, what are you doing in a place like this?"

"I'm having ice cream."

"Mom's going to find out. You know she will."

Fred scowled. He couldn't help it. "I'm a grown man, for Pete's sake. I ought to be able to have an ice-cream cone if I want one."

Sarah grinned up at Dane. Dane grinned back.

Fred changed the subject. "Where did you two meet? In school?"

Sarah's grin faded a watt. "Yes. Didn't Mom tell you about him?" She sounded put out.

"No," Fred admitted. "She didn't." And he knew why. She didn't want to worry him. Thought she had to protect him.

Sarah rolled her big brown eyes in disgust. "That's because she doesn't *approve*."

Imagine that.

"We had a medieval-history course together last year," Earring Boy explained.

Fred gave him a point for that. At least he *did* something.

The three people at the front of the line turned away from the counter holding their ice cream aloft. The line shuffled forward.

Fred shuffled with it. "Medieval history, huh? Is that what you're studying?"

"You mean, like, is it my major?"

"Something like that."

Dane shook his head. The chain danced on his ear. The

nose bob reflected a flash of light. "I graduated in history this year. I'm starting law school in the fall."

Law school? Fred couldn't have hidden his surprise if he'd tried.

Sarah noticed it. A scowl darkened her pretty face. "Yes, law school. He's going to be a criminal defense attorney."

Just what the world needed. Someone who looked as if he belonged on the streets putting criminals back on them. But Fred didn't voice his opinion. He just nodded and said the second thing that came to mind. "Sarah's uncle Joseph is an attorney. In New Hampshire. Corporate law, not criminal."

Dane nodded. "Yeah. She told me. That's not my thing, though—helping big corporations take over the world. I'd rather help the guys who need it."

Guys like rapists and murderers? Touching. Fred didn't say a word. And he refused to let anything show on his face. Besides, he supposed there *were* innocent people who found themselves in need of a defense attorney from time to time. He just hoped he wouldn't end up being one of them.

As if he could read Fred's mind, Earring Boy slouched forward and lowered his voice. "I heard about the murder you guys had here Friday night. Awesome."

Not the word Fred would have chosen, but he didn't argue. He didn't want to discuss the murder in front of Sarah, and he didn't want to talk to Earring Boy about it at all.

He moved another step closer to the counter. Close enough to finally read the blackboard.

Earring Boy must have sensed he'd said something wrong because he corrected himself quickly. "I don't mean awesome like I think murder's cool or anything. But awesome because it's happening while I'm here."

"Yes," Fred said. "Well."

"Sarah tells me you've helped the police with a couple of murder cases."

"I suppose you could say that," Fred admitted. He supposed he didn't mind Sarah bragging about him, or Earring Boy sounding impressed.

"So . . . ?" Dane lifted his dark eyebrows expectantly. They matched the roots of his hair. "Are you going to help out with this one?"

Fred shook his head quickly. "Not this time."

"Why not?" Sarah demanded. She sounded disappointed.

But not nearly as disappointed as she'd be when she learned her grandpa had been accused of the murder. He shrugged casually. At least, he hoped he looked casual. "No need to. Enos has everything under control." He inched forward and checked the ice cream in the front row of cardboard barrels. English Butter Toffee. Almond Mocha Fudge. Strawberry Cheesecake.

"But, Grandpa," Sarah protested. "Wasn't this guy your friend?"

Fred didn't know how to answer that. He didn't want to *lie,* but he certainly didn't intend to admit the truth. Not here, in front of so many people. "We knew each other in school," he said, and turned his attention to a container of Pralines & Cream. "Tell you what," he said, doing his best to sound jovial, "let me pay for your ice cream. You can each have two scoops."

Sarah smiled, but he hadn't thrown her offtrack completely. Her eyes warned him of that. "Thanks. You know what I want."

Fred did. She'd loved Neapolitan ice cream since before she could even walk. He'd never known her to order anything else. "What about you, Dane?"

Dane frowned in concentration, flicked his gaze between the menu and the containers a couple of times, then shrugged. "Pistachio, I guess. And Quarterback Delight."

"Okay. Do you want waffle cones or regular?" Fred could afford to be generous, especially if spending a few extra pennies would divert their attention.

"A waffle cone?" Sarah looked surprised. "I want one."

"I guess I'll have one, too," Dane said, scratching his goatee thoughtfully.

The people in front of them moved out of the way and Fred stepped up to the counter. He smiled at Pete Scott's new young wife, gave her the kids' orders, and added his own. A scoop of Almond Mocha Fudge and one of Caramel Pecan. In a waffle cone. Might as well live it up.

When he heard Dane ask Sarah something totally unrelated to ice cream or murder, he relaxed slightly and paid for the cones. He passed Sarah's and Dane's to them over his shoulder and took an experimental lick of his own. Cold. Creamy. Perfect.

Smiling, he led the way through the crowd toward the door, waited until Sarah and Dane had stepped through, and started outside. But at that moment someone stepped in front of him and he found himself face to chest with Deputy Grady Hatch.

Grady took an exaggerated step backward to let Fred pass.

Fred did.

Instead of going on about his business, Grady followed him away from the door. "So, Fred. How are you holding up?"

Fred scowled at him. He didn't want to discuss the murder in front of Sarah. No telling what kind of fool thing Grady might say. He took a lick of his melting ice cream. "I'm hot. How about you?"

"The same." Grady looked out over Main Street and wiped his brow. "It's a scorcher."

Sarah had followed Dane a few feet down the boardwalk. She perched against the handrail and laughed at something he said. But when she realized Fred wasn't with them, she glanced around to find him and saw Grady standing there. Grinning, she tugged Dane back toward them. "Grady. Hi."

Grady looked pleased to see her. Not so pleased by her choice of companions, but he hid his reaction well. "Hello, Sarah. Someone told me you were home for the summer, but I was beginning to think it was all a rumor."

"I know. I know." She laughed and ducked her head. "I haven't been out much." She looked back up at Dane and the sparkle returned to her eye. "This is my friend Dane Riggs."

Always the gentleman, Grady offered a hand to shake.

Dane gave him the same treatment he'd given Fred—the thumb wrap, the hand brush, the finger clutch. "How's it goin'? I hear you had a murder in town Friday."

Great. The kid wasn't only tacky, he was tactless.

Grady's eyes narrowed slightly. "Yes, we did. Where did you hear about that?"

"All over, man. It's the talk of the town. Everywhere we go, somebody's talking about it."

Grady nodded slowly, but he flicked a warning glance in Fred's direction, as if he thought Fred might suddenly be overcome by the urge to confide in Earring Boy.

Not much danger of that.

Earring Boy looked up the street and back again. "I guess it's understandable in a place this size. The gossip, I mean."

Not surprisingly, Grady scowled. He always got defensive when someone tried to make Cutler sound like a backwater town. Fred usually did, too. But he didn't feel like arguing about it today. He had more important things on his mind.

"People are the same all over," Grady said. "It doesn't matter where they live."

"True," Dane said thoughtfully. "But it's not like, say, Denver, where there's a murder every day."

Grady's scowl deepened. He didn't seem any more impressed than Fred by Sarah's choice of companions. "I don't think Denver's murder rate is quite that high."

Dane laughed through his nose. "I'm exaggerating, man. I know it's not that high. It's just that . . . well, in a place like this, you don't expect something like murder."

Grady obviously didn't appreciate that observation. He stiffened and drew himself up to his full height. "We have our share of excitement up here," he said, sharing a glance with Fred. "Sometimes more than our share."

Certainly more than Fred's share. But he didn't say that, either. Instead, he nodded toward the ice-cream parlor and tried to steer the conversation in a less threatening direction.

"So, you're heading inside?" He licked his ice cream again, just in case Grady needed encouragement.

Grady glanced over his shoulder as if he'd forgotten where they were. "Yeah. I thought I would."

But Dane wasn't ready to let the conversation end. "So, do you have a suspect yet?"

Grady's face reddened. "One or two."

One or two? Fred had to admit he liked the sound of that. He slanted a curious glance at Grady but didn't let himself ask.

Grady shifted his weight and looked away, as if he needed to decide how much, if anything, to say. "It sounds like LeGrande Macafee wasn't the world's best-liked person."

An understatement if Fred had ever heard one. But he kept his opinion to himself. "What makes you think that?"

Grady shrugged. "Nothing anyone actually said. It's just the way they act when they talk about him. Stiff—you know."

Fred did.

Grady pondered some more, shifted again, and gave his duty belt a twitch. "What do you know about Oliver Wellington?"

The question caught Fred by surprise. "Oliver? Not much. I only saw him at reunions. He's the world's most boring man, but I hear he's doing well financially."

"That's what I've heard," Grady admitted. "But I'm not sure it's true. What about Jeremiah Hunt?"

Fred studied Grady for a second before he answered. "I've heard he used to work for LeGrande, but he quit."

"Thea Griffin?"

That named stopped Fred cold. "Thea? She's a widow. Why?"

"They're all the people we know of so far who've had contact with LeGrande in the last little while."

The first two, Fred could believe. But Thea? He scowled at Grady. "Thea hadn't seen him in over fifty years."

"I didn't say she'd seen him," Grady said. "But according to LeGrande's secretary, she called him last month."

"Last month? Are you sure?"

"As sure as I can be." Grady wiped his sleeve across his forehead. "I've got to tell you, Fred, this case has me stumped. Our victim's a man nobody's seen in fifty years, but everybody has a reason to hate. Hell, the only person we can completely rule out is Percy Neuswander, and that's only because he couldn't have inflicted the wound from his wheelchair."

Dane pushed himself into the conversation. "So, everybody's a suspect?"

"Everybody but Grandpa and the guy in the wheelchair," Sarah reminded him.

Fred hoped Grady had enough sense not to set her straight, but he didn't want to take any chances. "Grady really shouldn't be talking about an ongoing investigation—should you, son?"

"No," Grady agreed. "And neither should you. Especially this time."

Fred could have kicked him for saying that. He willed Sarah to take no notice.

But it caught her attention, just as it would have her mother's. "Why *this* time?"

Belatedly, Grady realized he'd said something he shouldn't. He flushed and tried to backpedal. "No special reason."

Sarah knew him too well. She narrowed her eyes and dragged her gaze from Grady to Fred. "You *are* helping, aren't you, Grandpa? I knew it."

"I already told you I'm not," Fred insisted. "Like I said, I went to school with the guy. And I was at the reunion Friday night. Other than that, I'm not involved."

Grady tried to make up for his mistake. "You're jumping to a pretty big conclusion, Sarah. There are lots of reasons Enos doesn't want us talking about this case."

"Yes, but—" She broke off, confused. Her eyes narrowed

even further. "You both look like you're trying to hide something. I'm not a child anymore, you know."

As if to prove that, Earring Boy put a supportive arm around her waist.

"Nobody's saying you're a child," Fred assured her. But he could tell by the look on her face that he'd have to tell her something or she'd never stop asking questions. "The truth is, I'm the one who found the body."

Relief tempered the suspicion in her eyes. "Is that it?"

"That's it," Fred lied.

Grady bobbed his head enthusiastically. "Enos doesn't want him talking about it—to anyone."

"Whoa," Dane said. "You mean, like, there are things at the scene of the crime only Gramps and the murderer know about?"

Gramps? Fred snorted and sent him a withering look only a complete fool could misinterpret.

Grady's lips twitched as if he found something amusing. But when he saw Fred's glare, he sobered instantly. "Could be. We don't know yet."

Thankfully, Sarah seemed content with the explanation. She took another healthy lick of her ice cream and smiled at Dane. "See? Didn't I tell you my grandpa's a kick?"

Dane nodded, but he seemed to sense something Sarah didn't. He trailed his slow blue gaze across Fred's face, as if he could see inside him if he concentrated. "Yeah," he said at last. "Awesome."

Sarah didn't seem to notice. She stepped away to toss the rest of her cone into the garbage can, then turned back to face Fred again. "Isn't he great, Grandpa?"

Obviously, she wanted them to form a mutual admiration society. Fred did his best to oblige. "Wonderful."

She beamed, took Mr. Wonderful's arm again, and leaned against him. "I knew you'd hit it off. I just knew it."

Oh, yes. They'd hit it off, all right. Destined to become pals. Fred could feel it in his bones.

Grady chuckled softly and turned away so Fred couldn't see the grin on his face. Very funny.

Sarah kept smiling, delighted by the impending friendship. "Then, Grandpa, can I ask you a favor?"

Fred cocked an eyebrow at her. "What kind of favor?"

"It's not a big thing," she assured him quickly. But she widened her eyes and looked up at him the way she had as a child when she wanted something she shouldn't have.

Phoebe had been able to resist that look most of the time. Fred hadn't. Not once. Even when, as now, it sent curls of apprehension up his spine.

"It's just that Dane needs a place to stay while he's here," she said. "Mom doesn't think it would look right for him to stay with us. Benjamin and Deborah are spending the whole month with Dad, so there's lots of room, but she *still* won't let him stay."

Fred's smile froze in place.

Earring Boy tried to look sincere.

Sarah flashed a hopeful smile. "So, can he stay with you?"

Grady stole another amused look at Fred.

"With *me*?" Fred shook his head and tried to come up with a reason for refusing that wouldn't offend Sarah.

She widened her eyes a bit more. "It would just be for a couple of weeks."

A couple of *weeks*? With Earring Boy? Not on his life.

"He wouldn't be any trouble. We'd spend most of our time together."

That's what worried Fred. He could just imagine what Margaret would have to say if he let Earring Boy stay with him.

Grady snorted a laugh. "What a great idea. With Dane around to keep you company, you won't have to search for things to keep you occupied."

"I have plenty to do," Fred snapped. But the disappointment on Sarah's face tugged at his heart, and the determination in her dark eyes convinced him she'd find some way to keep Dane around if he refused. He tempered his response with a smile. "But that doesn't mean Dane's not welcome. I'd be glad to have him."

He excused the lie in the interest of family harmony. And the sudden grateful smile on his granddaughter's face almost made it worth the sacrifice.

Almost.

```
┌─                    ─┐

        twelve

└─                    ─┘
```

Fred poured his second cup of coffee of the morning and stared out the window at the lake. The sun winked off the water's smooth surface and a light breeze teased the tops of the trees lining the shore. He'd spent the past hour searching for his pills, but he still couldn't find them. And the sound of Dane moving around in his son Joseph's old bedroom down the hall grated on his already raw nerves.

On top of everything else, now he had to play host to Mr. Wonderful. Honestly, he didn't know how much more he could take.

Footsteps padded down the hallway into the living room. A minute later the television blared to life. Earring Boy had an addiction to the television that only his never-ending chatter could rival—as if Fred *wanted* to know what went on in his head.

It was a damned shame when a man couldn't even enjoy his morning coffee in peace. He just hoped Sarah would come after Dane soon and that she'd keep him busy the rest of the day.

Barely controlling his irritation, he left his coffee on the counter and pushed open the swinging door that led into the living room. A pair of huge bare feet propped on the arm of the couch greeted him. A second later Dane's face appeared at the other end of the couch. "Morning, Gramps."

Fred didn't answer immediately. He crossed the room, turned off the television set, and wheeled around to face him. "Let's get one thing straight right now. You can call me Mr. Vickery. I don't even mind if you call me Fred. But *don't* call me Gramps."

Dane's smile faded. "Sorry."

The apology made Fred feel a little better, but not much. He nodded toward the television and set another rule. "And leave the set off until noon, at least. You don't need it on so early in the morning."

Dane stretched two hairy brown arms over his head and sank back onto the cushions. "Sorry." He scratched the hair on his bare chest. "So, what's the plan this morning?"

Fred crossed to his rocking chair by the front window and settled himself into it. "I don't have any plans."

"Really? You're just going to sit here?"

"No." Fred retrieved the morning *Post* from the floor beside his chair and tugged off the rubber band. "I'm going to read my newspaper."

"Anything in there about your murder?"

"It's not *my* murder," Fred reminded him. "And I doubt there'll be a mention of it. It's a Denver newspaper."

Dane sat up and lowered his feet to the floor. "Check it out. Maybe there's something in there."

"There isn't." Fred lifted the paper to hide his face, but he could still see Dane from the corner of his eye.

"Then do you mind if I take a look?" Dane didn't wait for an answer. He stood, crossed the room, and tried to sneak a section of the newspaper from Fred's lap.

Fred slapped his hand on top of it. "You can read it when I'm finished."

Dane took a step backward and perched on the arm of the couch. "Okay, man. That's cool. I can wait." Apparently, he couldn't wait long. Within seconds he began to fidget. Another minute later he broke that uneasy silence in the room. "Have you heard anything else about the murder?"

Fred scanned the headlines on the front page. "I can't talk about it."

Dane ran his hand over his bleached hair. "Yeah, I know. But—"

Fred lowered the paper and scowled at him over the top of it. "You heard the deputy yesterday. I can't talk about it."

Dane rested his elbows on his knees and tilted his head so he could see Fred behind the paper. "Yeah, but I've been thinking."

No doubt his mother would be proud.

"I just can't figure out why anybody would want to kill an old man like that."

"Why not?" Fred lifted the paper again and turned the page. "You think just because he's old, nobody cares about him anymore?"

"It's not that." Dane leaned farther into Fred's line of sight. "It's just *where* it happened that bugs me. I mean, you were at the school in the middle of a reunion, right?"

Fred slanted a glance at him. "Right."

"And the only people there were a bunch of old—" Dane broke off and sent Fred an embarrassed smile. "Old class-mates."

Fred didn't bother asking what Dane had been about to say. He got the gist of it. He pretended interest in an article on foreign policy.

Dane didn't let that stop him. "So, doesn't it seem weird that somebody would wait fifty years or more to bump the guy off?"

It wouldn't sound weird if he'd known LeGrande.

Dane paced to the round oak table where Fred kept his family photographs. He picked up one of Fred and Phoebe with all four children standing in a fishing boat on Yellow-stone Lake. One of Fred's favorites.

Earring Boy didn't look impressed. He replaced the frame on the table and ran a hand across his scraggly chin hair. "When you found the body, did you see or hear anyone else around?"

"I think we'd better change the subject."

Dane frowned, but a spark of mischief lit his eyes. "Oh, come on. What will it hurt to talk to me? I don't know any of these people. Who am I going to tell?"

Fred shook his head. "That's not the point—"

"Come *on*. I saw the look on your face yesterday when we were talking to that deputy. You're just dying to get involved, aren't you?"

Fred sent him a look that had always convinced his children to toe the line. "It doesn't bother me in the least."

Earring Boy just leaned closer and grinned. "From what Sarah tells me, you're always right in the middle of stuff. So, why are sitting here in your rocking chair this morning instead of trying to figure out what happened?"

Instinct told Fred to leave the room, but he refused to let some punk kid bulldoze him in his own house. Slowly, he refolded the newspaper and dropped it to the floor again. But before he could say anything more, unfamiliar footsteps sounded on the front porch followed by a loud knock.

Silently thanking whoever had chosen to interrupt, Fred pushed to his feet and flicked a glance at Dane's bare chest. "Go get dressed. I don't want you lounging around the house half-naked."

Dane shrugged elaborately and stood to face him. "Want me to see who that is first?"

"No. I want you to put a shirt on." Fred crossed the room, waited for Dane to disappear inside the bedroom, then worked up a smile and pulled open the door.

But when he saw Ivan Neeley standing on the other side in uniform, his smile evaporated.

Ivan nodded once. "Fred."

"Ivan."

Ivan lifted his eyebrows, no doubt expecting Fred to invite him inside.

Fred didn't. He hadn't forgiven him for questioning Margaret or putting ideas about quitting into Enos's head. "What do you want?"

"I want to ask you a few more questions about the Macafee murder." The Macafee murder. As if Enos and the boys had a hundred unsolved murders on the books. Ivan always had liked to make himself sound important.

"I've already told Enos everything I know," Fred reminded him.

Ivan shifted position on his stocky legs and propped his hands on his duty belt, no doubt hoping to look threatening. "Yes. Well. I need you to tell me."

Fred scowled at him. "Does Enos know you're here?"

Ivan flushed and shifted position again. He looked for all the world like a little boy caught with his hand in the cookie jar. "Of course he knows. He asked me to talk to you."

Fred didn't believe that for an instant. If Enos had questions, he'd ask them himself.

Ivan drew himself up to his full, inconsiderable height. "Are you going to let me in? Or do I have to tell Enos you're uncooperative?"

Fred deepened his scowl. "I've never been uncooperative with you, and you know it. But I have a houseguest. I don't want to talk about this in front of him."

As if on cue, Dane came back into the room. He'd put on a shirt so wrinkled Fred figured he must have wadded it under his pillow and slept on it. When he saw Ivan, excitement brightened his face. He closed the distance between them and hovered behind Fred's shoulder.

Ivan divided a disapproving glance between them. "Who's this?"

"Dane Riggs." Dane extended his hand as if he intended to shake Ivan's. Fred stepped aside and let him perform his ritual on the hand Ivan offered. "I'm a friend of the family."

Not exactly the way Fred would have introduced him, but he didn't argue. He enjoyed the shock on Ivan's face too much.

Ivan swept his gaze from Dane's head to his feet and back again. "Well, Mr. Riggs, I'll have to ask you to leave us alone. I'm here on official business."

Dane laughed triumphantly and thumped Fred on the shoulder. "So, they're asking for your help, after all. I knew they would."

Fred didn't see any reason to correct him.

Apparently, Ivan did. "We don't need help," he said with a sneer. "Especially from the main suspect in a murder case."

Fred could have belted him. Honestly. And he might have done so if Dane hadn't been standing there, if Ivan hadn't been on duty, and if he hadn't known how much worse losing his temper would make everthing.

Dane's smile faded instantly and disbelief replaced the excitement in his eyes. "Suspect? *Gramps?*" He let out an uneasy laugh. "No way."

Fred firmed up his stance and met Ivan's sneer squarely. "I didn't kill LeGrande Macafee." He spoke slowly, so Ivan could understand the hard words. "I found his body. I called Enos. I kept the others from disturbing the murder scene. I did everything a concerned citizen *should* do."

Ivan shook his head slowly. "Yeah, but you had a motive, Fred. Nobody else did."

"Bullshit." The word popped out of his mouth before he had time to think about it. "Everybody had a motive. LeGrande made enemies everywhere he went. For hell's sake, Ivan. You've known me your whole life. You know I didn't kill anybody."

Ivan narrowed his eyes. "That's what you're counting on, isn't it? That we'll ignore the evidence because of who you are."

"I *want* you to look at the evidence," Fred insisted. "*All* of it." He tried unsuccessfully to quash the growing desperation in his voice.

Something he couldn't identify sparkled in Ivan's eyes, and Ivan held out a brown evidence bag. "Even this?"

"What is it?"

"A prescription bottle." Ivan's sneer grew. "We found it by the body. You might be interested to know whose prescription it is."

Ominous dread crept through Fred. He knew exactly what was inside without asking.

Dane gaped at him. "Is it yours?"

"It's his," Ivan said. "So, Fred, suppose you tell me how it got next to the murder victim."

Fred could barely make himself speak. "It must have fallen out of my pocket when I took his pulse."

"Oh?" Ivan widened his eyes in obvious disbelief.

"For hell's sake—" Fred began.

But Dane cut him off. "I don't know Gramps very well," he said slowly, "but I think you're wrong about him."

Ivan snorted a laugh. "Yeah? Well, think what you want."

That did it. The slender thread holding Fred's temper in check snapped. He met Ivan's gaze straight on. "The damned pills fell out of my pocket when I checked his pulse," he said again, a little louder this time. "You don't have one bit of hard evidence against me. There's no murder weapon with my fingerprints on it. No witness who saw me kill the son of a bitch."

A flicker of uncertainty moved through Ivan's gaze. "Not yet, but—"

Fred straightened his shoulders a bit further and spoke with far more confidence than he felt. "Are you here to arrest me?"

"Not yet."

"No." Fred raised his voice a notch. Through the haze of anger, he noted the surprise on Dane's face and the furious red creeping into Ivan's. But that didn't stop him from having his say. "You're not going to arrest me because you don't have a case. You're here to harass me, because you think it will make you look important."

Ivan puffed out his chest and tried to look tough. "I'm here to question a murder suspect."

"I've already answered your questions," Fred shouted. "But since nothing I've said has made it through your thick skull to your brain, I'll tell you once more. I did *not* kill LeGrande Macafee."

Dane let out a slow whistle.

Ivan put a threatening hand on his sidearm. "I could drag you down to the station and ask my questions there."

Fred held out both hands to make it easier for the whelp to cuff him. "Do it, then. Let's go." He was tempting fate, but he couldn't stop himself.

Dane put a restraining hand on his arm. Fred shrugged it off.

Ivan stayed completely still for a few seconds longer, but some of his bravado faded. "You're pushing it, Fred. You know that."

"Maybe," Fred snapped. "But so are you. It's bad enough that you even suggest me, but it's worse than you frightened my daughter half to death. I'm warning you, Ivan, if I hear you've disturbed my family again or dragged my name through the mud, I'll have your butt in a sling. So, unless you can produce some real evidence against me, we're through here."

Ivan took a step backward, made one more attempt to look intimidating. It didn't work. "If you did it, I'll prove it."

"Go ahead and try," Fred yelled. "You'll make yourself the laughingstock of the whole county." Without giving Ivan a chance to respond, he slammed the door hard enough to make the window rattle. It gave him an odd satisfaction. And the sound of Ivan's retreating footsteps made him feel even better.

Behind me, Dane let out another low whistle. "Awesome."

Fred ignored him and tried unsuccessfully to still the trembling of his hand. Ivan had gone too far. But the case against Fred was gathering steam. Doc was right. If anyone else in Fred's family had been in this kind of trouble, he wouldn't have let anything stop him from asking questions or trying to prove their innocence. And it was high time he stopped counting on someone else to clear him.

Swearing softly, he snagged his keys from the table where he'd dropped them last night.

Dane stepped in front of him. "Where are you going?"

"Out."

"You want me to come with you?"

"No. I want you to stay right here until you hear from Sarah."

"Are you sure?"

"More than sure. And I don't want you saying a word to

her or her mother about what just happened. They don't need to know."

"They won't hear it from me."

"If anyone calls, tell them you don't know where I went."

"I *don't* know," Dane reminded me. "Where *are* you going?"

Fred wrenched open the front door and stepped out onto the porch. "I'm going to take care of business." He didn't clarify. Dane knew too much already. And he didn't want to take the chance of the kid letting something slip.

Fred knew he'd be asking for trouble by taking this step. But it didn't seem to matter. No matter what he did or didn't do, trouble seemed determined to find him.

It came down to two options. He could sit in his rocking chair and wait for Ivan to arrive with the handcuffs, or he could do something to prove himself innocent.

But Fred had never been much good at sitting, and he didn't have the patience to wait. He had to find some way to shift the odds back in his favor. He had no idea where to begin looking. But he couldn't let that stop him. He'd faced tougher odds than this before, and he'd managed to come out on top. He'd just never had quite so much at stake.

thirteen

Fred ground the Buick's ignition to life, shifted into reverse, and turned around to check behind him before he backed out of the garage. Just as he started to accelerate, something darted into the path of the car.

Swearing aloud, he slammed on his brakes and narrowly missed hitting Dane. He shoved open the car door and glared at the kid through the opening. "What the hell do you think you're doing?"

"Coming with you, man." Dane rounded the back of the car and planted himself in front of the door. "Sarah just called. She has to do something with her mother, so she said I should hang with you."

"I don't want you to hang with me," Fred snapped, and tried to shut the door again.

Dane blocked him. He ran his hands over his two-toned hair and smiled. "Well, okay. I'll go back inside and call her again. I'll just explain that you're going somewhere."

That made Fred hesitate. He didn't want Dane to come with him. He didn't want Margaret to know he'd gone somewhere in the Buick—she'd know what that meant. And he *certainly* didn't want to leave Dane alone in his house. It didn't leave him with much of a choice, but of all the evils, letting Dane come along seemed like the least offensive.

Sending the kid a grudging nod, he shoved the car into

park. "Go inside and put on some shoes. And a decent shirt. One that doesn't look like you slept in it."

Dane's grin widened. "Yeah. Sure." He bolted across the sidewalk, jumped onto the front porch, and disappeared inside.

Time was, Fred had been able to move like that. But no longer. It was hell to get old. Within minutes Dane came through the front door again. Thankfully, he'd not only changed into a clean black T-shirt, but he'd also put on a respectable-looking pair of jeans. Grinning, he sprinted back toward the car and slid into the passenger's seat. "Where to?"

Fred put the car into reverse again. "To see an old friend."

"Cool. Why?"

"So I can find some other old friends."

Dane shifted sideways in his seat and ran a hand across his hair. "Friends from the reunion?"

Fred nodded, checked for oncoming traffic, and backed onto Lake Front Drive. "Yes. But let's get one thing straight right up front. I do the talking. You're just along for the ride."

"Sure. Okay."

He sounded agreeable enough. He even looked agreeable. But Fred wanted to make sure he understood. "I'm serious. Not a word. No matter what I say, you don't say a word."

"Got it."

Fred relaxed slightly, slowed when he neared the intersection with Main Street, and waited for Sophie Van Dyke to pass by before starting around the corner.

Dane faced forward again and smoothed a hand across his stomach. "So what you mean is, when you're scamming people, you don't want me to give you away."

Fred turned too far, overcorrected, and glared at Dane when he finally got the wheel under control. "I don't scam people."

"Oh. Right. Then why do you want me to keep quiet?"

"Because she doesn't know you, and you're . . ." He

waved a vague hand in front of him. "She doesn't know you."

"Yeah, but you're the number-one suspect in the murder."

"I'm one of the suspects," Fred admitted.

"That guy who came to the house said you're number one."

Fred scowled at him. "That's only because the widow accused me of killing her husband in front of the entire reunion."

"And because your prescription bottle was by the body."

Fred deepened his scowl, but he couldn't deny it. "And because my pills fell out of my pocket when I checked his pulse."

Dane let out a low whistle. "When you do something, you do it all the way, don't you?"

Fred felt a smile tug at his lips. He couldn't stop it. "I try to."

Laughing softly, Dane slouched in his seat. "So who's this old friend we're going to see?"

Fred hesitated before answering, but it took him only a second to realize it didn't matter. Dane would find out soon enough. He slowed to let Kirby Manning pull out of the bank's parking lot. "Her name is Ardella Neuswander."

"And who is she?"

"The class busybody."

Dane chuckled. "I guess every class has one, huh?"

"People are people," Fred told him, "no matter how old they are or where they live."

"Okay. Who was your class nerd?"

"Nerd?" Fred chuckled. "I guess that would have been Jeremiah Hunt."

"And the boring guy?"

He didn't need to think about that one. "Oliver Wellington."

Dane nodded slowly, as if he needed to remember the names. "The smartest one in your class?"

"Thea Griffin. And the most popular was my wife, Phoebe." He spied Summer Dey watching him from the window of The Cosmic Tradition, but he didn't panic. If anyone else had seen him, he'd worry. The realization that he trusted Summer to keep her mouth shut caught him by surprise. He pushed the notion aside and concentrated on driving.

"Who was your class jock?" Dane asked.

Fred checked the windows of the Bluebird as they passed for signs of Enos or one of his deputies. He didn't trust them not to follow. Luckily, he didn't see anyone watching. Convinced the coast was clear, he accelerated and drove into the forest. "Ardella's husband, Percy, was our star athlete. He's in a wheelchair now."

"No kidding?" Dane slanted an interested glance at him.

"No kidding. They live down in Granby."

"And that's where we're headed, right?"

"Right."

"And we're just going to drop in on them?"

"It works better that way."

Dane's grin worked its way across his face again. "The element of surprise?"

"Something like that."

"Why don't you just call her?"

"I don't like the telephone," Fred said with a shrug. "You can't see a person's eyes or the expressions on their face. Sometimes it's not so much what they say as how they say it. Or even what they don't say."

Dane nodded. "Body language."

"Exactly." Fred steered the Buick around a hairpin curve and stole a glance at the young man. "You can tell a lot about a person by their body language."

"Oh, yeah. I know all about that." Dane straightened in his seat. "What about the other people you're trying to find?"

"Grady asked me about three people yesterday," Fred reminded him. "I figure it would be smart to start with one of them."

Dane nodded solemnly. "Makes sense. And we're going

to see Ardella because you don't know where to find them, but she does."

"Right."

"But if she thinks you're the murderer, how are you going to convince her to tell you?"

"I'm still working on that."

"So, which one of the others are you going to see first?"

"I guess that depends on which one lives closest."

"And which one do you think murdered the guy?"

"None of them."

Dane's eyes rounded in confusion. "None of them?"

"I can't imagine any of them committing murder," Fred admitted. If one of his classmates killed LeGrande, he'd also left Fred to take the rap. Fred couldn't believe that of anyone. "I think I know who did, but I can't prove it—yet."

"Who?"

"LeGrande's son, Roger."

"His son?" Dane shook his head in amazement. "Man, that bites. What makes you think he did it?"

"Because I saw him there. I witnessed a fight between them." And because he couldn't imagine anyone else capable of the act. But honesty forced him to admit silently that any one of his former classmates could have done it if LeGrande had upset them enough.

Dane broke into his thoughts. "But you didn't actually see him kill the guy, right?"

Some of Fred's natural good humor faded. He'd been asked that question one too many times, and every time a bit more of his certainty evaporated. "No. That's why we're on our way down the mountain." Saying it aloud for the first time made it more real somehow. But if not Roger, then who?

The Jeremiah he remembered wouldn't have had the nerve. Oliver had the nerve, but Fred honestly couldn't imagine LeGrande letting down his guard around him long enough to let Oliver get the best of him.

And Thea? Fred tried to force the idea out of his mind. He didn't want to believe Thea had anything to do with

LeGrande *or* the murder. He tried telling himself Grady had misunderstood LeGrande's secretary, that Thea hadn't called LeGrande's office last month, that he hadn't seen the hatred in her eyes when LeGrande walked into the reunion. But he had to face reality. Now, more than ever before, Fred couldn't afford to let sentiment blind him.

Half an hour later Fred pulled into the Neuswanders' driveway and shut off the ignition. He didn't get out of the car immediately, but sat for a moment trying to gear up for the conversation ahead.

A concrete ramp slanted from the double driveway to the wide front door. Hanging baskets filled with pink flowers swung in the breeze. A gray cat dozed in the shade of an orange-berried bush. The place looked homey. Comfortable. So why did he feel so apprehensive?

Because Dane had a point—one Fred hadn't seriously considered before. Ardella might refuse to talk to him. She might slam the door in his face. Well, Fred just couldn't let that happen. One way or another, he had to convince Ardella she could trust him.

He pushed open his door and climbed out into the heat. To his relief, the breeze had already lowered the temperature by several degrees.

Dane unfolded himself, stood, and took a slow look around. "This reminds me of my grandma's house."

He looked so wistful, Fred couldn't help but ask, "Do you see her often?"

"No." The softness in Dane's expression vanished. He started up the ramp.

Fred couldn't help but wonder why. But now wasn't the time to ask. Stuffing his hands into his pockets, he followed the boy to the front door. By the time he made it to the top of the ramp, Dane had already rung the bell and Ardella answered just as he came to a stop.

The air around her smelled like cookies—spicy-sweet and chocolaty. She wiped her hands on the apron tied around her waist and smoothed the back of her honey-colored hair. When she saw Fred, her eyes widened and she took a step backward. "Fred? What are you doing here?" She didn't look pleased to see him.

Fred tried not to let it bother him. He pasted on his friendliest smile and tugged open the screen that stood between them. "Ardella. Mind if I talk to you for a few minutes?"

She glanced over her shoulder, then shook her head quickly. "No. No, of course not. I just didn't expect to see you and your friend." Her eyes lit on Dane and she stiffened, as if she expected him to mug her on the spot.

Fred put a hand on the boy's shoulder. "This is Dane Riggs. He's dating my granddaughter."

Ardella's expression tightened even more. She stepped away from the door to let them enter. "Come in. Percy's in the backyard."

"I don't want to disturb him," Fred assured her. "I just need to ask you a couple of questions." He stepped inside and waited while she closed the door. The narrow living room looked like Ardella—busy. Knickknacks and framed photographs crowded almost every surface, but the wood beneath them gleamed. A piano littered with sheet music stood against one wall and a jungle of green plants overran a table near a side window.

Ardella waved them toward the sofa and perched uncomfortably on a reclining chair. She turned a smile on them, but it looked forced. Nervous. "What can I help you with?"

Fred sat beside Dane, folded his hands together, and made an extra effort to look nonthreatening. "You don't need to worry, Ardella. I didn't kill LeGrande."

She let out a nervous titter. "Oh, heavens. I never thought you did."

It was a lie, and they both knew it. But Fred didn't contradict her. He nodded, as if he believed her. "I'm glad to hear that because I need your help."

She pulled back sharply, laughed again, and stopped herself by pressing her lips together. She darted another nervous glance toward the kitchen door, as if she wished Percy would come in and rescue her. "What kind of help?"

Fred leaned forward slightly. "I've got to prove that I'm innocent."

Her eyes darted from Fred to Dane and back again. "How are you going to do that?"

Dane sent her a friendly smile.

Fred matched it. "By talking to everyone who was at the reunion that night. That's where you come in."

She put one hand to her breast and laughed again. "Me? I don't understand."

"I need addresses and phone numbers. I figure you're the most likely person to have them all."

She shook her head quickly. "I can't give them to you."

Fred tried not to let his frustration show. "Why not?"

"Because."

Fred had heard more convincing reasons in his lifetime. He tried a joke. "What's the matter? Are you worried that I'm going to kill someone else?"

Ardella's hand fluttered, her gaze faltered, and she lied again. "No, of course not. But people have entrusted me with their personal information. I can't give it out without their permission. Not even to you."

Dane made a noise in his throat.

Fred pretended not to hear it. He pulled in a breath and let it out again slowly, and he tried to keep his voice steady. "This is important."

Dane leaned forward and added, "It's a matter of life or death, ma'am."

"I understand that," Ardella said, "but I just wouldn't feel right."

Dane caught her gaze and held it. "We certainly understand the position you're in, ma'am. But would you feel right about Fred going to jail for a crime he didn't commit?"

Ardella shook her head, this time more slowly. For a heartbeat, Fred thought Dane had won her over. In the next, she firmed her resolve even more. "No, of course not. But if Fred's innocent, he's not going to be arrested."

She had no idea how wrong she might be. Fred thought furiously, trying to decide which tack to take next.

Dane leaned back on the couch and cocked one ankle across his knee. "You don't believe he's innocent?"

"I didn't say that. But you have to admit, Fred, you do have a temper."

Dane barked a laugh. "Gramps? He's a teddy bear."

Fred tried to look warm and fuzzy.

Ardella's gaze darted between them again. "Well, he wasn't a teddy bear when we were younger."

"We're not talking about when we were younger," Fred reminded her. "We're talking about last Friday night."

"Well, yes, I know. But we all know how you felt about Phoebe, and after what LeGrande said about her—" She broke off and shook her head as if the rest went without saying.

Fred held back a sigh of frustration. "I didn't like him lying about her, but I didn't kill him."

"You hit him."

"But I didn't kill him. Someone else did. I'm not the only one LeGrande wanted to talk to. I'm not the only one who hated him, you know that as well as I do."

Ardella nodded reluctantly. "He wasn't exactly the nicest fellow in our class."

Now they were getting somewhere. Fred leaned a little closer. "He told me he wanted to set things straight with certain people before he died."

"Yes, I know." Ardella relaxed a bit more. "He told me about the cancer. And I knew he had things on his mind. I could tell that when I talked to him on the phone."

That pricked Fred's interest. "Did he give you any idea what he had on his mind or who else he wanted to talk to?"

Ardella folded her hands in her lap. "No. He didn't say a word. He just sounded distracted."

"Do you have any guesses?"

She sighed softly. "Oh, no. No. I wouldn't presume to guess about something like that."

Not aloud, anyway.

"So, what *did* you talk about?" Dane asked.

Fred used one foot to gently remind him of his promise to keep his mouth shut.

Ardella didn't seem to mind the question. She made herself comfortable in the chair and gestured with one hand. "Oh, this and that. He asked about some of our old classmates." Her eyes narrowed again. "He asked about you, Fred. And Phoebe."

Fred hadn't been expecting that. "Did he? What did he ask?"

"Nothing special. He just wanted to know whether or not you'd be at the reunion. Of course, I told him about Phoebe passing, but he must have forgotten. That's why I was so surprised to hear him ask you about her."

LeGrande hadn't forgotten, Fred thought bitterly. He struggled to keep his anger from showing. "Who else did he ask about?"

"He asked about Iris, of course. You can imagine why he'd want to know if she planned to come."

"His ex-wife," Fred explained to Dane, then turned back to Ardella. "Did you tell her LeGrande asked about her?"

Ardella shook her head. "No. I probably should have, but I didn't want her not to come. I didn't know if LeGrande was coming for sure. He hadn't made up his mind at that point. And I certainly didn't expect things to turn out the way they did."

Fred wondered if a warning to the rest of them could have prevented the tragedy. Probably not. If LeGrande had made up his mind to put a false shine on his reputation, he'd have found some way to do it. "Who else?" he prompted.

Ardella toyed with an apron string. "He asked about Jeremiah Hunt. Of course, I assumed he was concerned because of the trouble they had a few years back."

"You mean, when Jeremiah quit working for him?"

Ardella's eyes clouded. "No, I mean when LeGrande fired him."

"I thought he quit," Fred said, more to himself than to Ardella.

"Is that what he told you?"

"I didn't actually talk to him," Fred admitted. "Someone else told me."

Ardella ticked her tongue against the roof of her mouth. "Gossip. I can't abide it."

Fred made a noncommittal noise. Dane flashed a grin, then averted his face so she couldn't see him.

Ardella didn't seem to notice. "It was sad, really. It happened just six months before Jeremiah was scheduled to retire. Of course, that left him without a pension. He's been trying to get by on a little savings and Social Security. You can imagine how hard that would be."

Fred's heart skipped a beat. Dane's head whipped around again.

"I don't know exactly what Jeremiah did to get fired," Ardella said softly. "LeGrande was reluctant to say anything bad about him."

Fred could just imagine.

"But I know Jeremiah's had a rough time financially since then. In fact, I was surprised he could afford to come to the reunion."

Fred's heart skipped again. A man who'd lost his job six months before he could draw his pension just might be angry enough to murder the man he considered responsible.

Ardella warmed to her theme. "And Thea, of course. He asked about Thea."

Fred's elation faded. "Thea? Do you have any idea why he'd ask about her?"

Ardella's brows knit. "I suppose it's because they dated for a while. He asked about Coralee, too. And a couple of the other girls."

"Anyone else?"

Ardella tapped her finger to the side of her mouth and thought for a second or two. "Oliver Wellington. And it seems like he asked about someone else, too, but I can't remember—" She broke off, thought for a moment, and smiled slowly. "Oh, yes, I do. He asked about Al."

"Al?" Fred sat back and stared at her. A dull ache started in his forehead. "Al Jarvis?"

Ardella nodded and held up one hand as a barrier. "Yes, but don't ask me why. I don't know. I don't even remember them being friends."

"They weren't," Fred assured her.

She bobbed her head in satisfaction. "That's everyone. If LeGrande asked about anyone else, I don't remember."

Fred rubbed his forehead, but it didn't stop the pounding. "What about his children? Did he say anything about them?"

"No. He didn't talk much about anything personal."

"Did you happen to see his son at the school that night?"

"His son?" Ardella looked confused. She thought for a second, then shook her head. "No. But, then, I was so busy, I wouldn't have."

Just Fred's luck. Of course she wouldn't have. "I understand why you don't want to give me addresses," he said. "But if you could even give me telephone numbers, it would help."

She hesitated, and Fred thought she might actually agree. But she shook her head again with such determination, he knew she wouldn't change her mind. "The only thing I can suggest is to check at the Columbine. I know Thea had a room there, and the last time I talked to her, she was planning to stay for the funeral Thursday." She stood and looked down at him. "That's where Stormy Macafee is staying, too."

Interesting. He wondered if the new Mrs. Macafee would feel up to answering a few questions, or if he'd be letting himself in for trouble if he tried to talk to her. He pushed to his feet and did his best to smile. "Thanks for your time, Ardella. I appreciate the help."

She worked up a scowl. "Well, now it's your turn to do me a favor. I don't want you to tell anyone I talked to you."

He didn't promise. He couldn't. He just nodded Dane toward the door and left Ardella standing there and staring after them.

Bone-deep sadness filled him, but a little bitterness and resentment got in there with it. For days, he'd resisted the idea that one of his classmates might be guilty. Apparently, they had no such trouble believing the worst of him.

fourteen

Fred made the drive from Ardella's house to the Columbine Inn in silence. Thankfully, Dane had enough sense not to interrupt his thoughts, offer his opinion, or find any other reason to speak. Fred made a mental note to thank him later. Later, when his emotions made sense again. When he'd stopped riding the roller coaster of disgust, anger, self-pity, and morbid curiosity.

He pulled into the hotel parking lot, circled the large U-shaped building once, and found a parking space near the office. Only then did he break the silence. He nodded toward the new family restaurant on the other side of the lot. "I want you to wait over there while I talk to Thea."

He expected Dane to argue. To his surprise, the kid nodded once and stepped out of the car. "Sure thing, man. Just don't forget me."

Fred pushed aside an unwelcome flicker of warmth, reminded himself he didn't approve of the kid, and hurried toward the inn's lobby. Arctic air rushed out to meet him and set his knees twinging as he crossed the small foyer toward the front desk.

He knew better than to ask for Thea's room number. The most he could hope was for the desk clerk to put him through to her room on the telephone. But his conversation with Ardella had left him feeling a bit battered, and he wasn't at all convinced he'd even get that.

A dark-haired woman of about thirty stood behind the

chest-high desk, tapping on a computer in front of her. She glanced up as Fred approached, put on a friendly expression, and stopped typing. "Good afternoon. May I help you?"

"I hope so," he said, doing his best to look equally friendly. "I'm looking for one of your guests. Thea Griffin."

"Thea Griffin?"

"That's right. Can you connect me with her room from one of your telephones?"

The woman shrugged lightly. "Of course I could."

Great. Something was finally going his way.

"But it wouldn't do any good."

Fred scowled. "Why not?"

"Because she's not in her room. I saw her leaving a few minutes ago."

Fred held back a sigh of frustration. "I don't suppose you know when she'll be back?"

"No, sir."

He started to turn away, then decided to take a chance. "What about another one of your guests? Stormy Macafee."

The clerk's smile slipped. "Macafee?"

Fred nodded. "She may be registered under her husband's name. LeGrande Macafee. Is she staying here?"

The smile faded altogether. "Yes. But . . ."

Fred put a bit more warmth into his smile and leaned an elbow on the counter. "Her husband and I went to school together. They're here for our reunion. Would you mind putting me through to *her*?"

"I'm afraid I can't do that, sir. Mrs. Macafee has asked us to hold her calls today."

That didn't surprise him. Not really. He shifted his expression from friendly to concerned. "I understand, but I really need to talk with her. It's important."

The clerk's entire face worked itself into a frown. "I don't know if you've heard about her husband. . . ?"

"I know about the murder." Fred kept his tone confidential. "It's a terrible thing, isn't it?"

"Then surely you understand why Mrs. Macafee doesn't want to be disturbed."

Fred supposed he did. He couldn't say he'd feel any differently if he were in her shoes. But he wasn't in her shoes. And his own were getting more uncomfortable by the moment. He leaned a little closer. "It's about her husband's death. I wouldn't bother her otherwise."

The young woman glanced over her shoulder at a closed door behind her. Probably the manager's office. For an instant Fred thought she might give in. Instead, she gave her head another determined shake. "I'm sorry, sir. I can't put you through to Mrs. Macafee for any reason. The only visitors she's seeing are the sheriff and his deputies, and her doctor."

Fred certainly didn't want to run into any of them.

The clerk seemed to sense that. She sent him a tight smile. "Now, if there's nothing else I can help you with . . . ?"

"No. Thanks. Maybe I'll grab some lunch before I head back home again." Fred started toward the outside doors, but she called after him just as he reached for the handle. "Sir?"

Wondering if she'd changed her mind, he turned back quickly. His knees gave a painful throb. He ignored it and worked up his best smile. "Yes?"

"If you're really looking for Mrs. Griffin, I saw her going over to the restaurant about five minutes ago."

Well, why couldn't she have just said so in the first place? He glanced at the restaurant again and smiled slowly. Finally, something was going his way. He tried not to look overly excited. He didn't want the clerk to get any funny ideas about him or mention his visit to Enos or one of his deputies. "Is the food over there any good?"

The young woman looked surprised by the question. "At the Kettle? Yes, it's very good—if you like old-fashioned home cooking."

"Love it."

"Well, then. Enjoy your lunch."

Fred thought he just might. He pushed back out into the afternoon heat. This time, as he crossed the parking lot, he realized the scent of something cooking hung in the air. He couldn't identify it, but his stomach knotted painfully, reminding him he hadn't eaten all day. On top of that, the ache in his head had grown worse.

He increased his pace, covered the distance to the restaurant, and tugged open the outer door. Inside, the scents became easier to identify—roast beef, something spicy, and pie. He could definitely smell pie.

He swept his gaze over the dining area, cut in half by a long counter that stretched from just inside the door to the far wall. Tables and booths filled the rest of the room, some occupied, but most empty. Soft music drifted from speakers in the ceiling, the kind that encouraged people to linger over their meals.

Dane sat at the counter alone. Jeremiah Hunt had his nose buried in a newspaper at a table across the room. Coralee and Burl DiMeo sat in a corner booth, each so deep in thought they didn't even notice him. And Thea Griffin sat at a table in front of the window.

Perfect.

She smiled when she saw him and waved him toward her table.

He didn't even hesitate. Smiling broadly, he crossed toward her. From a distance, she looked fine, but as he drew closer he saw dark circles shadowing her eyes and deep lines etching her face. She looked small. And old. And frightened.

"Well, hello," she said when he drew closer. Her smile wiped a few years from her face, but anxiety still dulled her eyes. "This is a nice surprise. What are you doing here?"

"Just getting lunch. What about you?" He took the chair across from hers and glanced out the window. Perfect view. The motel on one side, the rest of the restaurant on the other. He could see everything from here.

"The same." Thea closed her menu and leaned back in her seat. "I'm surprised to see you so far from home."

"Far? I don't even live fifteen miles from here."

She wagged a hand at him. "I know, but you always were such a stay-at-home."

A waiter appeared out of nowhere, placed a menu on the table in front of him, and filled his empty glass with water. Fred leaned back in his seat to give the young man space to work. "You came two thousand miles for the reunion," he reminded Thea. "Driving fifteen for lunch doesn't seem out of line."

She smiled a thank-you at the waiter, tilted her head to one side, and turned the smile back on Fred. "You're right, of course. Do you come here often?"

Fred thought about saying he did, just to prove a point. But he didn't want to actually *lie*. "No. I thought I'd try something new for a chance."

To his surprise, Thea laughed. Across the room, Coralee DiMeo jerked her head around and squinted to see them better. She lifted one hand in a halfhearted wave. Burl followed her gaze, but when he saw Fred, he scowled darkly and said something that made Coralee look away quickly—as if just looking at Fred might contaminate her somehow.

Thea didn't seem to notice. She shook her head quickly, and Fred caught a glimpse of the young girl he'd once known. "You?" she said. "Try something new? I don't believe it."

Fred did his best to ignore Burl and Coralee. "Why in the world not?"

"Because." She laughed again, softer this time. "You're a creature of habit. You always have been."

"It's entirely possible that a man could make a few changes in fifty years." His voice came out sharper than he'd intended.

But Thea didn't seem to notice that, either. "Yes, I suppose it is." She put a hand on his arm and smiled into his eyes. "Don't frown at me like that. I'm not trying to insult you."

Her touch made him uncomfortable. He drew his arm

away—slowly, so he wouldn't offend her. "I'm not insulted."

Her smile softened and a few of the clouds left her eyes. "See? You're still the same old Fred. And I still adore you."

Fred glanced away quickly. He had no idea what she meant by that, and he didn't think he wanted to know. Some things were better left alone.

"You're embarrassed." Her voice held the same teasing note she'd once used on him.

Fred didn't like it one bit. "I'm not embarrassed."

"Yes you are." Her smile widened and her eyes sparkled. "I'm flattered."

Fred's face grew warm. He didn't know how to respond to that. He only knew he needed to turn the conversation around before it got away from him. He adjusted the napkin and silverware on the table in front of him. "I need to ask you a few questions," he said quietly, "about LeGrande."

Just as he'd expected, the teasing light in Thea's eyes died. "LeGrande? What about him?"

"How well did you know him?"

Was it just his imagination, or did she stiffen slightly? "Not well. Why?"

"Had you talked with him recently?"

"Me?" She laughed without humor. "Heavens no. Why would you ask that?"

"Then you didn't try to contact him a month before the reunion?"

This time her shoulders straightened, her lips thinned, and her chin lifted. "No. Of course not."

Without calling her a liar, Fred didn't know how to respond.

Thea glanced around the restaurant, letting her gaze drift over the other members of their class. "LeGrande was a bit of a . . ." She hesitated over the word. Fred thought of a few he could supply, but he kept his mouth shut. Better to keep his opinions to himself. After a long moment she sighed softly and sent him a halfhearted smile. "Well, LeGrande was LeGrande. I don't know how else to put it."

"Yes, he was."

"And this whole thing is frightening." She let her gaze linger on his face. "I still can't believe it. Or that Stormy thinks you did it. Last Friday was one of the most awful nights of my life."

"It wasn't one of my better nights, either," he reminded her.

She shuddered at some memory and toyed with the edge of her paper napkin. "I don't think I'll ever forget the sound of Stormy screaming. It was the worst thing I've ever heard."

Fred let silence hang between them for a moment. He knew Thea was trying to divert him from his original question, but he decided to go along with her—for the moment. "What about Stormy? How is she taking it?"

"She's been hysterical. Absolutely hysterical." Thea rearranged her silverware on her napkin with trembling fingers. "Bernard Huggins has stopped by a couple of times with the sheriff. I guess he probably gave her something to calm her down." She glanced up at him again. "He's certainly gotten old since the last time I saw him."

Doc *had* aged, and not well. But Fred didn't want to talk about him. "I know Stormy's upset, and with good reason, but I didn't kill her husband."

"I know you didn't."

"I wish I could convince her of that." Fred spoke slowly, testing the waters before he went too far. "Have you seen her this morning?"

"No. I stopped by her room earlier, but she's still too upset to see or speak to anyone. She wouldn't even open the door."

Disappointment mingled with a flicker of hope. Fred tried not to look or sound overly interested. "Then you know what room she's in?"

"Yes." Thea eyed him warily. "Her room's just a few doors down from mine."

Fred nodded casually, as if the news meant nothing to him.

Thea pursed her lips and narrowed her eyes. But before she could question him, the waiter materialized beside the table again. "Are you two ready to order?"

Fred breathed a silent sigh of relief. He wanted to talk about LeGrande's murder, but on his own terms—not Thea's.

Thea tore her gaze away, smiled up at the young man, and ordered a salad. Fred didn't think twice. Doing his best to ignore his hunger pangs, he ordered his favorite—country-fried steak with mashed potatoes and extra gravy. And coffee. A full pot.

The young man jotted both orders on a small pad without even commenting on Fred's choice or warning him about his cholesterol level. Heaven. Fred made a mental note to come here more often.

The instant the young man walked away, Thea's scowl returned. "Why do you want to know which room Stormy's in?"

Fred lifted both shoulders and took a drink of water. "Like I said, I'd like to talk with her. I'd like a chance to convince her I didn't kill LeGrande."

Thea narrowed her eyes a bit further. "I don't believe you. If that's all you wanted, you could leave her a note. I know you, Fred. I've seen that look on your face before. Tell me what you really want."

She'd known him over fifty years ago, but she didn't know him now. At least, that's what he told himself. He didn't like thinking he was so transparent.

When he didn't answer immediately, she leaned a little closer. "Is it about your fight with LeGrande?"

The question knocked some of the wind out of his sails. "I wouldn't mind asking her a few questions," he admitted.

"What kinds of questions?"

Fred studied her for a minute, trying to decide if she was being nosy or defensive. He couldn't tell. "Just questions."

She pulled back and stared at him. Hard. "You know, don't you, that the sheriff and his deputies have been asking questions about you. And Burl DiMeo keeps giving you the evil eye."

Fred slanted a glance at Burl. Sure enough, he chose that moment to send Fred another stony look. Fred turned slowly back to face Thea. "What did the sheriff ask you?"

Thea's frown deepened another notch. "About the history between you and LeGrande, and about what happened when LeGrande first came into the reunion."

"What did you tell them?"

"I told them the truth."

"Which was—"

"That you and LeGrande had never been friends, but that as far as I knew, you hadn't seen him in over fifty years."

"And . . . ?"

"And I said I couldn't imagine anything that happened fifty years ago would still be bothering you so much that you'd kill a man over it."

Fred didn't even try to hide his relief. "You're right."

Thea leaned a little closer and lowered her voice even further. "But I'm not sure I believe that."

"Why not?"

"Because there *is* one thing that would still upset you enough to get you riled." She spoke so softly, Fred could hardly hear her.

He tried to laugh, but it came out sounding choked. "What?"

"Phoebe. Everyone saw how you reacted when LeGrande started talking about her. Everyone knew how upset you were. I don't know what happened between the two of them, but I *do* remember how much Phoebe changed after she and LeGrande split up."

Nonsense. Phoebe hadn't changed because of LeGrande. He tried to say so, but his throat had tightened so much he couldn't get the words out.

Thea didn't let up. "What did happen between them?"

"Nothing." One word, that's all he could manage. He wanted to sound forceful, determined, sure of himself. Instead, he sounded weak and even frightened.

Thea's expression shifted subtly. She studied him for a long moment. Too long. Something uncomfortably close to pity drifted through her eyes.

"Nothing happened," he said again.

"Fred . . ." There it was again. She felt *sorry* for him.

Fred could put up with a lot of things, but he couldn't tolerate Thea's pity. "This is ridiculous," he snapped. "You're letting your imagination run away with you."

Thea put a hand over one of his. "Fred, listen to me. Everyone knows *something* happened between Phoebe and LeGrande. Don't you realize that by denying it, by hiding it, you're making things worse for yourself?"

Fred jerked his hand away from her touch. Her words echoed relentlessly through his mind. Everyone knew something happened between Phoebe and LeGrande. Everyone remembered the change in Phoebe. Everyone, it seemed, except Fred.

He couldn't talk about it anymore, and he refused to listen to another word. He staggered to his feet and muttered some excuse for leaving.

Thea gaped at him. Dane scowled, but he didn't move. Burl and Coralee stared at him. Even Jeremiah lowered his newspaper to watch. But Fred didn't care. He wheeled around and hurried out of the restaurant into the blistering afternoon heat.

fifteen

Fred tried to hurry across the parking lot, but the cold air inside the restaurant had stiffened his joints and his knees protested every step. He heard Thea come out the door behind him, but he ignored her and kept walking.

"Fred?" Her voice caught up with him. She sounded worried.

Fred didn't care. He cursed his aging body and tried to walk a little faster. But his blasted knees wouldn't cooperate.

"Fred, wait." Her voice sounded ominously close. Apparently, arthritis hadn't gotten the best of her yet.

He pulled his keys from his pocket and tried to unlock the Buick's door, but before he could fit the key into the lock she snagged his shirtsleeve.

"Wait, Fred. We need to talk about this."

Fred didn't need anything of the sort. He yanked his arm from her grip and tried again to reach the door lock.

Thea brushed his hand away and planted herself in front of him. "What is the matter with you?"

Fred didn't bother answering.

"Talk to me," she demanded.

"There's nothing to talk about."

"I'm trying to help you. Can't you understand that?"

"I don't need your help."

"Well, you need *someone's*." Her entire face set itself in stone. Stubborn woman. No wonder he'd stopped dating her. She tilted her head to one side and studied him carefully. As if in slow motion, her eyes widened. "You don't know, do you?"

"Don't know what?" Fred purposely kept his voice gruff. Maybe it would discourage her.

It didn't. She'd grown more persistent in her old age. "You don't know what happened between Phoebe and LeGrande. *That's* why you're so secretive about it." She didn't even wait for him to deny the accusation. "Phoebe never told you whatever it was, did she?"

More than anything in the world, Fred wanted to tell Thea she was wrong. But he couldn't seem to form the words.

"Oh, Fred." She reached for him again, this time with a gentle hand. "I can see in your eyes how hurt you are."

"Don't," he warned. To his dismay, the word came out thick with emotion. He ran one hand along the back of his neck and grimaced when he realized his collar had become damp from perspiration.

To his relief, she pulled her hand away and the pity in her eyes evaporated. "All right. You don't know what happened between Phoebe and LeGrande. Then what did LeGrande do to upset you the second time?"

"It's not important."

"It was important enough for you to get into another fistfight with him."

"It wasn't a fistfight," he snapped. Not technically anyway. LeGrande hadn't hit back. "Frankly, I'm tired of defending myself. All I want right now is to find the man who killed him."

"Maybe it wasn't a man."

That comment caught him off guard. "What do you mean?"

"I mean, LeGrande had two wives there last night, and neither of them looked very happy."

"One wife, one ex-wife," Fred reminded her.

Thea waved the reminder away. "Whatever. Iris was not at all pleased when he showed up. You saw that. And Stormy was obviously upset with him, too."

Fred quirked an eyebrow at her. "You think one of them killed him?"

"Maybe." Thea gestured toward the restaurant. "Or what about Jeremiah Hunt? Did you see *his* face when LeGrande walked in? Or Oliver Wellington? Or, for that matter, Coralee?"

The last name caught Fred off guard. He flicked a glance at the restaurant's windows gleaming golden in the afternoon sunlight. "Coralee?"

"She and LeGrande dated for a long time. Don't you remember? And their breakup was anything but friendly."

Fred gave each of those names some thought. Iris. Stormy. Jeremiah. Oliver. Coralee. He met her gaze and held it. "And you."

Fear darted through her eyes. She blinked and it disappeared. "Me?"

"You called him at his office last month. Why?"

She tried to laugh, but failed miserably. "How do you know about that?"

"I have my sources."

"And you think *I* killed him?"

"I didn't say that. I'm just asking why you called him."

Her gaze faltered and color flooded her cheeks. "It was personal. It had nothing to do with his death."

"Then tell me why."

She rounded on him unexpectedly. "Why should I? You won't talk to me."

Fred couldn't argue with her. He rubbed the back of his neck again and let out a deep sigh.

Thea must have sensed his tension fading. The color drained from her cheeks and she managed a weak smile. "We're straying from the point, anyway. Neither of us killed LeGrande. If you want my opinion, I think we should march right back over to the restaurant and have a chat with Jeremiah Hunt. And when we're through talking to him, we'll talk to Burl and Coralee."

"I'll talk to Jeremiah. *Alone*."

Her smile faded. "Don't be silly. You need me with you."

He didn't need anything of the sort, and he opened his mouth to tell her so.

But she cut him off before he could get a word out. "Don't argue with me. You're obviously too upset to think clearly."

If anything upset him, her pushiness did. He worked up a reassuring smile. "I'm fine."

"Of course you are."

Fred tried another argument. "Look, Thea, I appreciate your offer. Really. But I'll be a lot less conspicuous if I do this alone."

She laughed aloud. "You can't honestly believe that. Really, Fred. Those people in there think you killed Le-Grande. Just how inconspicuous do you think you'll be if you start asking questions about him?"

Fred supposed she had a point, but that didn't mean he wanted her around. Every time he asked questions, he got answers even he didn't want to hear.

Thea took both of his hands in hers and met his gaze steadily. "If you approach them alone, you'll scare them off. But they're not afraid of me, and if I'm with you, they'll feel safer. And you can sit there with that grumpy old look on your face and pretend that you're irritated with me for talking about it at all."

There wouldn't be much pretense about that, but Fred had to admit—grudgingly—that her idea had some merit.

She must have sensed his resolve weakening. "Okay? Will you let me help you?"

"Why do you want to?"

"Because we're friends. Because we once meant something to each other . . ." She let her voice trail away, then drew a deep breath and finished. "Because, if *I* were the one in trouble and you knew about it, you'd move heaven and earth to help me." She freed one of his hands and held hers up, as if she thought he might protest. "Don't deny it. You've always been more worried about other people than yourself."

Her words touched him. They sounded like something

Phoebe might have said. Maybe. He didn't know what Phoebe might have said anymore.

Thea released his other hand and tilted her head. "So, do we have a deal?"

"I suppose." He still didn't like the idea, but he didn't argue. Once Thea made up her mind about something, there was no stopping her. And if she'd decided to ask questions about LeGrande's murder, Fred would be safer to tag along than to turn her loose on her own. Besides, she just might be right.

He trailed her back across the parking lot, tugged open the heavy glass door for her, and followed her inside.

Burl and Coralee looked up as they entered. Dane laughed at something a pretty, young waitress said. Jeremiah sat behind his newspaper, surrounded by dirty dishes. Fred couldn't see anything but the bush of silver-gray hair at the top of his head and his gnarled fingers clutching the newspaper.

Without hesitating even for a second, Thea started toward him. Fred followed her through the maze of empty tables and came to a halt beside her.

Jeremiah must have heard them approaching. He must have sensed them standing there. But he didn't acknowledge them by so much as a twitch of a finger.

Thea flicked an annoyed glance at Fred and positioned herself beside the table where Jeremiah couldn't ignore her.

He did anyway.

Fred cleared his throat.

Jeremiah had to work a little harder to ignore that, but he managed.

Thea gently pushed down his newspaper with one hand. "Jeremiah? Do you have a minute?"

He couldn't ignore that, and he didn't. His entire face wrinkled into a deep scowl. "I'm busy, Thea."

Jeremiah hadn't ever been the outgoing sort, but this was downright antisocial, even for him. "We just want to talk to you for a minute," Fred told him.

Jeremiah unfolded a couple of his wrinkles and flicked an annoyed glance at him. "What about?"

Without waiting for an invitation, Thea sat across from him. Fred didn't hesitate to join them.

Jeremiah's scowl tightened again, but he didn't protest.

Thea laced her hands together on the table and beamed a smile at him. "I just haven't had a chance to talk to you yet, and when we saw you sitting here, I told Fred we really should say hello."

Jeremiah didn't look thrilled, but at least he didn't tell them to leave. He spent a couple of seconds refolding his newspaper, then set it on the table beside him.

Thea patted the back of her hair and let out a sigh. "It's unusually warm for this time of year, isn't it?"

Fred mumbled something about the heat, but he didn't expect Jeremiah to put up with them for long, and he didn't want to waste precious time talking about the weather.

Jeremiah glanced out the nearest window, then turned back with a shrug. "I suppose so."

Thea turned her smile up a notch. "I always find the heat draining, don't you?"

Another shrug, this time followed by an impatient frown. "I don't mind. It's better than the cold."

Fred tried to catch Thea's gaze so he could signal her to ask the important questions before Jeremiah came up with an excuse to leave.

She didn't pay even the slightest attention to him. "Where are you living now, Jeremiah?"

He looked surprised by the question, but he answered anyway. "I'm in Golden."

Thea nodded, as if that triggered something in her memory. "Yes, that's right. I remember Ardella telling me that. And you're retired?"

Fred flicked a glance at her, a little startled by how well she'd worked in that question.

Jeremiah shook his head. "Not entirely. I still work a few hours a day."

That surprised Fred, but he tried not to show it. "What do you do?"

"I'm in public relations." Jeremiah sounded normal, but something flickered in his eyes that made Fred wonder.

Fred couldn't imagine Jeremiah working with the public in any capacity. Not successfully, anyway. "Is that what you've always done?"

Jeremiah shook his head slowly. He pulled in a deep breath and focused on the newspaper beside him. "No, only the past few years."

Thea shifted in her chair beside him. Jeremiah kept his gaze averted.

Fred nodded, as if that explained everything. "What did you do before that?"

Jeremiah dragged his eyes away from the newspaper and met Fred's gaze. "What is this, twenty questions?"

"No," Fred assured him with a friendly smile. "Just catching up."

Jeremiah's wrinkles went to work again. "Well, I don't want to catch up. Now, if you'll excuse me—" He grabbed his newspaper and started to slide out from behind the table.

Thea put out a hand to stop him. "Wait. We didn't mean to upset you."

Jeremiah paused on the edge of his seat. "I'm not upset."

No. Obviously not. Fred pretended to believe him. "We're all a little edgy, I guess."

Jeremiah's shoulders slumped slightly and some of the harshness left his face. "I guess so. With good reason."

Thea sighed softly. "With *very* good reason."

Jeremiah stopped trying to get away and lowered the newspaper to the table again. He leaned back in his seat, poured a fresh glass of water from a carafe on the table, and took a long drink. His hand shook, but Fred didn't know whether nerves caused it or if old age had gotten the best of him.

"Are you going to the funeral Thursday?" Thea asked when Jeremiah stopped gulping water.

Jeremiah split a glance between them. "I haven't decided yet. Are you?"

Thea answered before Fred could even open his mouth. "We'll be there. And I wish you'd come, too. I'm worried that a lot of people will stay away."

Jeremiah lifted one bushy eyebrow. It looked like a caterpillar. "You're probably right. A lot of people probably will stay away. After all, LeGrande *was* a bastard." The instant that word left his mouth, he smiled an apology at Thea. "Sorry. It just slipped out."

Thea waved away his apology. "Why do you say that?"

Jeremiah snorted a laugh. "Because it's true."

Fred didn't argue. He rubbed his chin and tried to look thoughtful. "Didn't I hear somewhere that you worked with him for a while?"

"I worked *for* him," Jeremiah said, but he seemed reluctant to admit it.

"What did you do for him?"

"Bookkeeping."

That fit the picture Fred had of him a little better. A job like that would drive Fred crazy, but it would suit Jeremiah.

"My husband was an accountant," Thea said. "He loved that sort of work. Did you?"

"I enjoyed it," Jeremiah admitted.

"How long were you with LeGrande?" Fred asked.

"Thirty-three years."

A lifetime. In Fred's opinion, thirty-three minutes with LeGrande was too much to put anyone through.

"What made you decide to change?" Thea asked. "I can't imagine Stewart ever doing anything else."

"I had my reasons," Jeremiah said.

Fred supposed getting fired could be considered a reason. Apparently, Jeremiah didn't intend to admit it, but Fred didn't know whether it was simply a matter of pride or to cover a motive for murder.

Fred thought about pushing him, then decided against it. He had other questions to ask and he didn't want to lose

Jeremiah now. "In thirty-three years you must have gotten to know him fairly well. And his family."

Jeremiah's expression tightened again. Something about that question made him nervous. "Not that well. We didn't see much of each other. I worked for LeGrande. We weren't friendly."

"Did you work for him when he and Iris split up?" Fred tried to keep the question casual, but something about it made Jeremiah's scowl deepen.

"Yes."

"Did you ever meet his children?"

Jeremiah looked confused by the question, but he nodded. "Yes."

Good. Now they were getting somewhere. Fred locked his hands together on the table. "Did you happen to notice any of them at the school Friday night?"

Jeremiah looked from Fred to Thea and back again. "His kids?"

"Yes."

Jeremiah took so long to answer, Fred expected him to say no. Instead, to his astonishment, Jeremiah nodded. "Sure. I saw his oldest boy for a minute."

Fred's pulse skipped a beat. "Roger?"

Jeremiah nodded. "Yes. Why?"

"Because I overheard him arguing with LeGrande that night, and I think—"

"You think he killed LeGrande?" Jeremiah finished for him.

More than a little relieved, Fred sat back in his seat and nodded. "I do. I've been looking for someone else who saw him there so I can convince the police—"

Again, Jeremiah cut him off. "That he's the murderer? I can't help you."

Fred straightened suddenly. "Can't? Or won't?" Thea put a warning hand on his arm. He shrugged it away.

"Can't," Jeremiah said. "I did see Roger on Friday night, but he didn't kill LeGrande."

"How do you know?" Fred demanded. "He had a fight

with LeGrande shortly before the murder. The kid hit him more than once and—"

"And then he left," Jeremiah said almost triumphantly.

"Left?" Fred stared at him. "He left?"

"He left," Jeremiah said with a firm nod. "That's when I saw him. He came storming out of the school madder than a hornet, got into his car, and drove away."

"That could have been after the murder," Fred pointed out.

Jeremiah shook his head. "He left before the murder. I saw LeGrande when I went back inside. He was still alive."

sixteen

Stunned, Fred sat back in his seat again. Jeremiah must be mistaken. Roger *couldn't* have left the school while LeGrande was still alive. That would mean someone else had to be the killer. One of their classmates. One of his friends. Someone who'd kept silent when Stormy accused *him*.

Not a friend at all.

Thea put a hand on Fred's arm and leaned forward to look at Jeremiah. "Are you sure?"

"Of course I'm sure."

She turned her gaze on Fred. "You look upset. Are you all right?"

"I'm fine." And he was, if he ignored his disappointment and his growing irritation with her habit of touching him every time she took a breath. He shifted in his chair and managed to draw his arm away in the process. The air conditioner sent a blast of cold air down his neck. He shifted again and focused on Jeremiah. "Where was LeGrande when you saw him?"

"In the hallway, walking toward the men's room."

"Did he say anything?"

"To *me*?" Jeremiah shook his head. "He didn't see me."

"And you didn't say anything to him?"

"Hell no." Jeremiah snorted a laugh. "I didn't want to talk to him at all."

From the corner of his eye, Fred watched Thea drop her

hand into her own lap. He relaxed a bit. "What happened next?"

"I don't know," Jeremiah admitted. "I just wanted to avoid him, so I went back into the gymnasium."

"You didn't see anyone else in the hallway?" Fred asked.

Jeremiah shook his head and spooned an ice cube from his glass. "Nope. Nobody."

"You didn't see me?"

Jeremiah put the ice cube into his mouth, adjusted it carefully, and shook his head again. "No. Why? Were you there?"

Fred nodded, but he didn't elaborate. Instead, he struggled to readjust his thinking. But he'd been so certain about Roger, he had difficulty shifting gears. His head pounded from hunger and confusion. "If Roger didn't kill LeGrande, who did?"

Jeremiah lifted both thin shoulders in an elaborate shrug. "Your guess is as good as mine. He screwed over enough people in his lifetime, including half our graduating class, it shouldn't be hard to find someone who wanted him dead."

Fred plucked a package of crackers from a basket half-hidden beneath Jeremiah's napkin, tore it open, and popped one into his mouth. And he decided to push Jeremiah a bit. "What about you? Did he 'screw you over,' too?"

"Me?" Jeremiah laughed away the suggestion. "No. LeGrande and I weren't exactly friends, but I had nothing against him."

"You worked for him for thirty-three years and got fired six months before you were supposed to retire, but you didn't have trouble with him?"

Splotches of color dotted Jeremiah's cheeks. He drew himself up sharply. "Where did you hear that?"

"I have my sources."

"You've been asking questions about me?"

"One or two."

Jeremiah glared at him. His face might have been carved from stone. "Why?"

Fred glared back. "Because some people are taking Mrs.

Macafee's accusation seriously, and I'm not going to sit around twiddling my thumbs while people judge me and find me guilty of something I didn't do."

A muscle in Jeremiah's jaw jumped. The color in his cheeks deepened. "Well, *I* don't think you killed him, so why are you checking up on me? Why don't you ask questions about somebody who really hated him?"

"And who would that be?"

Jeremiah let out another laugh, but this one sounded less confident. He let his gaze drift toward Thea, then jerked it back again. "I don't think I should name names."

For some reason, Thea had lost her animation. She sat with her hands laced in front of her, her face cold and hard. Fred had no idea what had brought about the change—unless he'd offended her by drawing away. But he didn't have time to worry about that now.

He polished off the second cracker and pulled another package from the basket. "Look, Jeremiah. Someone at that reunion killed LeGrande. It wasn't me, and you want me to believe it wasn't you. So, who do you think it was?"

Jeremiah pulled back slightly and raked his gaze over Thea again. "I don't know."

A slow flush crept up Thea's neck and into her face. Strange. Maybe Fred hadn't brought about the change in her after all. But something had.

Fred thought back over the last bits of their conversation, hoping to find something unusual in what Jeremiah had said, but nothing leaped out at him. He leaned a little closer and lowered his voice. "You knew LeGrande better than the rest of us."

"I didn't know him," Jeremiah insisted. "Not well, anyway."

"You saw him more recently than I did," Fred argued. "You worked with him. If he had trouble with someone in our class, you'd be more likely than I would to know about it."

Jeremiah shrugged lazily, but the expression in his eyes looked anything but casual. "Okay," he said after a long moment. "What about Oliver Wellington? There was some sort of trouble between him and LeGrande a little while back. And Iris, of course." He cocked a caterpillar eyebrow at Fred. "How far back do you want me to go? LeGrande thought he was quite the ladies' man in high school. He went with the girls and tossed them aside like yesterday's trash when he was through—didn't he, Thea?"

The flush on Thea's face deepened. "I suppose so." Her voice came out sounding brittle. Maybe even a little worried. Jeremiah had obviously touched a nerve.

Fred supposed one of LeGrande's romantic exploits might have led to murder—except they'd all happened half a century ago. No, the motive *had* to be something more recent. "What kind of trouble did Oliver have with him?"

Jeremiah worked up another shrug. "I don't know details. I don't even know if it's true. Just a rumor I heard around the office."

His elusive answers grated on Fred's nerves. "What was the rumor?"

"I just heard that Oliver was upset with LeGrande for some reason. Whatever it was happened around the time LeGrande made his big killing on the stock market. Before that, I used to see Oliver around the office at least once a week. After that, he almost never came around."

Interesting. "Do you know where I can find Oliver now?"

"He lives in Steamboat Springs, I think."

"What about Iris?"

Jeremiah knit his caterpillar brows together. "Hell, you know about Iris. LeGrande cheated on her and then dumped her for a younger woman."

"What was the gossip around the office then?"

Jeremiah wagged a hand in front of him. "The usual. We all knew about Stormy before Iris did. She was always in the office, always hanging around. It was pretty obvious what was going on."

"How did Iris react when she found out?"

"It was ugly. Really ugly." Jeremiah's eyes narrowed. "You know, you could get yourself in trouble, digging into people's secrets like this. You know the old saying, don't you? Curiosity killed the cat."

The words sent a chill through Fred. He locked gazes with Jeremiah. "Is that a threat?"

"A threat?" Jeremiah barked a laugh. "No, it's a friendly warning. You've always been too curious for your own good, Fred. But you can't be too careful. None of us can."

"I doubt there's a serial killer working his way through our graduating class," Fred told him.

"I never said there was," Jeremiah snapped. "But I was out in the hallway not long before the murder. And, frankly, I'm not willing to take any chances."

"You think the murderer saw you?"

"Who knows? But I do know I've said too much already." He stood quickly and snagged up his newspaper and the bill for his meal. "Hell, for all I know, it could have been Burl or Coralee over there. And I'd rather not have anyone know I've been talking to you about it."

He pivoted away and started toward the cash register. Fred thought about trying to stop him, then decided to let him go. Obviously, he'd said all he intended to say.

But his words made Fred think twice about letting Thea tag along with him and involve herself in the investigation.

"Well?" Thea said when Jeremiah had put some distance between them. "What do we do now? Talk to Burl and Coralee? Or Oliver?"

Fred shook his head. "Neither. Now you tell me why you got so quiet while Jeremiah was talking about LeGrande."

"Why I—?" Thea leaned back in her seat, as if she needed some distance between them to see him clearly. "I don't know what you're talking about."

"Don't lie to me, Thea."

She tried desperately to look confused, but the crimson flush that crept up her neck and into her face gave her away. "I'm not lying," she protested, but her words lacked conviction.

Fred shifted in his seat to face her. "You don't bluff very well. Something Jeremiah said upset you. What was it?"

Thea lowered her gaze and studied her fingers for a long moment. An uneasy silence fell between them, broken only by the clatter of dishes coming from inside the kitchen.

"What happened between you and LeGrande?"

She stayed silent so long, Fred thought she'd refuse to answer. She flicked a couple of furtive glances at him, then let out a long sigh. "We went out once. Right after you and I stopped seeing each other."

The answer surprised him. "How did Jeremiah know about it?"

"LeGrande had a big mouth."

"What *was* it about that guy that made all you women so crazy about him?"

Thea tried to smile. "We were young. And he seemed to have everything. He was good-looking, intelligent, athletic. . . ." She let her voice trail away, and she worked up another halfhearted smile. "He was also a real jerk."

"*I* could have told you that."

"You did." She focused on Jeremiah's empty glass as if it held the secret of the universe. "You know how it is, though. Men can sense the truth about other men *long* before a woman can—and the other way around, too. But when we're young, we write it off as jealousy or something equally foolish."

Fred supposed that was true. It had certainly been true in LeGrande's case. "What happened between the two of you?"

Thea kept her gaze riveted on the glass. Even in the air-conditioned restaurant, beads of condensation trickled down its sides. She wiped one away with a trembling finger. "I guess it won't hurt to tell you. After all, it happened forever ago." She took a deep breath and let it out again slowly. "We went to a Valentine's Day dance at the school. Everything was fine at first, but afterward he tried to get a little too friendly."

Fred froze in his seat.

Thea's lips quivered slightly. "When I told him no, he got angry. Very angry. And pushy." She hesitated, then added, "Forceful, if you know what I mean."

Fred could only stare at her. His stomach lurched and anger burned through his veins. "He forced you?"

She nodded, but the effort took everything she had. "Afterward, I got out of his car and started to walk home. He came after me and told me to get back in the car, but I refused. He finally got tired of arguing with me and left me there."

"And you walked home?"

She slanted a glance at him. "No. You don't remember?"

Remember? Fred hadn't known anything about it. He shook his head slowly. "No."

"You and Phoebe saw me walking and offered me a ride home."

Fred searched his memory, but he drew a blank. "You didn't tell us what happened, did you?"

She smiled gently. "No. But I think Phoebe guessed. Remember? When we got to my house, she came inside with me and sent you home alone."

That rang a bell. A very soft, vague bell. He could almost remember that. He remembered being hurt and confused—and even a little angry. But he hadn't let Phoebe or Thea see that. "I had no idea."

"I know you didn't. I didn't want you to know."

"Then why did you call him last month?"

"Because Ardella told me he was thinking about coming to the reunion."

"And you didn't want him to come."

"I told him to stay away or I'd tell everyone what he'd done." She managed a weak smile. "I spent most of my life being afraid of LeGrande, but I guess Stewart's death made me realize he couldn't hurt me anymore. I finally stopped being that frightened young girl."

Fred's stomach twisted again. "Why didn't you ever tell me what happened?"

"I didn't tell anyone."

"But I—" Fred began, but his throat tightened again and kept him from finishing.

"You would have beat the hell out of him," she said with

a thin smile. "And then everyone would have found out about it. I didn't want anyone to know."

"Oh, Thea—"

"Don't feel sorry for me. I can't stand it." Wistfulness filled her eyes, softened her face, and stilled her hand on his. "You know, there was a time when I'd have given anything to have you feel sorry for me. Or to care about me the way you cared about Phoebe."

Had he seemed so heartless to her? Had he *been* heartless? "I cared about you," he said weakly.

"Yes." Her lips curved in a sad smile. "But not the way you loved Phoebe. Never the way you loved Phoebe."

"No." He wouldn't deny the truth.

She pulled her hand away and made a visible effort to put the moment behind her. "Ah, well. I had a good life with Stewart. He loved me, and I loved him. It just wasn't the kind of storybook romance I dreamed about when I was a girl. But, then, how many of us get that?"

Not many. But Fred kept that thought to himself. Saying it aloud wouldn't help.

"So?" Thea straightened in her seat and met his gaze steadily. "Now that I've answered your questions, what's next?"

"Next, I talk to Oliver. But not yet. I need to think for a while."

Thea stood and smiled down at him. "I guess that means you don't want me to come along."

Fred shook his head. "I failed you once. I won't let myself put you in jeopardy."

She put a hand on his shoulder. "You didn't fail me, Fred. It wasn't your fault at all."

"I should have known."

"I'm all right, Fred."

"I'm glad." He smiled up at her, but his lips felt stiff and unwieldy, and he couldn't deal with the pain of knowing she'd suffered such a horrible thing and the guilt of realizing he'd been too wrapped up in his own world to notice.

seventeen

Fred walked slowly down the grassy hillside beside the church, dimly aware of the damp lawn and spongy ground underfoot from the afternoon thunderstorm. The sun listed toward the western mountains, painting the evening sky with its inky brush and stretching shadows across the green lawn.

His mind reeled, as it had all the way back up the mountain, with the story Thea had told him and the horrible possibility she'd forced him to face. Dane had chatted all the way home, endlessly, about this and that, the waitress at the restaurant, his plans with Sarah, the pouring rain. You name it, he'd talked about it. But Fred hadn't been able to listen.

He needed to make sense of his life again. Strange that a man could live seventy-three years believing he knew himself and his loved ones, then, in an instant, lose everything. Always, no matter what else happened in his life, Phoebe had been a sort of foundation for him. Even after her death, her memory had been there for him. But tonight, for the first time in his life, Fred felt completely alone.

Chipmunks and birds chattered happily in the nearby trees, celebrating deliverance from the day's heat. The sound taunted him. A car's engine slowed on the road behind him, but he didn't look back. He just hoped whoever it was hadn't noticed him, or if they had, they'd leave him alone.

At the bottom of the hill, he walked between headstones toward the one that marked Phoebe's final resting place. He rarely came here—he saw no need for that. Phoebe wasn't here, and he hated pretending that she was. But sometimes lately, when trouble hit as it had now, he came to talk to her.

He stopped beside the stone that marked her grave, locked his hands behind his back, and studied the inscription there. He'd loved this woman as he'd never loved another human being in his life. He'd spent forty-seven years as her husband, and he'd believed they'd been honest about everything. But now a strange unease filled him—as if he were visiting a stranger.

Kneeling on the cool, wet grass, he brushed leaves and grass away from the stone. But the action loosened something inside. He sat back on his heels and gave in to his overwhelming despair.

He rarely cried over Phoebe—not in public, anyway—but he couldn't seem to stop. He imagined Phoebe as she'd been when he first fell in love with her—her heart-shaped face, her deep brown eyes, her soft smile. She'd been beautiful as a young girl, but not nearly so lovely as she'd become as a woman. With every passing year she'd grown more beautiful in Fred's eyes. Every gray hair, every tiny wrinkle, every extra pound had only endeared her to him more.

She'd hated the effects of age. She'd frowned at her face in the mirror and colored her hair and watched the scales, trying, she said, to keep herself attractive for him. Nothing he'd ever said, none of the assurances he'd given her, had convinced her that nothing could have made her unattractive in his eyes. Nothing. He'd loved her spirit, not just the body that had contained it, and he'd believed, perhaps foolishly, that he'd known the woman she was intimately.

Apparently, he'd been wrong. He hadn't known her. Not completely. And he couldn't rid himself of the pain that knowledge brought.

He touched the cold marble with one hand. "What happened between you and LeGrande?" he asked. His voice came out gruff with emotion. "Why could you tell Al and not me?"

He waited, listening as he sometimes did, for an answer or the sense of peace he'd come to expect when he thought of the woman he'd spent his life loving. But today, it didn't come. Not even the soft whisper of a breeze in the nearby trees.

"Was I such a bad husband that you couldn't trust me?" The words caught in his throat and tears blurred his eyes. "I tried to be the kind of man you needed, but I didn't know."

Nothing.

He dashed away the tears, pushed back to his feet, and voiced aloud his biggest fear. "Was there anything else you didn't tell me? Because if there was—" His voice caught again and the words hung there in the heavy evening air.

When a soft hand touched his shoulder, Fred jumped half out of his skin. With his heart tap dancing in his chest, he whipped around, ignoring the twinge in his knees, half expecting to see Phoebe standing there.

Instead, he found himself looking into Margaret's worried eyes—the eyes that looked so much like Phoebe's, Fred thought his heart would break.

"Dad?" Concern filled Margaret's voice. "I was on my way home when I saw you walking down the hill. What are you doing here?"

Fred tried desperately to smile, but he could tell by the way her eyes darkened that he failed miserably. "Just visiting your mother."

"Why?"

He couldn't answer that, so he countered with a question of his own. "Why shouldn't I?"

"Because you never come here unless something's horribly wrong."

She knew him too well. But he didn't admit that aloud. "Nothing's wrong." To his relief, his voice came out sounding almost normal. He glanced over his shoulder at his own name and date of birth chiseled beside Phoebe's, at the unfeeling marble waiting for the final entry. "I guess this reunion has made me miss your mother more than usual."

Margaret didn't immediately say anything to that, but he could feel her watching him, studying him, trying to read his expression.

He didn't look at her.

Unfortunately, she was too much his daughter to accept such a feeble-sounding explanation. She let out a sigh and stepped in front of him. "You miss Mom every day. What's really going on?"

Fred shook his head and tried to look puzzled.

But it did no good. Margaret saw right through him. "Something's wrong," she insisted. "Something's worrying you, and I don't believe it's just the reunion. It's not the murder, either, so don't try to tell me that. It's something more."

He tried desperately to come up with a reasonable explanation, but his mind remained a stubborn blank.

"It's about Mom, isn't it?" Margaret demanded. "That's why you're here."

Fred shook his head quickly. Too quickly. Even *he* could tell that.

Disbelief flashed in her dark eyes. "Tell me."

"There's nothing to tell." Nothing he wanted her to hear, anyway.

"I don't believe you."

"Well, you're just going to have to."

"No, I don't." She reached out to touch him again.

Fred sidestepped her. He wouldn't stand here and let her badger him with questions. Turning his back on her, he took two steps toward the hill.

"What are you running away from?" she shouted after him.

Fred wasn't running away.

But a sudden flash of insight brought him back around to face her. Margaret always became overly concerned about him when she had problems of her own. He'd seen it happen time and again—as if dealing with his problems could help her forget hers.

He closed the distance between them and rested both hands on her shoulders. "Why won't you tell *me* what's bothering *you*."

Her eyes widened almost imperceptibly, then narrowed again. The breeze that had been so conspicuously absent only moments before ruffled the hair around her face. "This isn't about me. It's about you."

Fred didn't believe that for a second. "Is it one of the kids? Is Webb pestering you?"

Margaret shrugged away from his touch. "Webb's not bothering me. He couldn't be happier about the separation."

Good. If you asked Fred, separating from Webb was the best thing Margaret had ever done. "Do you miss him?"

Margaret laughed weakly. "God, no." Her expression softened subtly. "No. I don't. But I guess the kids do." She tucked a lock of hair behind one ear and let her gaze travel to the tops of the trees. "Benjamin's been acting out in all sorts of strange ways—taking the car and disappearing for hours at a time, shouting at me whenever he does come home, snapping at Deborah for no reason at all. And Deborah's crawled into a shell. I can't seem to get through to her. I hate wondering what's happening between them at Webb's apartment, wondering what he's doing to help them, and knowing he's probably only making everything worse."

Fred understood only too well. He knew she had to let the children visit their father—the court would order her to—but he hated thinking what the visits would do to them.

Now that she'd started, Margaret couldn't seem to get it all out fast enough. "And Sarah—" She sighed heavily and shook her head. "She refuses to even see Webb. She'd rather stay home and torture me. She's head over heels *in love* with Dane." She said the name as if it left a bad taste in her mouth.

"Sarah *is* old enough to fall in love," he reminded her gently. "You were married at her age."

"I made a mistake."

"With the person you chose, maybe," Fred said. "Not with the institution of marriage. Dane's not a bad kid, he just looks a little strange."

"Not a bad kid?" Margaret's eyes narrowed and her lips thinned. "Do you know what I found in Sarah's room this morning?"

Fred shook his head slowly.

She reached into her pocket and pulled out a small plastic holder filled with several tiny pills.

Fred took the container and studied it for a few seconds. Obviously, it was a prescription of some sort, but he didn't know what kind. He met Margaret's gaze again. "What is it?"

"Birth control."

Birth control? Little Sarah? Impossible. But the miserable expression on Margaret's face told him it wasn't impossible at all.

He handed the pills back to Margaret. "And you didn't know about it?" Stupid question, but he didn't know what else to say.

"No." The word snapped like taut wire between them. "Of course I didn't know. I would *never* have given my permission for her to get them."

"She's twenty-one," he reminded her. "She doesn't need to ask your permission." This wasn't quite the shock for him it must have been for Margaret. He'd been through this stage with his own children. He still didn't know if any of them had had sex before marriage—he hadn't wanted to know. His approval or disapproval wouldn't have stopped them, just as Margaret's wouldn't stop Sarah.

Time was, when his children were younger, he'd thought he could influence their decisions. Now he knew better. Phoebe'd told him over and over again that the three best things he could do were teach them how to make their own decisions, give them a place to turn when they backed themselves into a corner, and never say I told you so.

She'd been right about all three. He supposed he should be glad Sarah was taking precautions—against pregnancy, at least—and he certainly hoped against other, more frightening things as well.

He tried voicing that thought aloud—cautiously. "I suppose it's a good thing she's being careful."

Margaret glared at him. "She wouldn't have to *be* careful if she used her head." She paced a couple of steps away and folded her arms across her chest. The waning sunlight showed traces of auburn in her dark hair. "She knows better than this, Dad. *She's* the one in control of this situation. She *has* to be strong enough to say no when some guy with raging hormones tries to push her into—" She broke off and made a face. "Well, you know."

Something in what she said made him uneasy. "Girls have hormones, too," he pointed out.

Margaret made a noise of disgust. "Not like *that*."

He looked deep into her eyes and saw the frustration and hurt there. But the trouble ran deeper than that. He could feel it in the air. He tilted her chin with one finger and made her look at him. "Maybe I'm old-fashioned, and maybe I raised you to be, but I don't think Sarah's ready for that. I'd like to see her wait until she gets married. Sex complicates everything—"

"Sex *ruins* everything," Margaret snapped before he could finish. She jerked her chin away. A deep red flush stained her cheeks. "She doesn't have to give in to him."

"Maybe it isn't about giving in," he suggested.

Again, that noise of disgust escaped her and her eyes flashed with that peculiar golden light. She waved her arms in agitation. "Guys can't control their urges. Any little thing can set them off. But she doesn't have to give him what he wants. And if he's going to behave *that* way, she shouldn't have anything to do with him."

"Of course men can control their urges, for heaven's sake—"

She shook her head hard enough to make a lock of hair fall into her eyes. "I knew you'd get defensive. But the bottom line is, it's up to Sarah to keep the boys she dates in line."

Fred couldn't remember ever hearing anything so ridiculous in his life. Nor could he imagine where she'd gotten that idea. "I was raised to believe just the opposite," he told her. "I was raised to believe that the man is the one responsible for keeping things under control."

"How? Once you guys start getting . . . excited, you can't control anything."

"That's not true."

Margaret let out an exasperated sigh. "That's not the point, anyway. The point is Sarah. I tried to raise her right and instill a few values into her. How could she *do* this?" She waved the pills at him as if he needed a reminder.

Fred stepped in front of her and forced her to meet his gaze again. "I don't understand. Are you saying that good girls don't have those urges?"

Another nod, this one hesitant.

Fred cupped her chin in his hand. "Those urges are normal." He kept his voice soft and his touch soothing. "Everyone has them. Surely, you had them, too."

She flushed brilliant red. "Yes, but look where they got me."

Fred couldn't argue with that, but something hidden beneath her words disturbed him. "Is that why you married Webb? Because you—" He broke off, let out an embarrassed laugh, and tried to find some less disturbing way to discuss the subject with his daughter.

Margaret flicked an almost hostile glance at him. "Well, I certainly wasn't going to give in if we weren't married. Mom would have killed me." She turned away from him again. "I wish she was here. She'd know what to say."

Her words stung. Phoebe *had* been better at this sort of thing than he'd ever be, but Phoebe wasn't here. Fred was on his own. His inadequate own.

He shoved his hands into his pockets and thought furiously. His fingers brushed the coins there and encountered something else he couldn't identify for a moment. A heartbeat later he realized he'd pocketed Summer's rocks along with his change.

What had she said again? That they'd help balance his emotions and restore harmony to his relationships? Hogwash. He'd never been less balanced or his relationships less harmonious than they were at this minute.

Margaret plowed her fingers through her hair and stepped back into the shadows. "Mom would know how to help Sarah understand why it's so important to keep those feelings bottled up. Sarah won't listen to me."

Fred swallowed what he'd been about to say and stared at her. "Bottled up? Is that what your mother told you?"

"Yes." She sounded almost hostile.

"Your mother told you all of this? That girls are responsible for keeping boys in line? That boys can't control their urges?"

Margaret nodded, but some of her certainty evaporated. "Before every date I went on."

All-too-familiar nausea rolled in his stomach. He knew with sickening certainty what had given Phoebe that idea, but he wondered why he'd never heard this before. "So, if a boy and girl find themselves in a compromising situation, it's the girl's fault for letting it get out of hand?"

Another wary nod.

Fred took a steadying breath and tried to rid himself of the deep pain in his heart. "Margaret. Sweetheart." He pulled in another breath and let it out slowly. He was heading into uncharted territory, and he'd need to watch every step. "Your mother was wrong."

Margaret's eyes flew open so wide, Fred might have found her expression funny if the subject hadn't been so serious.

He took another cautious step. "Having those kinds of feelings doesn't make a girl bad."

She shook her head and backed a step away. "I knew you wouldn't understand."

"But I do understand." Far better than she could imagine. "Sarah's fallen in love—"

Margaret backed another step away. Everything about her tightened—her lips, her jaw, her shoulders, the look in her eyes. "She's *not* in love. And I won't let her throw her life away for some boy who can't control himself."

"Like Webb couldn't?"

"They're all the same."

"Was Enos the same?" He shouldn't have asked, but he couldn't seem to help himself.

"Enos never tried anything with me." Anger flickered in her eyes again, but this time Fred suspected a different reason behind it.

"So, because Enos knew how to keep his urges under control, you didn't believe he found you attractive."

She didn't respond to that. She didn't need to. The look in her eyes answered for her.

Sick despair filled him. He rubbed his face to buy some time and tried frantically to decide what to say next. "Sweetheart, do you hear what you're saying? You're condemning half the male population for behaving one way, and the other half for behaving just the opposite."

She glared at him. "Don't be ridiculous."

"Listen to yourself," Fred insisted. "If *this* is what your mother taught you—"

"Don't!" She backed away from him quickly. "I can't believe you're doing this."

Her reaction stunned him. "Doing what?"

"Talking bad about Mom." She backed another step away. "You've *never* done that before."

"I'm not talking bad about your mother," he assured her.

She didn't look even slightly reassured. "What in the hell is going on with you lately?"

For half a heartbeat Fred wished he could tell her. For the space of a breath he wished he could drop his burdens at someone else's feet. But he couldn't. "Nothing's going on with me," he said.

Margaret shoved the birth-control pills back into her pocket. "All my life you've taught me to tell the truth. Even when it's not easy, you've made me be honest—with you, with Mom, with *everyone*. I didn't realize until now that the same rules don't apply to you."

"That's not true," he said, but he didn't even convince himself.

"Then *tell* me." She propped her hands on her hips and stared at him, waiting for something he couldn't give her, almost daring him to refuse.

But he couldn't give answers he didn't have. He couldn't explain something he didn't understand. He couldn't help her deal with something that ripped him apart whenever he thought of it. In the end he had no choice but to turn away and walk up the hill.

eighteen

Praying Margaret wouldn't follow him, Fred hurried through the gathering shadows toward his car. He hadn't noticed the Reverend Simper's car outside the rear door when he arrived, but it stood there now beside a dark-colored Lincoln.

Great. Perfect. The last thing in the world he needed was the Reverend Simper pestering him. He was in no mood.

He moved deeper into the shadows and pulled his keys from his pocket for a quick getaway. Before he could reach his car, the rear door to the church opened and a woman stepped out into the dusk.

She turned back to say something, no doubt to the reverend, but she spoke too softly for Fred to hear what she said. He didn't immediately recognize her, but he could tell she wasn't any of the women he'd normally associate with the church—Emma Brumbaugh or Becky Grimes or Sheila Vane.

To his relief, the Reverend Simper didn't come outside. The door closed behind her, but she didn't immediately walk away. Instead, she stood for a moment with her head bent. A flame flickered in the darkness and a moment later the faint scent of cigarette smoke reached Fred.

Stormy Macafee.

Instinct urged him to approach her. Common sense warned him to stay away. He argued silently with himself until she started walking toward the Lincoln, then made his decision quickly. If he didn't at least try to talk with her, he might never get another chance.

He hurried across the parking lot, making no attempt to walk quietly. If she truly believed he'd murdered LeGrande, he didn't want to startle her.

Even so, she didn't hear him until he was almost upon her. When she did, she wheeled to face him, dropped her cigarette, and let out a thin cry.

Fred held out both hands in front of him and tried to look harmless. "Mrs. Macafee, I wonder if I could talk to you for a few minutes."

She took a couple of unsteady steps away and pulled the strap of her bag up on her shoulder. "Stay away from me."

"I'm not going to hurt you. I just need to talk to you."

She shook her head and fumbled inside her purse for her keys. "Get away from me or I'll scream."

Fred took a step back, but he didn't leave. "I'm not going to hurt you, Stormy, and I didn't kill your husband."

She hesitated for less than a breath, then started digging through her purse again. But Fred had seen her uncertainty and he knew she believed him on some level.

She looked far more upset than Fred had expected, and he realized for the first time how much he'd let what Roger said about her affect him. She didn't look like a money-grabbing tart, she looked like a grieving widow, and Fred's heart went out to her.

"I know this is a horrible time for you," he said, "and under normal circumstances, I wouldn't disturb you. . . ."

Fresh tears pooled in her eyes and tiny lines formed around her mouth. "Then go away. I don't want to talk to you. I don't want to talk to anyone."

Fred could certainly understand that. He kept his eyes locked on hers and his voice gentle. Soothing. "I know. But I'd like to help you."

"Help me?" Confusion took the place of some of her anger, and the lines around her mouth deepened. "How?"

"I'd like to help find the person who did kill your husband."

Her dark eyebrows winged into her frosted hair. "So the truth is, you want *me* to help *you*."

Well, yes. But Fred didn't want to admit that. Instead, he said, "I'd just like to ask you a few questions. You may know something that could help both of us."

The tears started again. Fast and hard. "I don't know anything. If I did, I'd have told the sheriff already."

Fred shifted his weight and stuffed his hands in his pockets. "You may know more than you think."

She shook her head quickly. "I don't."

"Do you still believe I killed LeGrande?"

She started to nod, stopped, and gave her head another weak shake. "I don't know. You *did* hit him."

"I did, but I wasn't the only one who fought with him that night. Are you aware that LeGrande had a fight with his son that night?"

Curiosity got the best of her. She flicked one more wary glance at Fred, then nodded toward the Lincoln and motioned for him to get inside. "I'll give you five minutes."

Fred didn't think twice. He slid into the passenger's seat and shut the door behind him.

Stormy slipped behind the wheel and sent him a wary glance. "LeGrande had a fight with Roger? How do you know that?"

Funny she should ask about Roger. Fred hadn't mentioned *which* son. He clasped his hands together, rested them on his knees, and tried not to look threatening in any way. "First, let me say how sorry I am for your loss."

She nodded and glanced away. Either she truly grieved for her husband, or she deserved an award for her acting skills. But the pain in her eyes told him LeGrande's death had hit her hard.

He kept his voice soft and soothing. He didn't want to upset her any further. "LeGrande told me about his health problems. I know he came back to Cutler to straighten things out with several people."

Stormy's gaze flicked back to his and the tears overflowed again. She yanked several tissues from a dispenser on the seat and pressed them to her eyes. "He told you about the cancer?"

"Yes, he did."

She lost control again, held the tissues to her eyes, and gave in to her grief.

Fred waited. After several long seconds she gave one last shuddering sob and worked up a pitiful smile. "I'm sorry," she whispered. "It's just so unbelievable. I thought we had time. . . ."

Fred could certainly understand that. Time had been his best friend and his worst enemy during Phoebe's battle with cancer. He might have said so, but he didn't want to even mention Phoebe's name. "I overheard part of LeGrande's argument with Roger, but I have no idea how it started. Do you have any idea why LeGrande wanted to see him? Or what they could have been fighting about?"

Stormy gave that a moment's thought, but Fred detected a hint of uneasiness that hadn't been there a moment before. "I have no idea. LeGrande hadn't spoken to any of his kids in years."

Fred didn't believe her. He'd heard Roger's warnings for LeGrande to stay away from his family *and* for Stormy not to call his house. But he didn't intend to call her a liar. He wasn't ready to lose her yet.

Stormy brushed a stray lock of hair from her eyes and pulled a pack of cigarettes from her purse. With trembling fingers, she pulled out one and stuck it between her lips, but she paused before she lit it. "Do you mind if I smoke?"

Fred shook his head. He'd rather she didn't, but he wasn't about to tell a grieving widow she couldn't smoke in her own car. "I'm trying to find someone else who saw Roger at the school that night. I take it you didn't see him?"

"Why? Do you think *he* killed LeGrande?"

Fred didn't want to make accusations. He just wanted information. "I don't know what to think. I'm checking every possibility." He paused, then shifted to face her better. "Do you think he could have?"

She slanted a curious glance at him and lifted her shoulders in a casual shrug. "Sure. He *could* have."

"But you don't think he did?"

She shook her head quickly and barked a bitter laugh. "No. If Roger was going to kill anybody, it would have been me."

"Why is that?"

She waved one hand in a gesture obviously calculated to look casual. Smoke drifted from her cigarette through the darkened car. "Those kids blame *me* for stealing their father away from their mother. And they think I've somehow manipulated him to leave me all his money." She made a face and repeated, "Money. That whole family is obsessed with it."

Money had a way of doing that to people, Fred thought, but he didn't want to sidetrack her.

She inhaled deeply from her cigarette and waited to speak until she exhaled again. "What they don't understand is, most of the money LeGrande and I have is what we made through L&S Enterprises, *after* we got married." Another airy wave of the hand. "Oh, he had *some* when he was married to *The Bitch*, but it wasn't until he and Oliver started investing that he really started making a lot."

"Oliver . . . ?" Fred leaned a little closer. "You mean, Oliver Wellington?"

Stormy nodded and took another long drag. Another exhale. "Oliver used to give LeGrande investment advice. The trouble is, *she's* got LeGrande's kids convinced that he had the money hidden somewhere before the divorce and that half of it belongs to her."

"But he didn't?"

"No, he didn't."

"Is that why LeGrande wanted to see Roger? To work out the money problems?"

"I don't know." She gazed at him steadily with her wide blue eyes. Too steadily. She didn't even blink.

"He didn't tell you?"

"No. He didn't tell me anything. I knew he had things he

wanted to get settled, but that was all. I figured they were all things with you people."

Fred hesitated to ask the next question, but considering the things he'd heard Roger say about her, he had to know. "How was your relationship with LeGrande?"

She glared at him. Ash fell from her cigarette to the floor of her car. "How dare you ask that question. I loved my husband."

"I'm sorry," he said quickly. "I'm just trying to make sense of everything that's happened and everything I've heard."

"Oh?" She lifted her eyebrows again. "And what have you heard about me?"

"About you?" Fred pretended to think so he could buy some time. He decided on a vague answer. "Well, of course, we've all known Iris for years. . . ."

She made a noise with her teeth and looked away in disgust. "Yes, I'm well aware of that. I wasn't exactly welcomed with open arms on Friday night."

"Yes. Well."

"What are they saying about me?"

Fred hesitated, then decided to take the bull by the horns. "I've heard a few people wondering why a young, beautiful woman like you would marry someone so much older."

She jerked the cigarette toward her. "For love, Mr. Vickery. It's as simple as that. And now he's gone." Tears filled her eyes again and her breathing became shallow and uneven.

He gave her another few seconds, then asked the question he'd come to ask. "Have you seen or talked to Roger since you came to town?"

"No. I've only met him once, and I haven't seen him in years." She flicked her cigarette out the window and sent him a trembling smile. "Roger is a mean man, Mr. Vickery. He's just like his mother."

Fred thought it more likely he took after his father, but he didn't think Stormy would appreciate the comparison. "Did LeGrande know how you felt about his son?"

"Of course he did. I didn't make any bones about it. Those kids hurt him terribly, and I hated watching what their anger did to him."

"How did he feel about that?"

"He understood. Of *course,* he understood. If I'd had my way . . ." She broke down into painful sobs again.

Fred waited, patiently, wondering whether the tears were real or a way to change the subject.

"I'll admit," she said after a few minutes, "I tried to get him to forget all about them. Not because I was jealous of them or anything like that, but because every time he thought about them or tried to make contact he got hurt all over again."

Fred had certainly seen that happen before, but he didn't interrupt.

"Of course," Stormy went on, warming to her theme now, "I think their mother had a big hand in it, too." As it had before, her voice grew brittle when she spoke of Iris. "She told those kids that I stole their father away—as if anyone can *steal* a human being. What she's conveniently forgetting is that their marriage was in trouble before I ever came along. LeGrande just never had a reason to leave until he met me." She paused, waited for Fred to say something.

He didn't.

She scowled deeply and argued, "Women leave. Women aren't afraid to step out into the great unknown. But a man can be miserable, and he'll stay right where he is unless something better comes along."

Fred thought about Margaret's marriage. That's exactly what had happened there. Margaret had finally been the one to put an end to it. Webb would have stayed forever.

"When a man finally does leave," Stormy said, "when he decides to find a little happiness, everyone blames the *other woman* for snatching him from the bosom of his family. Well, I'm here to tell you, a man who's happy can't be snatched."

Fred thought there was probably some truth in that, but he didn't want to let the conversation drift any further into those waters. He worked up a reassuring smile. "Then you think it's possible Iris killed LeGrande?"

"No."

"No?"

"No, Mr. Vickery, I don't think she killed him. The Bitch wanted my husband's money too much. Now, if LeGrande had changed his will to include those kids again, I might believe it. But as it stands now—no, I don't think so."

"Then, who do you think did?"

The question wiped away the rest of Stormy's anger. Her face contorted with fresh pain. "I don't know. Other than the Bitch and her children—and *you*—nobody had a reason to kill him. He hadn't even seen any of you people for over fifty years, except Oliver, of course. And Jeremiah Hunt."

Fred took a chance with his next question. "Why did LeGrande fire Jeremiah six months before he was scheduled to retire?"

"He and LeGrande had professional differences."

"Professional differences that LeGrande couldn't endure for six months?"

She stiffened, and Fred knew he'd offended her. "No matter what you may think, Mr. Vickery, my husband wasn't a monster. If he felt it necessary to fire Jeremiah, it was. I don't know the details. You'd have to ask Jeremiah."

"I have," Fred admitted. "He wouldn't say."

Stormy's lips curved into a satisfied smile. "Doesn't that tell you something?"

Not necessarily. Fred decided to shift gears. "Tell me about Oliver."

Stormy's face tightened. "That bastard? What do you want to know about him?"

Her reaction surprised him. "Why do you say that?"

"Why? You haven't heard?"

"Heard what?"

"I told you that Oliver used to give LeGrande investment advice. What I didn't tell you was that when things didn't go his way, he turned on LeGrande."

"What do you mean?"

"I mean," she said stiffly, "he threatened my husband on more than one occasion."

Then why on earth had she accused Fred of the murder? He pulled in a steadying breath and made sure he'd heard her right. "Oliver threatened him? What kinds of threats? How long ago?"

"I don't know the details," she said again. It seemed to be a recurring theme. "All I know is, Oliver suddenly stopped coming around. LeGrande was upset about it at the time, but he didn't say much. He didn't want me to worry. And, like I said, it was years ago." She reached for another cigarette, changed her mind, and sighed. "If you'll excuse me, I really would like to be alone."

Fred bit back his disappointment. After all, he'd gotten much more than he'd expected. "Thanks for talking to me," he said as he pushed open the car door. "I know how difficult it was for you."

She nodded weakly, lowered her head, and dabbed her face with the tissues again. "I just want whoever took LeGrande away from me to pay."

Fred closed the door between them and watched her drive away. She certainly seemed genuine, but he wasn't quite ready to cross her off his list. Maybe because she'd lied. Or maybe because he just couldn't imagine anyone loving LeGrande Macafee that much.

nineteen

"So, what are we doing today" Dane pushed his breakfast plate to the center of the table, leaned back in his chair, and brushed a hand across his clean shirt as if it felt unfamiliar so early in the morning.

It probably did, but Fred gave the boy credit for at least putting something on. He tossed off the rest of his coffee and stood. *He* had plans to visit Oliver Wellington. They didn't include Dane. "Aren't you doing something with Sarah?"

"No, man." Dane tilted back in the chair, lifting its two front legs from the floor and resting its back against the wall. "Her mom's wigged out about something, and Sarah thinks it would be better if we don't get together today. I'm beginning to wonder why she even wanted me to come up here."

Fred spent a moment scraping his uneaten food into the trash and imagining the scene between Margaret and Sarah. There'd been tears, he knew that for certain. And shouting. And accusations.

He wondered how long it would take Margaret to come storming through the kitchen door to confront Dane. If she followed her usual schedule, twenty minutes, tops. He glanced at the kid as he crossed to the sink. "Sarah didn't tell you what her mother's upset about?"

Dane shook his head. "No. Do you think she's making it up? Do you think she's trying to give me the brush-off?"

"I don't think she's making it up," Fred said honestly. "But I don't know what she's thinking." He knew perfectly well what Margaret wanted. He also knew how persistent she could be. He wondered if, after a night and a day listening to her mother, Sarah would send Dane packing.

Much as he hated to admit it, Sarah could pick a worse young man. Dane might look odd, but he had a good head on his shoulders, and he seemed to genuinely care about her. Fred might not approve of the direction Sarah and Dane's relationship had taken, but he didn't think the boy deserved a dose of Margaret's temper so early in the morning— especially without warning.

"Well, don't just sit there banging my wall," he said gruffly. "Let's get these dishes done. We've got things to do."

Grinning, Dane lowered his chair to the floor again with a heavy bump. He stood quickly and scooped his plate from the table. "All right. Where are we going?"

"To Steamboat Springs for a chat with Oliver Wellington."

"The boring guy?"

"The boring guy who had some kind of trouble with LeGrande Macafee and threatened him somehow."

Dane's eyes widened. He slid his plate onto the counter beside Fred and leaned against the cabinet. "No kidding? You know where to find him?"

"Jeremiah Hunt told me he lives in Steamboat Springs."

"You've got his address?"

"No," Fred admitted. "We'll just look it up in the phone book when we get there." He stole a glance at the wall clock. Seventeen minutes. They couldn't afford to waste any time. "Bring over the pans, will you? I want to get moving before it gets too late."

Dane pushed away from the cabinet and started across the kitchen. "So, do you think Oliver killed him?"

"I don't know what to think," Fred admitted. He worked the stopper into the sink, started the water, and added a squirt of dish soap. "The only two people I'm sure *didn't* do it are Percy Neuswander and Roger Macafee. Unless Percy got LeGrande on his knees before he hit him, he couldn't have inflicted the blow from his wheelchair."

Dane handed him the frying pan and slid the pancake turner into the soapy water. "You *don't* think Roger's guilty now?"

"No. I finally found someone who saw him that night, but he also saw him leaving while LeGrande was still alive."

Dane relaxed against the counter again. "Okay. So, it could had been Oliver. And it could have been Jeremiah. And it could have been that lady you were with yesterday—Thea. What about that other couple we saw at the restaurant. Could one of them have done it?"

"Burl and Coralee?" Fred shrugged and scrubbed egg from a fork. "I doubt it. Coralee used to date LeGrande, but that was over fifty years ago. No, I'm convinced the motive has to be something more recent. Even hatred loses its power after fifty years."

"But you were still angry enough to hit him."

Fred flicked a glance at him. "Not over anything I knew about fifty years ago."

Dane grabbed a towel and started drying the dishes. "Okay. But what if you aren't the only one who learned something new on Friday? Something new about something old."

Fred stopped washing for a second, remembered the ticking clock, and started again. "I suppose that's possible."

Dane went on as if he hadn't spoken. As if he needed convincing. "If LeGrande came to the reunion to set things straight before he died, then he probably stirred up a lot of old stuff. Stuff you don't even know about."

Fred rinsed a plate and handed it to him. "It's possible."

"I'll tell you something. I spent a while in that restaurant yesterday, watching people and listening a little bit. There's something going on with those two."

"With Burl and Coralee?" Fred slid the frying pan into the water. "What makes you think so?"

"First of all, they didn't say a word to each other the

entire time they were in there. Not even, you know, 'nice weather' kind of talk."

"They've been married at least fifty years," Fred reminded him. "Maybe they didn't have anything to say."

Dane shook his head quickly. "No, man. There's something going on. Trust me. I can't explain it, but it's just a feeling I got from watching them."

"Did you overhear anything?"

"They didn't *say* anything," Dane reminded him. "Nothing. Hell, they barely even looked at each other."

Fred tried not to read too much into that. After all, compared with a new young love like Dane and Sarah's, a comfortable old relationship like Burl and Coralee's might seem wrong. But he wasn't foolish enough to discount any possibility, no matter how remote.

He glanced at the clock again, rinsed the last of the dishes, and unplugged the stopper. "You can leave the rest to air-dry. Let's get out of here."

"Why are you in such a hurry?"

Fred shrugged and started toward the living room for his keys. "Because we've got a long drive ahead of us."

"All right." Dane trailed after him. "What about Thea? Did you find out why LeGrande wanted to see her?"

Fred found his keys on the bureau by the front door, slipped them into his pocket, and nodded. "I think so."

"So, what was it?"

"I can't talk about it."

Dane's brows knit. "That bad, huh?"

"That bad."

"Okay. What about the other guy Ardella mentioned— Al. Have you found out anything about him?"

Fred shook his head and started back toward the kitchen. "Not yet."

"Maybe you should talk to him. Do you know where he lives?"

Fred pushed through the swinging door into the kitchen. "I do."

"Where? Is it close?"

"Fairly." He opened the back door and waited for Dane to step outside.

"Well, then? Let's go see him while we're out seeing people."

Maybe they should, but Fred wasn't at all sure he wanted anyone else around when he talked to Al—not even Millie. He wasn't sure he wanted to talk to Al at all.

He must have hesitated a moment too long. Dane arched his eyebrows and tilted his head to one side. "You don't want me around when you talk to him?"

Fred locked the back door and tried to look as if he didn't care one way or the other. "I can talk to him later."

Obviously, Dane didn't believe him. "So, who is he? A friend of yours?"

"Something like that." Fred nodded Dane toward the garage and followed him inside.

"All right," Dane said with a shrug. "You don't want to tell me, I can understand that." He made a visible effort to look unconcerned, but Fred could see right through him. He'd hurt the boy's feelings.

He worked up a smile and leaned his arms on the roof of the Buick. "Al Jarvis is my brother-in-law. He's a pest. Drives me crazy most of the time."

A ghost of a smile tugged at Dane's lips. "Yeah?"

Fred nodded. "If he had some problem with LeGrande that none of us knows about, it must have been something serious." He shrugged and added, "He's been my brother-in-law for fifty-two years. Even if I don't like him, I figure I owe it to him to ask him privately."

Dane's smile grew. "All right. I'm cool with that."

Fred checked his watch again and scowled. Two minutes or less. "Come on," he said, sliding behind the wheel. "Let's get out of here."

He started reversing before Dane even had the door shut and pulled onto Lake Front Drive while the kid was still fussing with his seat belt. He held his breath until they rounded the first curve, until he knew that even if Margaret did show up, she wouldn't be able to see them through the

trees, then settled back in his seat for the drive. And he tried
to convince himself they'd have smooth sailing from here
on out.

Fred slowed the Buick in front of a small white house on
a tree-lined street and glanced at Dane on the seat beside
him. "Is that it?"

Dane checked the address against the note he'd written on
his palm and nodded. "That's it, man. But I thought you said
this guy had a lot of money."

"That's what I was told," Fred admitted. He trailed his
gaze across the chipped paint, the weed-infested flower
beds, the cracked, uneven driveway sprouting weeds. He
tried to remember who'd told him that, but his mind came
up blank. All he could think about was the moment in the
school corridor when Oliver had pinned his arms behind
his back. And he couldn't help wondering if Oliver had
known, even then, that Fred wasn't guilty.

Dane snorted a laugh. "Well, if he has money, he sure as
hell doesn't spend much of it."

Fred started to respond, but when he noticed the curtain
in the front window twitch, he stopped himself and opened
his door. "Somebody's watching us. I'd better go to the door
before they get nervous. You stay here."

"Aw, come on."

"No." Once before, Fred had put his grandson, Benjamin,
in danger. He wouldn't repeat the mistake again.

He pushed the button to roll down the electric windows,
tossed Dane the keys, and climbed out from behind the
wheel. "If I'm not back in half an hour, go get help."

Dane grinned at him. "Cool."

Not cool at all. And hopefully not necessary. Walking
quickly, he crossed the lawn toward the front porch.

Before he could reach the bottom step, the door flew
open and Oliver stepped outside. He pulled he door shut
behind him, folded his arms across his ample middle, and
planted himself on the edge of the porch. "What are you
doing here?" He kept his voice low and darted a glance over

his shoulder, as if he wanted to keep someone inside from hearing them.

Fred tried to look friendly, but the scowl on Oliver's face made it difficult. "I just need to ask you a few questions."

Oliver shook his head and firmed up his stance. "You have no business being here after what you did."

"I didn't do a blasted thing," Fred snapped.

"That's what you say."

"It's the truth," Fred insisted, raising his voice a notch. "I found the body, dammit. I didn't kill him."

Oliver motioned for him to be quiet and glanced over his shoulder again. Sweat dotted his nose and upper lip. He looked nervous. "I don't want you here."

"Answer my questions, and I'll leave."

Oliver glared at him. "I could call the police."

Fred called his bluff. "Go ahead. I don't mind asking what I want to know in front of them. They'll probably be as interested as I am."

That got Oliver's attention. He stepped off the porch and closed the short distance between them. "You're still trying to play innocent?"

"I *am* innocent, you idiot." Fred raised his voice again. If Oliver wanted to shut him up, he'd have to start talking.

"Keep your voice down," Oliver commanded. "My grandkids are inside."

"Fine. Just tell me what I want to know."

"Don't try to push me around, Fred. I'm not going to stand for it. You're on my property, invading my privacy."

"Just tell me about the threats you made to LeGrande, and I'll give you all the privacy you want."

Oliver's eyes widened. He let out a harsh laugh and wiped the sweat from his lip. "Threats? I don't know what you're talking about."

"I understand you had a falling-out over some investment advice you gave him."

Everything about Oliver stiffened. "I never gave Le-Grande investment advice."

"Never?"

"Never. Now get off my property."

Fred had no intention of leaving without answers. "Why do you suppose Mrs. Macafee thinks you did?"

"I don't know why she thinks anything," Oliver snapped. One of his chins wobbled. "She's always been melodramatic."

Fred smiled slowly. "Really? You do know her, then."

Oliver froze for a second, then tried again to pull himself together. "I know *of* her."

Fred cocked an eyebrow. "You know enough of her to know she's melodramatic?"

Oliver wagged a hand in front of his face. "Gossip. You know how it is. You hear things."

"You must hear more than I do," Fred muttered. "Of course, I suppose all those trips to his office probably helped."

Oliver shook his head. Dark stains appeared under his arms. "I don't know where you heard that. I never went to his office."

Heat and frustration worked together to snap Fred's patience. "You're lying, Oliver. It's written all over your face. I *know* you did business with LeGrande. More than one person can testify to that. I know you gave him investment advice. And I know that you threatened him after one of the investments went bad."

Oliver took an involuntary step backward. "That's absolute bullshit. Whoever told you that is lying." His eyes flicked across Fred's face with no particular pattern. His chin quivered.

Fred didn't have the time or the patience to play games. "Look, Oliver, I'll be honest with you. If I've heard about your business with LeGrande, the sheriff's heard about it, too."

Some of Oliver's confidence evaporated.

"You know the sheriff is a friend of mine."

Oliver nodded slowly. "I heard that."

"If you tell me about the trouble between you and LeGrande, and if you didn't kill him, maybe I can put in a good word for you. If not, you'll be on your own when he comes to question you."

Oliver's face turned a blotchy red. "What makes you think he'll come to question *me*?"

"*I'm* here, aren't I? He can't be far behind."

Oliver's shoulders lost a little of their starch. He glanced behind him again, then jerked his head toward the driveway. "Let's move away from the house. I don't want my grandkids to hear any of this."

Fred didn't have any objection to that, but he kept one eye on Oliver as they walked. After all, whoever killed LeGrande had done it from behind.

To Fred's relief, Oliver behaved himself all the way to the driveway. There, he made another attempt to pull himself together. "All right. I'll admit I used to go to LeGrande's office. But I never gave him investment advice. That's the first thing you've got to believe."

Fred didn't have to believe anything, but he didn't bother pointing that out. "Then why is everyone under the impression you did?"

"LeGrande must have told them I did."

"Why would he do that?"

"Your guess is as good as mine. Who knows why LeGrande did anything?"

Fred shook his head. "LeGrande might have been a liar, but he always had a reason for what he said. Usually a selfish one."

"Well, he didn't have a reason this time," Oliver insisted.

Fred didn't believe that for an instant. "Why did you go to his office? Did you have business together?"

Oliver hesitated, took several deep breaths, and argued silently with himself.

Fred was quickly losing the rest of his patience. He could see Dane in the car, watching every move they made. A breeze stirred the air and brought with it the faint scent of rain.

Oliver didn't say a word.

"Did you do business together?" Fred asked again.

Oliver shook his head, but he kept his gaze averted, and Fred knew it was a lie.

He threw up his hands. "Fine. Tell it to the sheriff, then."

"For a while," Oliver muttered.

Fred turned back to face him again. "What?"

"I said, we did business together for a while. Biggest mistake I ever made, let me tell you."

Fred could have told him that. He moved a little closer. "What kind of business? Investments?"

"I knew him too well to get involved in something like *that* with him. LeGrande had no scruples."

Another lie. Fred could practically feel it. "Tell me the truth," he warned.

"That *is* the truth, Fred. I swear to God."

"I don't believe you." Fred started to turn away again. "I don't have time for games. Maybe the sheriff will have better luck getting it out of you."

"Wait." Oliver's eyes widened. He darted another nervous glance at the front of the house and tugged Fred a little farther away. "All right. Yes. He wanted to put together an investment partnership, and I thought it sounded like a good idea."

This was more like it. "So you did it?"

Oliver nodded miserably.

"LeGrande came out smelling like a rose, and you're living here? Why?"

"We didn't form the partnership right away. That came later. At first, LeGrande said he just wanted to keep in touch. We had lunch together. Drinks. You know. Friends."

With LeGrande? Fred tried not to laugh. He'd always known Oliver was boring, but not stupid.

"Later, after he made all that money, he talked about the partnership."

"And you agreed."

Oliver nodded sheepishly. "Yeah. It wasn't smart, I know. But he was doing so well, and I was tired of living like this." He waved one stubby arm around.

"There's nothing wrong with this," Fred told him. At

least, there wouldn't be if he painted and pulled a few weeds.

"It wasn't like what LeGrande had." Oliver folded his arms again. Closing up. "I worked hard all my life, and still barely scraped by. I was over sixty years old. It was my time."

Apparently not, Fred thought, or they wouldn't be standing amidst the weeds now. "You had enough money to form a partnership?"

"No. But LeGrande said my experience would be my part. He put in the money."

"What happened then?"

"Nothing." Misery filled Oliver's eyes. A flash of anger followed it. "Nothing."

"Something must have happened," Fred argued, "or you wouldn't be trying so hard to hide it."

Oliver shook his head. "I'm serious, Fred. Nothing happened. LeGrande kept getting richer. I got enough to pay the rest of the mortgage on the house—ten thousand dollars. That's it." He let out a heavy sigh and struggled with himself for a few seconds, then said, "What I'm going to tell you now has to stay between us."

"I can't promise that."

"You have to, or I won't tell you."

He looked so miserable, Fred caved a little. "All right. I'll keep it to myself as long as it doesn't have anything to do with the murder."

Oliver nodded once. "Fair enough." But he still needed a few seconds before he could speak. "I didn't know about what he'd done until *after* I tried to pull out of the partnership. Hell, I didn't even realize what *I'd* done until then." He pulled in a deep breath and met Fred's gaze with a desperate one of his own. "I guess I had too much to drink one day at one of our lunches. I don't know. I don't remember. Apparently, I told him about a takeover bid my company was involved in. The information wasn't public knowledge yet. I had no business saying anything, but I thought we were friends."

That was his second big mistake.

"Of course, you can probably guess—LeGrande acted on the information I gave him. He bought up as much stock of the other company as he could. And when the takeover was finally announced and the stock skyrocketed, he made a fortune. *That's* how he made all his money. Off of my big fat mouth."

Fred believed him. It was just like LeGrande to use someone else that way, and just like Oliver to give him the fodder he needed. If he hadn't been in such a tough position himself, he might actually have felt sorry for Oliver. But he couldn't afford to let old ties soften him, even for an instant.

twenty

Fred stuffed his hands into his pockets, rocked back on his heels, and studied Oliver carefully. The hot summer wind teased his hair upward and made it stand out as if he'd been electrocuted. Distress deepened the wrinkles on his face and tightened his mouth into a deep frown. He looked distraught.

But Fred didn't completely understand why. "I agree, it wasn't a smart move, but it was hardly a tragedy."

"Not then," Oliver agreed. "Not until I became his partner and used part of that money to pay off the mortgage on my house. Once *I* benefited, it became insider trading. I could go to prison, Fred. For a stupid mistake I don't even remember."

This time Fred couldn't help feeling sorry for him. "So you threatened him?"

"A couple of times. But only because he threatened to expose me if I tried to back out of the partnership. He wanted to make sure I kept my mouth shut in the future."

That sounded like something LeGrande would do. Always thinking of himself.

"They were empty threats," Oliver whined. "He knew it. I knew it." He held his arms out at his side and presented himself for inspection. "Look at me, Fred. I've never done anything in my entire life. But when he walked into that reunion, I wanted to kill him. I did. I'll admit it. And when he told Stanley Bridges to ask me for investment advice, I knew what he was up to. He was going to expose me anyway."

"And set the record straight," Fred added softly.

"Yes, but only so he could look good at his funeral."

"What about his wife and children?"

Oliver laughed sharply. "LeGrande didn't care about anybody but himself."

That was certainly true. It had always been true. "Did you talk to him at the reunion?"

"No." Oliver shook his head quickly. "I wanted to. When I saw him leave the gymnasium, I waited a few minutes and went after him. But I never did find him. And the next thing I knew, Stormy was screaming and shouting that you'd killed him." He rubbed his forehead and let out a heavy sigh. "I'm glad he's dead. It's the first time in ten years I've felt safe."

Fred believed him. He didn't want to, but he did. "Okay. If you didn't kill him and I didn't kill him, who did?"

Oliver looked a little surprised for a second, then a relieved smile spread across his face. "You believe me?"

"I don't know what to believe," Fred hedged. "But you knew LeGrande a hell of a lot better than I did. I want to know who you think killed him."

Oliver gave that some thought. "It could have been Jeremiah, I guess. After all, look what LeGrande did to him."

"I know he fired him, but how many years ago was that? Would Jeremiah still be upset enough to murder him in cold blood?"

"Maybe." Oliver pursed his lips, as if what he was about to say tasted bad. "LeGrande fired him six months before he was set to get his pension. And for no reason."

"How do you know that?"

"How do you think? LeGrande told me. His pension fund was in trouble, and he wanted to save money." Oliver slanted a glance at him. "Jeremiah's wife died shortly after he got fired."

"I didn't know that."

Oliver nodded. "Yep. And Jeremiah's always blamed LeGrande for her death. He's convinced that if he'd had his pension, he would have been able to get better medical care for her."

"There's probably some truth in that."

"I'm sure there is. Hell, even getting the flu costs a fortune these days. Imagine trying to pay for a decent nursing home on nothing but social security. She had Alzheimer's. He couldn't take care of her himself. He had to work just to make ends meet. He had to put her into a horrible place, and it damn near killed him to do it."

Fred could only imagine. He couldn't imagine having to put Phoebe into a home. He hadn't even liked leaving her in the hospital overnight while she battled the cancer. "Jeremiah told me he's working," he said. "Something in public relations."

"Public relations?" Oliver let out a bitter laugh. "He can call it that if he wants to, but he's a greeter at damned Wal-Mart—for minimum wage."

Pity coiled through Fred. He forced it away. Jeremiah could easily be the murderer, but even if he wasn't, he obviously didn't want pity.

Oliver went on, oblivious. "Or, it could have been Iris. Or even Yale."

"Why do you think they might have done it?"

"Because of the money."

"What money?"

Oliver looked at him as if he'd never seen anyone so stupid. "*LeGrande's* money."

"But I thought LeGrande made most of his money after the divorce."

Oliver shook his head in pity. "He did. But he used money he owed Iris to make it. She and Yale know he did, but they can't prove it. But, since the kids are still named beneficiaries in LeGrande's will—"

"Are they?"

"I think so. They were."

"So, with LeGrande dead, the kids get the money."

"Exactly. A lot of it, anyway." He thought again. "Or maybe Stormy did it. After all, they had the world's worst marriage. She cheated on him from the minute he put that ring on her finger until the day he died."

That surprised Fred. "Then why would she kill him and not the other way around?"

Oliver let out a malicious laugh. "Because he found out and he was planning to divorce her."

That was certainly interesting. And certainly nothing like what Stormy had told him. "Do you know who she cheated with?"

Oliver laughed again. "Half of L&S Enterprises—the male half. Half the male population of Cherry Hills." His smile faded and he leaned a little closer. "Even his own son."

Fred drew back as if Oliver had hit him. "You mean Roger?"

"I mean Roger."

"How do you know that?"

"Because I saw them," Oliver said with a sneer. "I met Jeremiah at the Copper Penny the night before the reunion, and we saw them together. They looked awfully cozy."

Then Roger's story hadn't been a complete lie. Before he could ask anything more, the front door of the house opened and a young girl about twelve stepped out onto the porch. "Grandpa? Are you going to play Monopoly with us or not?"

Oliver's expression softened. "I'm coming, honey."

"Now? We're bored."

"Right now." He sent Fred a glance that left no doubt as to its meaning. He'd said all he intended to say. Fred wouldn't get another thing out of him.

He didn't even intend to try. He knew exactly how Oliver felt. He felt the same way when someone brought up the murder in front of Sarah. He smiled at Oliver's granddaughter. "Sorry for keeping your grandpa so long."

Oliver looked almost pathetically grateful. Without even

a backward glance, he crossed to the porch, took his granddaughter's hand in his, and led her inside.

Fred stood there until the door latched behind him, trying to put together everything he'd just heard. He wondered how much of all this Enos knew, and wondered if he should tell him. But the instant the thought formed, he pushed it away.

He knew how Enos would react if he found out Fred had been asking questions. He knew what Enos would do. But Fred had no intention of backing off, shutting up, or staying home unless or until Enos told him he'd been cleared of all suspicion. With Ivan on the case and Enos so distracted, Fred figured the chances of that happening were slim to none.

He stuffed his hands into his pockets and started back toward the car, where Dane waited, slouched in the seat and bobbing his head in time to the radio that was undoubtedly draining the Buick's battery.

When Fred's shadow passed across Dane's face, the young man bolted upright in his seat. "So? What did you find out?"

"I don't think he did it."

"No?" Dane glanced at the house and back again. "Then who did?"

"His wife, his ex-wife, her new husband, or Jeremiah Hunt. One of those four."

Dane frowned in confusion. "You're not narrowing it down very fast."

Scowling, Fred slid behind the wheel and cranked the Buick to life. "Thank you for reminding me. But I'm doing my best."

"I didn't mean that the way it sounded, man. It's just that we've got to be missing something."

"I agree," Fred said, pulling onto the street again. "But what?"

"Damned if I know." Dane turned his head and watched the houses they passed for a minute. "I think you ought to talk to your brother-in-law."

"No."

"Why not?"

"I told you already," Fred reminded him. "I want to talk to him alone."

"How are you going to do that with your sister around?"

It was a good question, but Fred didn't want to admit it aloud. "I'll figure out something. Don't worry about it."

Dane fell silent for another minute or two. Just when Fred thought he'd dropped the subject, he launched in again. "There's some other reason you don't want to talk to him."

"Oh?" Fred flicked an annoyed glance at him. "You can read my mind, now?"

"No. Not exactly. It's just obvious that you don't want to talk to him. If you did, you'd go to see him. I mean, you could always leave me in the car again. So it seems to me, you don't really want to talk to him."

"Nonsense."

Dane shrugged elaborately and turned his gaze away. "All right. If you say so."

It *was* nonsense, Fred assured himself. He'd talk to Al—eventually. He would. Just not yet. "I'll tell you where we *are* going," he said, trying to wipe away the flicker of self-doubt Dane's question had ignited.

"Where?"

"To the Copper Penny. Oliver told me he saw Stormy Macafee in there with her stepson the night before the murder."

"No shit?"

"No kidding."

"They were together?"

"Apparently."

"Whoa. I wonder what's up with that."

"So do I," Fred admitted. "And I figure now might be a good time to find out."

"Cool." Dane put one hand on his stomach and leaned back in the seat trying to look pitiful. "But can we stop for lunch first? I'm starving."

Fred realized with a start how hungry he was. Getting his

appetite back was a good sign, he told himself. A very good sign. Maybe he was finally on the right trail, after all.

Fred parked the Buick on Ash Street beneath the shade of an old spruce tree and glanced at the storm clouds lining the western rim of the valley. Dark liquid lines traced from the sky into the forest below. A stiff breeze stirred the tops of the trees and carried with it the faint scent of ozone.

Dane slanted a curious glance at him. "Why are we parking way over here?"

"Because I don't want anyone to know where we are."

"Why? Are you afraid they're going to think you've started drinking?"

"No," Fred said patiently. "Because I usually don't go to the Copper Penny, and if they see my car there, they'll know I'm asking questions about the murder."

Dane nodded thoughtfully.

Fred pushed open his car door and pulled in a deep breath of tangy air. A jagged flash tore through the distant sky, lighting the darkened clouds for a moment, then fading again. Thunder, too far away to do more than grumble, followed. The storm was still miles away, but Fred knew this country. Within the hour they'd be in the thick of it. He didn't mind. He loved the rain. Loved the smell of the air before and the scent of the earth after.

"We'd better roll up the windows," he warned Dane. "I don't want the seats to get ruined."

Dane complied, brushed a hand across his two-toned hair, and turned a broad grin in his direction. "Ready?"

"Ready."

Fred climbed out onto the street, pressed the automatic door lock, and looked around to make sure no one had noticed him. From here, he could see the backs of the shoe repair shop and High Mountain Realtors, but no one would notice his car from Main Street.

Kicking himself into high gear, he led Dane through the trees lining the Copper Penny's small parking lot and past the few cars parked there. He didn't see his son-in-law's truck anywhere. Good. If Webb had Benjamin and Deborah for the month, he'd damn well better be home with them instead of drinking his life away in a bar.

He did see an Audi near the front door which he recognized as belonging to Albán Toth, the Copper Penny's owner. That perked him up a bit. He'd known Albán for a good thirty years. If anyone would tell him the truth about Roger and Stormy, Albán would.

Tugging open the bar's door, he stepped inside behind Dane. He waited for a moment, blinking while his eyes adjusted to the dim lighting. A belabored swamp cooler made an effort to push the air around, but it didn't stop the cigarette smoke from filling Fred's nose and stinging his eyes. A song on the jukebox pounded its beat through the floorboards and up Fred's legs, and set Dane's head bobbing. A woman's laughter drifted toward him from a table in the far corner.

Still bobbing, Dane glanced around, obviously curious.

Fred concentrated on Albán, who stood behind the bar with a young woman in a short skirt. Neither of them looked happy. The creases in Albán's broad forehead along with his wide, jerky gestures warned Fred he wasn't in the best of moods.

The young woman propped her hands on her hips and scowled up at him, shaking her head hard enough to make a cascade of dark curls dance on her shoulders. She had the figure of a woman and the face of a child, and to Fred's eye, she didn't even look old enough to be inside the bar.

He glanced at Dane, fully expecting the young man to notice and appreciate her obvious charms. To his surprise, Dane didn't even give her a second glance.

Motioning for Dane to follow him, he meandered casually toward a stool at the long bar and perched uncomfortably on it. Dane settled on one beside him and dragged a bowl of pretzels toward him.

Wearing his automatic customer-greeting smile, Albán glanced up. But when he recognized Fred, his smile faltered.

"Fred?" He flicked a glance at Dane and back again. "What's up?"

"Up?" Fred took a pretzel and waved it in Dane's direction. "I'm just spending an afternoon with Dane, here. He's a friend of Sarah's."

Albán held out a hand toward Dane, endured Dane's thumb-gripping ritual with a smile, and glanced back at Fred in confusion. "So, you're just out and about, having a good time?"

Fred nodded and took a bite of the pretzel. "Yep. Thought he'd like to see Cutler's hot spot."

Albán's smile grew slightly. "I see. Well, what can I get you?" After living in Cutler for nearly thirty years, Albán had all but lost his native Hungarian accent. Only the faint *V* where a *W* should have been reminded Fred he hadn't spent his entire life in these mountains.

"A beer," Dane said without hesitation.

Fred shook his head and reached for another pretzel. "We'll both have coffee." When Dane opened his mouth to protest, Fred sent him a meaningful look. "No sense muddling your head with alcohol."

Dane's shoulders slumped, but he nodded reluctantly. "All right. Fine. Coffee."

"Coffee." Albán's eyes narrowed. He looked suspicious. "For both of you." When Dane managed another nod, he shrugged and turned away. "All right. Coffee it is. It'll be a minute. I need to make a fresh pot."

"No hurry," Fred assured him.

Albán turned away and took up his conversation with the young woman while he worked. "From now on," he warned, "the only free drinks in this bar are the ones *I* okay."

She let out an impatient sigh, but sketched an *X* across her ample chest. "I promise."

"All right, then." Albán waved a hand toward the table in the corner. "Get back to work."

She snatched up a towel and a tray and slipped out from behind the bar. She picked up a couple of clean ashtrays and sent Dane a saucy smile—one far too knowing for someone her age.

With grandfatherly protectiveness, Fred watched Dane's reaction. The kid smiled back, but Fred honestly couldn't see anything questionable in his reaction. Well, good. If Sarah had to get involved with a young man, Fred certainly hoped she'd choose one who knew how to be faithful.

Albán watched the young woman leave, then shook his head and muttered, "She's nothing but a kid."

Fred knew the feeling all too well. "How old is she?"

"Twenty-one. But she's still nothing but a kid." Albán palmed his straight blond hair and scowled. "Or maybe I'm just getting old."

Fred chuckled. He knew that feeling, too. "It happens to the best of us."

"Yeah. But lately it's happening way too fast. And it's happening to me." Albán filled two glasses with ice and water and placed them on the bar in front of Fred and Dane. "So? What's really up?"

Fred lifted both shoulders and hoped he looked casual. "Nothing much."

To his surprise, Albán laughed aloud. "I know you better than that, Fred. If you were really showing Dane around town, you wouldn't bring him here."

Fred tried to look outraged. "Why not?"

"Because you're not a drinking man." Albán shook his head, but he looked amused. "Every time you show up here, you've got some reason." He leaned both arms on the bar. "And what an odd coincidence that you're here just a few days after the murder at the high school."

Dane slanted a worried glance at Fred, then used his most charming grin on Albán. "No, man. Really. I asked Gramps to bring me here."

Albán barked a laugh. "Gramps?"

Dane flushed and sent Fred an apologetic smile. "I mean, Fred. I asked *Fred* to bring me here."

Albán shook his head again. "Good try, but I don't believe either of you. What do you really want?"

Fred hesitated for only an instant. After all, he'd known Albán for years, and Albán had never betrayed his trust before. He sipped ice water and decided to take a chance. "Were you here last Thursday night?"

Albán nodded slowly. "Yeah, for a while. Why?"

Dane's grin widened.

Fred breathed a sigh of relief. "I'm trying to find out about some customers who were here. A man about fifty. Tall. Dark hair with a little gray. Muscular build. Odd-looking eyebrows. He would have been here with a dark-haired woman about the same age."

Albán started nodding before Fred finished. "I remember them. He looked vaguely familiar, but I don't remember seeing her before."

Perfect. "I know who they are," Fred said. "I'm just trying to find out why they were here."

Albán shrugged and tried to look as if he didn't understand Fred's question. "They were both here for a drink, I guess."

"Funny."

Albán grinned. "Look, Fred, why don't you stop beating around the bush and just ask me."

"All right. Did they look like they were romantically involved?"

Albán leaned one elbow on the bar and met Fred's gaze. "Why do you want to know?"

"The man is the murdered man's son from his first marriage. He was at the high school, fighting with his father not long before the murder. The woman is LeGrande's current wife."

Albán smiled as if he'd just won a prize. "I knew it. You're doing it again, aren't you?"

"Doing what?"

"Making up excuses to get involved in a murder investigation."

"That's not what I'm doing," Fred insisted.

"Oh?" Albán quirked an eyebrow at him. "Then what are you doing?"

Fred didn't answer. He didn't know what to say.

Dane leaned forward and took another pretzel. "Why do you guys all treat Fred like he's some sort of criminal just for trying to clear himself?"

"Clear himself?" Albán stared at Fred. Hard. "You can't be serious."

Fred sent Dane a warning glare and nodded at Albán. "Yes, but you didn't need to know about that."

Albán shook his head slowly. "Enos can't seriously suspect you."

Dane ignored Fred and slanted forward. "I don't know about Enos, but that deputy sure does. He's a jerk, man."

Fred had to agree with him, and he had to admit Dane's ready defense of him did his heart good. But that didn't mean he appreciated the kid opening his mouth. "I thought we agreed I'd do the talking," he reminded him.

Dane shook his head so quickly, the chain in his ear hit him in the cheek. "Not when people don't believe you."

Fred shifted on the uncomfortable stool. "Look, Dane, I appreciate your faith in me—"

Dane held up a hand and shook his head even harder. "Look, you've been okay to me. Really okay. Nicer to me than my own parents, if you want to know the truth. And I'm sick of listening to people talk to you like you're some old man who doesn't know what you're talking about." He bolted off his stool and glared at Albán. "The guy's trying to clear himself, man. Why don't you just answer his questions and quit playing games with him?"

Fred groaned aloud. He couldn't help it. The last thing in the world he wanted to do right now was to offend Albán.

Laughter from the far side of the tavern broke the silence. The scent of fresh coffee filled the air. The song on the jukebox changed to something hard and heavy. Albán's jaw set, his lips thinned, and his eyes narrowed. He looked at Dane for a long moment. Too long.

And then, to Fred's surprise, he tilted back his head and laughed.

twenty-one

"I've got to hand it to you, Fred," Albán said, wiping his eyes with the back of his hand. "You do know how to pick your friends."

Dane made a noise in his throat. Apparently, he wasn't quite ready to forgive Albán.

Fred smiled slowly. "I guess I do, don't I?"

Albán chuckled for a minute more, shook his head slowly, and motioned Dane back toward his stool. "Sit down, kid. I'm on Fred's side." He turned his attention back to Fred and propped one hip against the sink behind the bar. "You want to know about the couple."

"Yes, he does," Dane said. Thankfully, he sounded a little less hostile.

Albán wiped his hands on his apron. "Like I said, they were here, but I didn't think they looked romantically involved. Or, if they were, they were having a lovers' spat."

Interesting. Fred took another sip of water. "They were angry with each other?"

"Most definitely angry with each other. I'd say they didn't like each other much."

Dane propped himself on his stool again and folded his skinny arms across his chest, just in case Albán got any ideas about becoming uncooperative.

Fred bit back a smile. "Did you hear what they said?"

Albán shook his head. "I didn't wait on them." He started

to reach for the coffeepot, then stopped and smiled over his shoulder at Fred and Dane. "But Crystal did."

Fred glanced at the young woman on the other side of the bar as she leaned across a table and picked up an empty bottle. "Is that Crystal?"

"Sure is." Albán poured two cups of coffee and put them on the bar in front of them. "Do you want to talk to her?"

Fred nodded and took a fortifying sip. Dane ignored his. Fred caught Albán's gaze and nodded almost imperceptibly. Might as well let the kid have what he wanted. He wasn't driving.

Albán caught Crystal's attention and motioned her back to the bar. She held up her index finger to signal she needed another minute and moved on to another table.

"She'll be here in a second," Albán said, pulling a beer from the cooler and replacing Dane's coffee cup.

Dane darted a surprised glance at Fred, smiled slowly, and took a short drink from the bottle without looking away.

Fred tried to look gruff. "You can have *one*."

"Hey, man, that's cool. But I'd have been okay with the coffee."

"I know that," Fred groused. "That's the only reason I told Albán to give you the beer." Not entirely true, but Fred didn't want Dane to think he'd gone soft.

Albán saw right through him, though. He chuckled and reached for a damp rag. "Yep. We wouldn't want you to think it had anything to do with you sticking up for him."

Before Fred could say a word in self-defense, Crystal came back to the bar, slid her tray onto the counter, and brushed her hair away from her face with one hand. "Yeah?"

Albán nodded toward Fred. "You haven't met Fred yet, have you?"

She shook her head, sent Fred a benign smile, and turned a much friendlier one on Dane. "Nope. *Or* his friend."

"His friend is taken," Albán warned her.

Crystal held up both hands and took a step backward. "I just said hello."

Albán snorted softly. "Right. Well, now I need you to answer whatever questions Fred has. They're important."

"Okay." She plowed her hand through her hair again. "Shoot."

"I'm trying to find someone who was in here Thursday night," Fred said. He gave her a brief description of Roger and Stormy, and smiled—a grandfatherly sort of smile. "Do you remember them?"

She nodded her curls back into her eyes. "The older couple? Sure, I remember."

The *older* couple? Fred shared a glance with Albán. Kids to him—old fogies to her. "I think his name is Roger."

She nodded again. "Yeah, that's right. Roger and Stormy. I waited on them."

"Did you happen to overhear any of their conversation?"

She lifted one bony shoulder in a listless shrug. "Maybe a little. They were arguing. Bad. I thought at first they were, like, married, but then I didn't think so. You know what I mean?"

Fred nodded, though he didn't know if he did or not. "Do you remember what they were arguing about? Or what made you think they weren't married?"

Another shrug, this time with a hesitant look in Albán's direction. "Not really."

"Try," Albán urged. "It's important."

"Well . . ." She replaced the dirty ashtray with a clean one, then leaned one hip against the counter. Her skirt hiked up even farther and showed more of her legs than Fred wanted to see.

He looked away and caught Albán doing the same. Dane turned around on his stool and faced the nearly empty room.

If Crystal noticed, she didn't seem to care. "I remember he said some pretty mean stuff to her. He was like, 'You're nothing but a money-grubbing whore.' "

Albán met Fred's gaze. "Nice guy."

"Very." Fred chanced a glance at Crystal. To his relief, her skirt had dropped a little. "Anything else?"

Crystal shook her head slowly. "I didn't really pay attention. I was just, like, waiting on them."

Fred didn't believe that for an instant.

Apparently, Albán didn't either. "It's okay, Crystal. Fred really does need to know anything you can tell him."

Crystal thought about it for a second, then nodded again. "Well, okay. I just don't, like, want anybody to think I was *trying* to listen."

"Nobody's going to think that," Fred assured her.

"Not for a minute," Albán said. "Sometimes you can't help overhearing people when you're working."

Crystal laughed softly. "Especially when they're fighting like that."

"Like what?" Fred prodded.

"Well, you know. He said stuff like that to her, and then she was like, 'You're a selfish little bastard,' and 'The only thing you've ever cared about is the money.' And he was, like, 'Well, you sure got what *you* wanted.' And then she was all, some other lady ruined him."

Fred leaned a little closer, trying desperately to follow her. "What other lady?"

Crystal frowned in concentration. "I don't remember. It was a flower. Poppy or Daffodil or—"

"Or Iris?"

"Yeah." Crystal brightened. "Yeah, that was it. Iris."

Albán furrowed his brow in silent question.

"Roger's mother," Fred explained. "LeGrande's ex-wife. What else did they say?"

Crystal brushed a curl out of her eyes. "That was about it, really. I didn't stand there listening all night."

All very interesting, Fred thought, but it didn't help much. "Did you by any chance overhear the woman—Stormy—making a pass at Roger?"

"A pass?" Crystal laughed aloud. "Not *even*. She couldn't stand him."

So Roger had lied to LeGrande about that. It didn't surprise Fred. Not really. Telling lies about a man's wife must have been the order of the day. He pushed aside a flicker of bitterness as the memory of LeGrande's lies returned to haunt him. He couldn't think about that now. He had work to do.

Albán cocked an eyebrow at him. "Does that help?"

"Not really," Fred admitted. "I wish it did."

Crystal cleared her tray and started to pick it up again. But she stopped suddenly and glanced back at Fred. "Oh, yeah. There was that old guy who came in, too."

"What old guy?"

Crystal shrugged an I-don't-know. "Just some old guy. He came in and sat at that table over there." She pointed to one in a corner near the jukebox. "It was kinda weird, you know? He came in and sat down and ordered a drink, and then he saw Roger sitting there and just freaked out."

Fred's pulse skipped a bit faster. "Freaked out? How?"

"Well, he was like, 'Who is that,' you know? And I was like, 'I don't know.' And he was all, 'Do you know his name?' And I was like, 'No.'"

"Do you have any idea who he was? What did he look like?"

She rolled her eyes as if she'd never heard such a foolish question. "I *told* you, he was *old*."

Fred tried not to show his mounting irritation, but it came out in his voice. "Did he have a face?"

She snorted a laugh. "Yeah."

"What did it look like?"

"*Old.* Wrinkled. You know."

Fred saw that face every time he looked in the mirror. Apparently, once the wrinkles set in, all faces looked the same to her. He resisted the urge to warn her she'd be faceless someday, and tried giving her vague descriptions of Oliver and Jeremiah. "Was he short and fat, or tall and thin?"

"Neither. He was, like, tall and heavy."

That set Fred back a step. "Tall and heavy? Are you sure?"

"Yeah."

Fred met Dane's gaze. "Tall and heavy?"

Dane shrugged. "I don't know, man."

Neither did Fred. That was the problem.

Crystal picked up her tray, positioned it on her shoulder, and looked at him one last time. "I know his name if that would help."

"Yes," Fred said, exhibiting as much patience as he could under the circumstances. "I think it would."

"I remember it because it was weird, you know?"

Fred could only imagine. In her mind, his own name might sound weird. He gave her a gentle nudge. "What was it?"

She smiled at Albán. "Do you remember that guy?"

Albán shook his head. He looked almost as impatient as Fred felt. "What was the man's name?"

"It sounded like him, you know? Burly."

Fred sat back so hard, he nearly fell off the stool. "Burl?"

"Yeah. That was it. Isn't that what burly means? Big like that guy was?"

Fred didn't answer. He couldn't. His mind raced, trying to make sense of it all. Burl BiMeo had "freaked out" when he saw Roger Macafee. But why? He'd never met LeGrande before, so Roger's resemblance to his father couldn't have meant anything to him. Had he recognized Roger from somewhere?

A thought hit Fred so suddenly, his stomach knotted. All this time he'd assumed LeGrande was the intended victim. They all had. But what if they were wrong?

Dane nudged him gently. "What's the matter?"

"I just had a thought," Fred said slowly, trying to let it gel in his mind. "What if the murderer got the wrong person? What if someone intended to murder Roger and killed LeGrande by mistake?"

Albán looked skeptical. "How would the murderer know Roger was going to be there?"

Fred waved his hand toward the tables behind them. "Maybe he said he would be when he was in here. Who knows? We've all been assuming the murderer got who he was after, but what if we're assuming too much?"

Dane didn't look convinced, either. "Why would some-body want to kill Roger?"

"I don't *know*," Fred snarled. "I just thought of it." He slid off the bar stool, tossed money onto the bar and pulled his keys from his pocket. "But I know where I'm going next."

Dane polished off his beer and pushed the empty away. "Let me guess. To Burl's house."

"To Burl's house," he agreed. He pushed away his coffee cup and stood. And he let the flicker of hope grow a little.

"Okay," Dane said as Fred pulled away from the side of the road. "Let's get back to business. You think Stormy killed LeGrande, thinking he was Roger. And when she went back into the foyer and realized it was LeGrande, she decided to blame you."

"I didn't say I believed it," Fred argued. The idea didn't sound nearly as convincing when Dane repeated it. "I said it's possible."

The windshield wipers slapped the rain away, but not for long. The storm pelted the car without mercy.

"Well, yeah. I guess it is." Dane shrugged. "But why didn't she recognize her own husband when she hit him over the head?"

"It wasn't well lit," Fred reminded him.

Dane shook his head. He didn't look convinced. "Why didn't she recognize him when he fell?"

"Maybe she hit him and ran away."

Dane sighed and looked out his window. "I don't know, Fred. Something doesn't sound right to me."

Something didn't sound right to Fred, either, but he wasn't ready to abandon his theory so soon.

Dane slanted a glance at him. "So, can I ask you a favor?"

"Sure." Fred figured he owed him one.

"Can we stop by your house for a few minutes before we go anywhere else? I haven't talked to Sarah since this morning."

Fred flicked a glance at him. The boy looked so lovesick, he couldn't help smiling. "Sure." In the next breath, he remembered Margaret would be on the rampage. "Before we do, though, there's something we need to talk about."

"What is it?"

"You said Sarah's mom was upset about something this morning."

"That's what she said. But like I told you, I don't know what."

"I do."

"Yeah?" Dane's eyes clouded and he folded his arms across his narrow chest. "Is it me?"

"Not directly," Fred said. But that wasn't entirely true. He tried again. "She found Sarah's birth-control pills in her bedroom yesterday."

Panic darted across Dane's face. "Shit."

Fred nodded. "Exactly. It's hit the fan."

"Sarah told me how she feels about . . . well, you know."

Unfortunately, Fred did.

"So, that's why Sarah couldn't see me today."

"I think so."

Dane looked away again, rubbed his face, and let out a heavy sigh. "You know, I love her."

"Do you?"

"Yeah." Dane slouched down in his seat and sighed again. "I'd marry her but she doesn't want to marry me."

Fred flicked his gaze away from the road long enough to take in the boy's dejected face. "Does she love you?"

Dane nodded, but he looked miserable. "She says she does. I *think* she does. But she says she doesn't want to ever get married."

That was news to Fred. "Did she tell you why?"

"Yeah." Dane slanted an uneasy glance at him. "She says she doesn't want to end up like her parents."

Fred supposed he should have expected that, but it caught him off guard. "I see."

Dane sat up a little straighter. "You know, my parents' marriage wasn't that hot, either. And they're divorced. But

I'm okay with the idea of getting married. I'm just not going to make the mistakes my old man did."

Spoken with the assurance of youth. "Easier said than done," Fred said with a tight smile. "I thought I could avoid my father's mistakes when I was your age, too."

"Yeah? What mistakes?"

Fred gave that some thought. "My father was a stubborn man who never listened to anyone else in his life." He worked up a smile. "I loved him, don't misunderstand me, but I never felt really close to him. It was my mother who held the family together. I swore I wouldn't be a thing like him. That I'd be kind and gentle and patient and I'd listen. Then the kids came along and I opened my mouth one day, and out came my father's voice. Even without trying, I became just like him. And my wife was the one who held our family together."

"Yeah?"

"Yeah." Fred turned onto Lake Front Drive and drove slowly toward home. "It happens. Your parents make mistakes. You'll make mistakes. Guaranteed."

"And my relationship with Sarah—that's a mistake?" He sounded defensive.

"I didn't say that."

"You think we're wrong, don't you?"

Fred shook his head. "It's not about right and wrong, Dane. Margaret doesn't want to see Sarah get hurt."

"I'm not going to hurt her."

"Oh, yes you will," Fred told him. "You won't mean to, but you will. You won't be able to help it. And she'll hurt you."

"You're wrong. She'd never hurt me."

Fred pulled into the driveway, stopped, and faced Dane squarely. "If I had a dime for every time I hurt my wife, I'd be a rich man. I never meant to hurt her, but I did. And she hurt me. But we loved each other anyway."

Dane looked away and refused to meet his gaze again.

Fred didn't let that bother him. "You take a man and a woman and put them together and you're going to have trouble. Can't help it. There's all sorts of things going on—we don't think the same, we don't act the same, we don't want the same things."

"Sarah and I do."

Fred ignored him. "And when you add sex into the mix, you just increase the risk, that's all. It's harder to walk away from someone you've been that close to if it's not the right thing. Harder to let someone walk away from you."

Dane slanted a glance at him. He looked moderately interested.

Fred took that as a good sign. "Think about it. Tell me if I'm right. If Sarah broke up with you now, what would it do to you?"

"Kill me."

Not literally, but Fred didn't quibble. "And if she'd broken up with you before?"

Dane shrugged, but he didn't answer.

It didn't matter. Fred knew he'd gotten his point across. "What happens if Sarah gets pregnant—in spite of the pills?"

"I'll make her marry me."

Fred chuckled. "If you think you can make Sarah do anything, you don't know her very well." He sobered again and put a hand on the kid's bony arm. "Sarah's mother made a mistake when she was younger, and she's been paying for it her whole life. She doesn't want to see Sarah in the same boat." He held up a hand to stop the argument he knew was coming. "Not that I think you're a mistake. But Margaret's distrustful of all men right now. You just happened along at a bad time, that's all."

"So, you're saying I should just forget about Sarah?"

"I didn't say that at all. I'm just trying to—"

"Well, I can't give her up. I love her." Dane shoved open his door and jumped out of the car. He held out his hand and wiggled his fingers impatiently. "Let me have your keys."

Fred pulled them out of the ignition and dropped them into the boy's outstretched hand. Dane ran across the lawn and jumped onto the porch. Within seconds he disappeared inside.

Fred thought about following him, then decided to wait. Let the kids have their privacy. He settled back against his seat and watched the rain splatter against the windshield. He let the drumming on the roof of the car soothe him.

He sat that way for a long time, until the flash of headlights lit the driveway behind him. Margaret, he told himself. Or Sarah in her mother's car. He straightened slowly and worked up a smile as the car pulled into the driveway beside his.

The rain blurred his vision, and it wasn't until the driver of the other car climbed out that Fred recognized him. Not Margaret. Not Sarah.

Al. Alone. Without Millie.

Fred closed his eyes and pulled in a deep breath. Dane had been right earlier. He had been avoiding this. But he supposed the time had come to face the truth, whether he wanted to, or not.

twenty-two

Fred climbed out of the Buick and motioned Al toward the house. Rain pelted him and soaked his thin cotton shirt almost immediately. He walked as quickly as his old knees would move, hunched his shoulders as if that would keep the rain from touching him.

In his eagerness to phone Sarah, Dane had left the front door open, but Fred couldn't see him in the living room. He must have gone into the kitchen to make his call.

Shivering slightly, Fred yanked open the screen and stepped inside. Al trailed him and started to speak even before Fred could shut the door behind him. "Wasn't expecting this."

"I can't imagine why not," Fred groused. "We've had afternoon thunderstorms every summer for as long as I've been around." His voice sounded sharp and irritated, even to his own ears. Angry with the messenger, he supposed. Al had something to say, and Fred didn't want to hear it. Plain and simple.

Al slanted a glance at him. He'd obviously heard it, too. "Any luck finding LeGrande's murderer?"

Fred waved the question away and crossed to his rocking chair. "I'm not looking for LeGrande's murderer," he reminded him. "I'm only trying to clear myself."

Al laughed and followed him into the room. He lowered himself gingerly onto the couch and draped one arm over its back. "Say whatever you want to. I know you better than

that." He sobered again and let his gaze rest on a photo of
Phoebe on the oak table. "I tried calling earlier. You weren't
home."

"I've been busy. Just got back, as a matter of fact."

"I know." Al sent him a sideways glance. "I was up on
Main Street, watching for you."

Fred didn't know how to respond to that. He shifted his
gaze to the window and watched the rain. "Where's Millie?"

"Home. I want to talk to you alone."

"We're not alone," Fred informed him. "Sarah's boy-
friend is in the kitchen." As if that would stop Al from
saying what he'd come to say.

Al groaned—an old man's groan that spoke of aching
joints. "Then I'll be quick before he comes back into the
room."

Fred shook his head. "Whatever it is, I don't want to
discuss it with Dane around."

"You don't want to discuss it at all."

No, he didn't.

"I want you to know, what LeGrande said to you the night
of the reunion wasn't entirely true."

Not *entirely* true? Sudden, unreasoning panic filled Fred.
He tried to think of some way, *any* way to keep Al from
going on. He pushed to his feet and put his back between Al
and his heart. "I don't see any reason to talk about
something that happened so long ago."

"Well, I do."

He heard Al come to stand behind him. Felt Al's hand on
his shoulder. Gave in to the urge to shrug it away. "If
Phoebe told you something and asked you to keep it secret,
you shouldn't break her trust now." His voice came out
pinched. Harsh. The words hurt his ears.

Al put his damned hand on his shoulder again.

Fred moved away from him.

"She didn't tell me anything," Al said softly.

The pity in his eyes made Fred's anger surge again. He
didn't need Al's damned pity. The situation was bad enough
without it.

"She didn't tell me anything," Al said again. He rubbed his forehead and took a deep, shuddering breath, as if this moment hurt him as much as it hurt Fred.

But it didn't. It couldn't. And he hated Al for pretending it did.

Slowly, Al met his gaze again. "I was there."

Fred's knees buckled, but he forced himself to remain standing. His heart seemed to stop beating, but his pulse thundered in his ears. "What do you mean, you were there?"

"I'd gone to the market for something—don't remember what now, it's been too long ago. I saw Phoebe there and talked to her for a few minutes. It was the day before the New Year's Eve ball in 1946. Remember? You were taking her to it."

Fred nodded slowly. Of course he remembered. He'd been so in love with Phoebe by that point, he couldn't see straight. Couldn't think at all. He'd been thinking about asking her to marry him, but he'd waited because she'd seemed so withdrawn for several months before that, he hadn't been sure of her feelings.

Al smiled softly. "She was so excited. I remember her telling me about the dress she'd bought, about the shoes. I remember little Janice Doolittle standing beside her, and Phoebe giving her a piece of penny candy from the bag she'd just bought."

Janice Doolittle. Fred hadn't thought of Janice Lacey by that name in years.

"LeGrande was working there, you know. He was stocking shelves and making comments about you while Phoebe talked. She got fed up with him—you remember how she could get?"

Fred remembered.

"And she left. The next thing I knew, LeGrande disappeared. I finished getting whatever I'd gone after, and went outside. I started walking home, but I heard something—a noise that didn't sound right. Sounded like a woman's voice. Upset. Frightened. Something banging, like a car door."

Al wiped his face and turned away. "Then it got quiet. I

almost ignored it. I had things on my mind. But the silence bothered me. I still, to this day, don't know why it did. But it did. I thought it had come from that alley beside the market, so I looked, just to make sure everything was all right."

Fred's heart did stop beating then. He was certain it did.

"I saw LeGrande's car, and I saw someone inside. The windows were fogged over, but I could see people moving around, and I knew, somehow, that something was wrong." He laughed without humor. "I was such a wimp, I still don't know what gave me the courage to walk down that alley and check. I can't imagine how I dared open that car door, but I did. I knew LeGrande could beat the tar out of me, but I did it anyway."

Fred willed him to stop.

He didn't. "He tried to rape her, Fred."

Raw hatred made his stomach pitch. Bile rose in his throat. Time slowed. Sounds magnified. Outside, the rain slowed to a drizzle. He blinked back the tears that came from nowhere. After his conversation with Thea, he'd been half expecting it. But hearing the words spoken aloud almost did him in.

Blind fury robbed him of reason. His throat tightened and burned. His lungs refused to work. He wanted to argue with Al, but he couldn't speak. He couldn't move. He had to wait, dreading whatever Al planned to say next.

But Al fell silent and his kind, old eyes misted over.

Fred studied him for what felt like forever. "And you stopped him." No wonder Phoebe'd always had such a soft spot in her heart for him. No wonder LeGrande had backed down when Al stood up to him at the reunion.

Al lifted one shoulder in a self-deprecating shrug. "By chance."

Fred still needed to clarify, for his own peace of mind. "That's how you knew? Phoebe didn't tell you?"

Al's eyes widened in surprise. "Of course not. Why would she tell me? I was nothing to her."

Fred shook his head and looked deep into Al's eyes. "You were her friend."

Al waved the suggestion away. "Not at the time. She was nice to me, but she was nice to everyone. You know how she was."

Fred did. Oh, yes, he did. He pulled in a shaky breath and forced himself to admit, "She never told *me*."

"I know. We talked about it once, afterward. Only once in more than fifty years. *She* didn't want to talk about it at all, but I bugged her until she finally did. You know how I can be."

In spite of the pain, Fred sent him a thin smile. But he didn't agree aloud.

"She wanted to pretend it never happened," Al explained. "She didn't want you to know."

"Why? Did she think I'd lose my temper and do something to LeGrande?"

"No." Al looked surprised by the question.

"That has to be it. She didn't trust me."

"Trust you?" Al looked shocked. "It had nothing to do with her trusting you. She was afraid you wouldn't trust her."

Fred wondered if he'd heard him wrong. "She thought *I* wouldn't trust *her*? Why on earth not?"

"She thought it was all her fault—that she'd done something wrong, something that gave LeGrande the wrong idea. She believed that, because she'd gone out with him a few times that she'd led him on somehow."

"I'm sure LeGrande told her that," Fred croaked.

"I think you're probably right," Al admitted. "But she was afraid you'd think less of her and decide she wasn't good enough for you. She was so head over heels in love with you, she couldn't bear the thought of losing you. She talked me into keeping it a secret. Maybe I was wrong—" He broke off and looked at Phoebe's picture again. "I don't know anymore. But she was nice to me, even when the rest of you treated me like a pest, so I agreed."

The slow flush of embarrassment crept up Fred's neck into his face. He'd probably been more guilty of that than anyone else he knew, but for some reason he'd assumed Al hadn't noticed. He'd always thought of Al as locked in his own world. "She kept that horrible secret because she was afraid of losing me? I thought she just put up with me."

Al almost laughed. "Well, you were wrong. You know, Fred, I don't think you have any idea how much Phoebe loved you."

Fred couldn't make himself respond to that. But he thought maybe Al was right. Learning the truth, after all these years, added a new dimension to his relationship with Phoebe he'd never even suspected.

Al rubbed the back of his neck and took a step away. "You know, I envied you back then. You were the kind of guy I wanted to be. So sure of yourself."

Fred blinked in response. "I wasn't sure of myself at all."

Al's eyes widened. "You were a scrapper. You knew how to stand up for yourself."

"I was—" He broke off and searched for the right word. He couldn't find it. "I was insecure. And the only reason I stood up for myself was because I was afraid of what my dad would say if I didn't."

Al chuckled. "Your dad was a piece of work, all right. You remind me of him in a lot of ways."

Fred didn't know if he should take that as a compliment, or not. He rubbed his face and looked out the window again at the sun working its way through the dark clouds and the steam rising from the lawn. "Yes," he said. "Well."

Dimly, he became aware of sounds coming from the kitchen. Of Dane's voice raised in anger or frustration. Of the telephone jangling as he slammed the receiver.

Al heard it, too. He darted a glance over his shoulder, then back at Fred. "Sounds like you've got more trouble on your hands."

Fred nodded. "It never ends, does it?" He slanted another glance at Al and forced himself to ask, "Does Millie know about what you told me?"

"No. Like I said, other than that one time with Phoebe, I never spoke of it again. And I won't, either."

Fred nodded, but he knew in his heart that *he* would. He

had to. For Phoebe's sake, and for the sake of their daughter and granddaughters, he couldn't let her misplaced guilt touch even one more life.

At that moment the kitchen door slammed open, and Dane stormed into the living room. Red-faced. Angry. When he saw Al standing there, he ground to a halt.

Fred knew their faces probably betrayed them, just as Dane's gave away the emotions churning within him.

Dane didn't seem to notice. He pulled in a breath, held it, and released it slowly. "I'm leaving in the morning."

Fred didn't ask why. He didn't need to. He thought about arguing with the kid, but Dane's face warned him he wouldn't get very far. The situation required tact, finesse. "You're leaving me high and dry, huh?"

"Well, I sure as hell can't stay here."

Al mumbled something under his breath and started for the door. Fred couldn't understand most of what he said, but he heard Millie's name. Imagine. After all these years of thinking Al a dimwit, Fred had to admit he was wrong. He followed Al to the front door and laid a hand on his shoulder in silent thanks.

Al smiled back at him. The gratitude and genuine affection in his eyes touched Fred deeply. Without taking time to think, he yanked Al closer and wrapped his arms around his brother-in-law's bony shoulders. A quick hug, that's all, but more affection than he'd ever shown Al in his life. He cleared his throat and managed to voice his thoughts aloud. "Thanks, Al. You've been a good friend."

Al waved his words away, but Fred knew they'd pleased him. He watched Al walk, slump-shouldered, toward his car until Dane spoke almost in his ear.

"What was that all about?"

"Nothing," Fred said with a shrug. "Just some old family business." He turned to face the kid again. "You know," he said, hoping he sounded casual, "if you leave in the morning, you'll be leaving me on my own."

Dane didn't seem to care. "Somebody else can go with you, man. I don't stay where I'm not wanted."

"Who said you're not wanted?"

"Sarah." He ground out her name between his teeth.

Fred shook his head. "I don't believe it."

"You think I'm lying, man? Call her."

"I never said you were lying," Fred assured him. "If you say she doesn't want you, I believe you."

"That's what she says." Dane paced a couple of jerky steps away, then back again. He propped his hands on his hips one second, then flung them to his sides again the next.

"Well, then," Fred said, as if that settled everything. "I guess that's that."

"It's her mother's doing."

Fred tried to look surprised. "You think so?"

"I *know* so."

"But you're still leaving." Fred pretended to ponder that for a moment. "Well, I guess you're right. It's probably just as well. It probably wouldn't have worked out, anyway."

Dane snorted a laugh. "Everything would have been *fine* if Sarah's mom hadn't gone snooping around in her room."

"Probably," Fred admitted, walking slowly toward his rocking chair. "I don't suppose it ever bothered Sarah to hide the truth from her mother."

Dane scowled at him. "Of course it bothered her. Sarah loves her mom—apparently, more than she loves me."

"Well," Fred said, groaning as he lowered himself into the chair, "I guess we'll never know what would have happened between you two now." He rubbed his chin thoughtfully. "'Course, there's always the other side of the coin."

"What other side?"

Fred propped his feet on his footstool. "It's not you Margaret objects to, it's the kind of relationship you're having with her daughter. She's afraid you're going to hurt her."

Dane jerked one hand through the air in front of him. "I wouldn't hurt her, but she won't even give me a chance."

"A chance at what?"

"To prove that I'm not going to hurt her."

Fred lifted one eyebrow. "Seems to me she's giving you that chance right now."

"No." Dane shook his head angrily. "She wants me out of Sarah's life."

Fred worked up a casual shrug. "Well, yes. But that doesn't mean you have to go."

"I'm not sticking around where I'm not wanted." His words sounded tough, but his voice pleaded with Fred to convince him otherwise.

Fred sat back in his seat and shrugged again. "I can certainly understand that. Why would you?"

"Exactly." Dane paced toward the couch and perched on its arm.

Fred picked up the paper from that morning and gave the headlines a once-over. "You and I know that you love Sarah, no matter what. If *they* don't believe that—" He broke off and left Dane to ponder the options.

"Sarah knows I love her."

"I'm sure she does."

Dane hmmphed his response to that.

Fred turned to the second page and resisted the urge to look at the kid. He went on as if Dane had offered another argument. "No, I agree with you. Absolutely. Why should you have to prove anything to Sarah or her mother?"

"I shouldn't."

"No, you shouldn't. You've told Sarah you love her, and that should be enough." He turned another page and pretended interest in a story about road construction on I-25.

"Yes, it should." Dane jerked to his feet and paced away again.

"I'm sure that if the tables were turned," Fred mused, "if you're the one who threw in a roadblock and things got tough, you wouldn't expect Sarah to stay."

Dane's step faltered. He mumbled, "No, I wouldn't," but he didn't sound quite as certain as he had a moment ago.

Fred pressed his advantage—casually. "When a relationship gets too difficult, the best thing to do is just get out."

"I don't expect it to be easy," Dane argued. "I'm not that stupid."

Fred turned another page. "I know you're not stupid. But I didn't think you were the type to give up, either. But if you're not sure Sarah's the right one for you, I don't blame you. I'd do exactly the same thing." He heard Dane stop pacing, felt him glaring at him. Fred ignored him. "Look at this," he said, nodding toward the paper. "It says here—"

Dane didn't let him get any further. "Sarah *is* the right one for me."

Fred lowered the paper and tried to look surprised. "But you're not willing to fight for her? You're not willing to set her mother's mind at ease and show them both that you love Sarah—even if that means doing without the physical relationship for a while?" He pretended to think about that for a few seconds, lifted the paper again, and said, "Well, then, maybe you're not the right one for her."

Dane still wasn't ready to give up the argument. Not entirely. "She should *trust* me, man."

"Why? Because you told her she could?"

Dane came back to the couch and put his scowling face in Fred's line of vision. "What do you mean?"

"Trust isn't a gift, son. It's something you earn. And you have a chance to earn it or lose it right now. It's up to you. You're the only one who knows what Sarah means to you."

Dane's scowl deepened. He rubbed the scraggly goatee on his chin. He glanced at the pictures on the round oak table, walked over, and picked up Sarah's graduation photo. "You know," he said at last, "she warned me about you."

"Warned you?"

"Warned me." Dane slanted a glance at him and a ghost of his grin returned. "She was right."

Fred didn't completely understand, but the look on Dane's face when he ran one gentle finger across Sarah's photographed cheek told him he should accept the compliment and not ask questions.

twenty-three

Fred drove slowly through the bumper-to-bumper tourist traffic in Glenwood Springs, watching for the sign marking the turnoff to Burl and Coralee's house. After being on the road for nearly three hours, his backside ached, his eyes burned, and his stomach demanded attention. He checked his watch—nearly noon already.

He hadn't dared set off for such a long trip without calling first, so he'd done something he rarely did—he'd phoned ahead. To his surprise, Coralee had agreed to see him. Burl, she said, would be out for a while this morning, but Fred could share lunch with her if he'd like. He'd accepted without enthusiasm at the time, but the thought of it now perked him up considerably.

He'd been out the door and on his way before Dane even thought about waking. He just hoped the kid would take advantage of the time alone to talk with Sarah again—and that Margaret wouldn't interfere too much.

Someone in a green Jeep Cherokee pulled out and whizzed around him going far too fast in such traffic. The Suburban in front of him stopped suddenly and tried to maneuver into a parking space that *might* comfortably house a Toyota.

Fred shook his head, exhibited extraordinary patience while he waited for the driver to figure out what an idiot with half a brain could easily see, and thanked the good Lord Cutler didn't have what some people considered its fair share of the tourist trade. If having a depressed economy meant peace and quiet, he'd suffer gladly.

After what felt like forever, the line of traffic inched forward again. A few blocks later he saw the sign he'd been looking for and turned onto the side street with a sigh of relief. He drove the remaining two blocks and turned in front of the DiMeos' small yellow frame house a few minutes later.

Roses drooped in a garden near the street, sadly in need of water, and the lawn looked as if it could use the attention of a lawn mower. Weeds had begun to take over the two other flower beds near the house. They hadn't gotten far yet, which told Fred the neglect hadn't been going on long.

He followed the walk to the front door and rang the bell. Coralee answered so quickly, he figured she'd been watching for him.

Her lips curved as she pushed open the screen door, but the smile didn't make it all the way to her eyes. "Come in. Come in. It's hotter than the dickens out there."

He followed her into the tiny living room and sat in the chair she indicated. The chair listed to one side, and the springs had definitely seen better days, but Fred tried to look comfortable.

She resettled herself in a rocking chair near the front window and rested her cane against a nearby table. Green and gray yarn trailed from a basket on the floor to a shapeless mass she'd left on a footstool nearby. She must have been knitting while she waited.

Against the far wall, a set of cheap wooden shelves housed a few books and glass figurines, but its predominant use was, obviously, to serve as a shrine to their son. Two small, limp flags on balsa-wood poles rose out of a glass vase, and a young man in uniform smiled out at the room and his mother from inside an ornate silver frame. Other objects too small for Fred to identify surrounded the photograph. His favorite things, no doubt.

Coralee noticed the direction of Fred's gaze and gave up all pretense of smiling. "Our son, Kenny."

Fred could have kicked himself for drawing her attention to him. He didn't want to start off by bringing back painful memories.

"He was a good-looking kid." Fred couldn't see him clearly from this distance, but he didn't figure that mattered. Coralee wouldn't argue with him.

To his surprise, she scowled slightly. "He was a good kid. Kind. Caring. Loving. That was Burl's doing, mostly. He raised that boy right."

"I'm sure you had something to do with it, too."

A hint of her smile returned. "I tried to be a good mother." She narrowed her gaze and cocked her head. "But that's not why you're here."

"No," he admitted. "No, it's not." He hesitated for a moment, unsure now how to bring up the murder, not at all certain how to ask about Burl's odd reaction to seeing Roger Macafee at the Copper Penny. He didn't want to upset her unnecessarily.

"You're here to talk about LeGrande's murder."

She didn't sound upset, but Fred didn't want to take any chances. He said only, "Yes."

"Why do you want to talk to me? I don't know anything."

"I ran into Burl the other day," Fred said. "He mentioned that you were out of the gymnasium when you heard Stormy scream. I'm hoping maybe you saw someone else in the hallways."

Her scowl deepened, and she shook her head. "I didn't see anyone. I already told your sheriff that."

"Yes, I know," Fred said gently. "Maybe I'm just grasping at straws, but sometimes you hear or see something you don't remember at the time because it doesn't seem important." He worked up a friendly smile. "I've spent a lot of time thinking about it since then, and I've remembered hearing footsteps. I didn't see anyone, but I'd be willing to bet they belonged to a woman."

"A woman? What woman?"

He shrugged and suggested, "Stormy Macafee."

Coralee's scowl changed subtly. "Foolish woman."

"Who? Stormy? What makes you say that?"

She raised her eyebrows as if he'd asked an incredibly stupid question. "She married LeGrande, didn't she?"

"Well, yes—"

"Enough said." Coralee smoothed her knotted hands over the legs of her pantsuit. "It seems a shame for you to make such a long drive just to be told I don't know anything. You could have asked me that over the telephone."

"Yes," Fred admitted, "I suppose I could have. But I didn't get a chance to visit with you at the reunion. Everything got out of hand, what with LeGrande showing up and then the murder."

"And the horrible things he said about Phoebe."

Fred stiffened, forced himself to relax. "He lied."

"Of course he lied." Coralee let out a bitter laugh. "LeGrande was a horrible liar. He'd say anything to get what he wanted."

Fred nodded thoughtfully, then ventured another question. "What do you suppose he wanted that night?"

Everything about her stiffened. "Why are you asking me? I don't have any idea what went on in that man's mind."

Under other circumstances, Fred might have believed her. But the flash of something he couldn't immediately identify in her eyes and the slight thinning of her lips told him she had an idea. He decided to try coming at her from a different angle. "His son was there that night. Did you see him?"

"His son? No." Coralle tried to look confused, but her voice sounded brusque—as if her patience was wearing thin.

Fred took a chance on another question. "Do you know which son I'm talking about?"

She stopped rocking. The color drained from her face. "What kind of question is that?"

Fred's turn to be confused. He tried not to show it.

Coralee gripped her cane and stood. "What are you doing, playing some sort of game?"

"No. Of course not," Fred said quickly, trying desperately to figure out what she meant. Maybe Burl had downplayed her emotional condition. Maybe losing her son had left her unhinged. She certainly *looked* unhinged. "LeGrande had two sons," he explained. "Roger and Gary. I wondered if you knew which one I saw at the school that night."

She let out a distrustful laugh. "Roger and Gary?"

Fred nodded. "Roger's the oldest. He's the one I saw. He had a fight with LeGrande."

Coralee stood there for a moment, head high, eyes narrowed, chin tilted skeptically. "That's what you're asking me? Whether I saw Roger Macafee at the school that night?"

"Yes." Of course. What else would he be asking? He'd pushed too far, but he didn't know how. Warning bells sounded in the back of his mind, but he couldn't understand why. Apprehension crept up his spine, but he couldn't explain it.

Slowly, almost reluctantly, Coralee untilted her chin. Her eyes cleared again. "No. I didn't see him there."

Fred let out a silent sigh of relief and stood to face her.

She waved him back to his seat. She might look like her old self again, but Fred didn't trust her any longer. "I promised you lunch," she said, moving slowly toward the kitchen. "I'll have it ready in a minute."

"I can't stay." He tried to sound apologetic instead of frantic, but it didn't work. He could hear the desperation in his own voice.

"You have to stay. I've already made the sandwiches."

Fred hesitated. More than anything, he wanted to leave. He didn't want to risk upsetting her again, and after the warning Burl gave him, he certainly didn't want Burl to come home and find him there. He trailed her toward the kitchen door and tried to come up with an excuse to leave that wouldn't offend her. "I've got a houseguest," he said at last. "I don't want to be away too long."

She pivoted to face him. "Honestly, Fred, it's only sandwiches and chips. Don't be such a fussbudget. Fifteen minutes one way or the other isn't going to make *that* much difference."

He told himself to relax. One quick sandwich and he could leave. He worked up a smile and turned back toward his seat, but the photo of Kenny caught his eye. Curious, he moved closer and bent to look at the smiling young man whose death had changed his mother so completely.

An army uniform, Fred recognized it. But the face that smiled up at him caught him off guard and froze everything inside. Dark hair. Broad, uncomfortably familiar smile. Eyebrows that winged upward at such an odd angle he'd seen them on only two faces before—LeGrande's and Roger's.

Everything fell into place with dreadful certainty. He slanted a glance at Coralee and caught her watching him. Her face changed again. Slowly. Anger mixed with fear in her eyes.

He straightened slowly and watched her start toward him, clutching the cane with its knobby head. The blunt instrument with the odd pattern Enos hadn't yet been able to match. His mouth dried. His heart thudded dangerously in his chest. His lungs expelled every breath of air they held.

Coralee reached the entry into the living room. "You honestly didn't know when you came here?"

Somehow, he managed to speak. "I didn't know."

She stood ramrod straight, and her fingers clutched the cane so tightly her knuckles whitened. "LeGrande was going to tell everyone that Kenny was his son. He said he wanted to set things straight before he died."

Another awful truth LeGrande had twisted to suit his own purposes. Fred thought he might be sick, but he tried to force away the feeling and stay alert. He didn't know what Coralee might do next. She'd killed once to keep her secret. Nothing said she wouldn't kill again.

Coralee pulled in a shaky breath and tried to hold herself together. "They call it date rape these days. We didn't have a name for it back then. It didn't happen so often."

"It happened," he assured her. "We just didn't talk about it."

Coralee sagged against the door frame, and tears filled

her eyes. She let her gaze travel to Kenny's picture and settle there. "When I first realized I was in the family way, I didn't want him. Can you imagine that?" She met Fred's gaze again. Guilt and remembered pain contorted her features. "I didn't want him. I've wondered so many times if that's why God took him away from me."

"No." He couldn't manage to get anything else out around the lump in his throat.

She sent him a grateful smile, but he could tell she didn't believe him. "Burl came along right about then. For some reason, he imagined himself in love with me."

"Burl does love you," Fred assured her.

"Oh, yes, *now*. But only because he doesn't know the truth about me. If he knew—" She broke off and shook her head. "If he knew . . ."

"If he knew, he'd love you even more," Fred promised.

"For lying to him about Kenny? No. He'd hate me, and I don't think I could bear that. He's all I have. And it would destroy him." She crossed the room to stand at Fred's side and picked up the picture of her son. "He adored that boy. Kenny was his whole life. I wanted to tell him before we got married, but I was too afraid. I wanted to tell him when Kenny was born, but I knew I'd lose him. And then it was too late."

She sighed with regret and met Fred's gaze again. "You have no idea how horrible it's been, keeping the secret from him all these years. Watching him with Kenny and not being able to tell him, lying down beside him at night and loving him so much I thought my heart would break, and I still couldn't tell him."

Fred's heart twisted. He imagined Phoebe carrying her secret all through their marriage, angry with herself, believing he'd reject her if he knew.

"Tell him now," he urged. He couldn't rid himself of the awful certainty that Burl had already figured out part of the truth when he saw Roger at the Copper Penny. Whatever he imagined had to be worse than the truth.

Horror widened her eyes. "I can't. You don't understand."

"I understand better than you might think." He put a gentle hand on her shoulder and forced himself to say what he knew he had to tell her. "LeGrande tried to rape Phoebe, too. He didn't succeed, but only because Al came along and stopped him."

Coralee stared at him, uncomprehending, for a moment. "Phoebe? *That's* what LeGrande was talking about? That's why you hit him?"

"No. I didn't know about it until yesterday. Believe me, it doesn't change how I feel about her. It only makes me sad that she didn't think I'd understand."

She averted her gaze and stepped away from his hand. "But she didn't lie to you about one of your children. Burl would never forgive me that."

"He might surprise you."

"No." She stepped away from him and shook her head frantically. "No. I won't tell him. I can't." As if on cue, a door opened and shut again somewhere in the back of the house. Coralee sent a frantic glance toward it, put the picture back on its shelf, slightly off center. She turned to Fred. "I won't tell him," she insisted.

Burl moved too quickly. He walked in carrying a plastic bag full of dry cleaning just as the last words left her mouth. He brushed a kiss to Coralee's cheek, narrowed his eyes at Fred. "Tell me what?"

"Not you," Coralee said, pasting on a smile. "We were talking about Percy Neuswander."

"Oh?" Burl started down the hall, glanced at the off-center photo of Kenny, and stopped short. He glanced from it to Coralee and halted in his tracks. "What aren't you going to tell him?"

Coralee forced a laugh. "Oh, just old class gossip."

Burl obviously didn't believe her. He slanted a pointed glance at the picture.

Fred's stomach lurched. He didn't want the truth to come out this way. She deserved a chance to tell him alone. But he couldn't make himself move.

Burl rounded on him. "What the hell are you doing here, anyway? I thought I told you to leave her alone."

Fred nodded. "I—"

"I want you to leave—now!"

Fred knew he'd feel the same way if he'd been in Burl's shoes. He wouldn't want anyone to disturb Phoebe or dig up the past she'd worked so hard to bury. But Coralee *had* murdered LeGrande. And Fred wasn't in the clear yet. Not by a long shot.

Burl grabbed his arm and tried to propel him toward the door. "Leave now, Fred, or I'm calling the police. They'll probably be very interested in what brought you here. After all, we only have your word that you *didn't* kill LeGrande."

Coralee gasped. Burl spun around to check on her.

Fred yanked away from his grasp. He willed Burl to tell Coralee what he knew. One piece of the truth might open the floodgates to the rest of the story. But Burl remained stubbornly silent. And Coralee, who'd protected her secret this long, made no move to confess it now.

Fred's heart went out to her. He didn't think Coralee presented a danger to anyone but the man who'd harmed her so many years before and then threatened to destroy what peace she'd been able to create for herself. But he wasn't by any means ready to take the rap for her. He had his own life, his own pain, his own family to think of.

Still, he didn't know if he had the heart to turn her in, or even if he should. He held up both hands to keep Burl away from him. "All right. All right. I'll go." He turned one last look on Coralee and added, "You know, Coralee, it never would have been too late for Phoebe to tell me what happened to her."

Coralee shook her head and backed a step away. Burl's brows knit. "What does Phoebe have to do with this?"

"I found out yesterday that LeGrande tried to rape her when we were all younger. She was afraid to tell me. Afraid I'd think less of her. Afraid she'd lose me, I guess."

Burl's craggy face softened a touch. "Rape?" He flicked

a glance at Coralee, and everything about him seemed to cave in on itself. "Rape?" he whispered.

Coralee held herself rigid for another second, but she must have been able to see the silent question in Burl's eyes and hear the pleading in his voice. "You knew?"

Burl wiped his eyes with his fingertips and nodded. "I always wondered."

"About Kenny?"

Burl nodded again. "He didn't look like me, Coralee. Not even a little. And we never did have another child, not even a hope. But it didn't matter to me. I loved you, and I loved him, and he was my boy."

"Then how . . . ?"

"I saw LeGrande's son the night before the reunion. He looked so much like Kenny, I didn't know what to do or say. I couldn't ask you. I knew you didn't want me to know. And it didn't matter." He took her shoulders gently and pulled her around to face him. "It didn't matter. Most of the time I forgot. Kenny was my boy. Even after I saw LeGrande's kid at the bar, I could still pretend it wasn't real. Until LeGrande walked into that reunion. And when he said he was going to set the record straight on some old things, I knew Kenny was one of them. If someone else hadn't killed him first, I'd have done it myself. I lost my boy once, and I wasn't going to lose him again."

Tears streamed down Coralee's tired face. She touched his cheek gently. "You knew all along, and you didn't hate me?"

"Hate you? Coralee, sweetheart, how could I hate you? You've given me love and life for fifty years. And you gave me my only child."

Incredible sadness filled Fred. Bone-deep weariness threatened to overwhelm him. She murdered a man to keep her secret quiet, but there'd been no need. No need at all.

He moved toward the door, fully intending to give them privacy. But before he could reach it, footsteps sounded on the other side, and someone pounded on the door. He glanced out the window, saw the patrol cars sitting at the curb, and turned back to face his friends. "It's the police."

Burl's head shot up.

Coralee sagged against him. "Oh, my God."

Burl wrapped a protective arm around her. "They're probably just here with more of their questions, Coralee. Don't worry. I'll get rid of them."

She shook her head, but the effort seemed to take more than she had to give. "You can't. Oh, my God, Fred. What am I going to do?"

Fred stood for a moment, uncertain, until the second knock sounded. "You're going to take Burl into the kitchen and explain everything to him," he said, moving slowly toward the door. "I'm going to talk to the police."

He waited until they'd moved into the other room, then pulled open the door. He knew what he should do. He knew what he wanted to do. But justice, he told himself, was justice. He had no real choice.

twenty-four

Fred pushed open the door of the Bluebird and stepped inside quickly to get out of the heat. Already, the sun had risen high enough in the sky to make walking uncomfortable and to reflect off the windows along Main Street and hurt his eyes with its glare. Inside, the cool air and artificial light brought welcome relief.

He waved to the folks at the counter—Grandpa Jones, working over a plate of pancakes. Sterling Jeppson, taking elaborate measures to keep from dribbling syrup on his tie. Grady on a stool near the kitchen where he could chat with his mother when she could spare a minute.

Other people nearly filled the dining area, folks seeking cool air and good food. Blessedly, no one had claimed his favorite corner booth. A good sign.

He slid into his seat and scanned the room. When he saw Margaret, who rarely ate at the Bluebird, on the other side of the dining area with Sarah and Dane, he drew back in surprise. But the conversation held her attention. She didn't seem to notice Fred. In fact, she looked uneasy—eyes slightly narrower than usual, lips pursed in disapproval, shoulders rigid—but at least she was there, talking.

While the jukebox whirred for a few seconds, Fred let his gaze travel over the rest of the customers. Pete Scott and his new young wife near one of the windows, Olivia Simms arguing with Roy Dennington, a few other people Fred didn't recognize. But he did recognize one woman who sat alone at a nearby table.

Thea Griffin. Imagine that. Years melted away, and the memories of evenings spent here together after taking in a movie or studying for a test rolled over him. She smiled when he noticed her, stood, and approached his booth almost hesitantly. The jukebox clicked to its next selection, and Elvis began to pelt out the soulful strains of Lizzie's favorite song, "Clean Up Your Own Backyard."

The memories left him a little unsteady, but he motioned for Thea to join him and tried to joke. "Fancy meeting you here."

She slid into the booth and folded her hands on the table in front of her. "I've been waiting for you."

"Really?" He didn't know what to make of that, but he tried not to show his uneasiness. "What made you so sure I'd be here?"

She chuckled as if he'd asked something ridiculous. "I told you, Fred, you've always been a creature of habit. You're even sitting in the same booth you always shared with Phoebe."

"Yes." The word caught in his throat. His visit to the cemetery that morning had left his emotions too close to the surface. He'd finally made peace with the truth, but now he wanted to put it behind him. "Yes," he said again, and the word came out stronger this time.

"I have to leave for the airport in a few minutes," Thea said. "But I wanted to see you once more before I go."

"Will you join me for breakfast?" An empty question. Fred could hear even in his own voice.

Thea must have heard it, too. She shook her head and smiled softly. "No, thank you. I really can't stay more than a minute. It's a long drive, and I don't want to be late for my flight." But she made no move to leave. Instead, her expression sobered slowly. "I heard what happened yesterday. Ardella called this morning and told me."

Fred didn't bother asking how Ardella had found out. But if she'd heard about Coralee, everyone in their class knew by now.

Thea lowered her gaze and studied her hands for a minute. "Is it true about Coralee?"

"I'm afraid so."

She lifted her eyes again and met his gaze steadily. "It was self-defense?"

"It was." The lie came easily. He'd had plenty of practice telling it over the past twelve hours.

"And you knew about it all along? You were there?" She sounded suspicious, and with good reason. But Fred didn't let it bother him. She might suspect the truth, but she wouldn't say anything to anyone.

"Yes."

Thea smiled slowly and pretended to believe him. "I always knew you were a good man."

The comment brought a flush of embarrassment to his cheeks. He could feel it. He glanced quickly at Margaret, watched her scowl at something Sarah said, and turned his smile back toward Thea. "I don't know about that."

She put her hand over his for only a moment. Strangely, he didn't resent the contact as he had a few days ago. "Well, I *do* know," she said softly. She pulled her hand away again and flashed a grin full of mischief. "You'll be interested to know that Ardella is calling everyone to let them know what happened. She told me she never suspected you for an instant. She knew from the first that you were innocent."

Fred slanted a glance at her. "Did she?" He laughed softly and shook his head. "Well, then, I suppose I can show my face at the next reunion."

Thea's smile softened again. "I hope you do. I'll look forward to seeing you again."

"I'll look forward to seeing you, too," Fred admitted. He meant it. This experience had taught him, perhaps better than anything had in his life, not to take friends for granted.

She waited, as if she expected him to say something more. For the space of a heartbeat he wondered if he should suggest they keep in touch. But honesty forced him to admit he wouldn't do it. He couldn't do that to Phoebe's memory.

Moving slowly, Thea slid out of the booth and stood

beside it for a moment. "Be good to yourself, Fred. You deserve it."

He nodded slowly. A flicker of doubt nagged at him, making him wonder if he'd ever see her again. At their age, they couldn't count on anything. But he pushed the doubts aside. He didn't want old age to suspect it had caught up with him. "You do the same."

With one last smile, she pivoted and walked away. Fred watched until she disappeared, and tried once more to put the misgivings out of his mind. It had been a good morning so far. He wouldn't let anything destroy it.

He turned over his coffee cup on its saucer and waited for Lizzie. But before the door closed behind Thea, it slammed open again and Enos barged inside. He stormed through the dining area, straight to Fred's booth, without sparing a glance for anyone else.

Scowling darkly, he slid into the seat Thea had vacated. "You and I need to talk."

Fred pushed away the cup and saucer and met his gaze evenly. He'd been expecting this. In fact, he was surprised Enos hadn't stopped by to yell at him last night. "About what?"

"About *what*?" Enos glanced around the room to make sure no one had heard him. When he saw Margaret, his expression altered subtly. He made an effort to pull himself together, and lowered his voice before he went on. "About this new game you've been playing called obstructing justice."

Fred cocked an eyebrow at him. "Why? Are you going to arrest me?"

"I should," Enos snapped. "I really should."

"Maybe you can toss me in jail next time," Fred offered. "If you're around next time."

Enos's scowl deepened. "Don't try to change the subject. We're talking about *you* right now."

Fred laced his fingers together on the table and waited. Might as well let Enos have his say. He wouldn't be happy, otherwise.

Enos leaned a little closer and demanded, "Do you have any idea how much trouble you could be in for what you did?"

"More trouble than being accused of murder?"

It seemed like a reasonable question to Fred, but Enos's scowl deepened a bit more. "I never thought you were guilty. You know that."

"Maybe not," Fred conceded. "But everyone else did."

"Not everyone," Enos reminded him. "You could have saved a lot of time and trouble, not to mention heartache, if you'd just told me the truth in the first place." He narrowed his eyes and studied Fred intently. "It *is* the truth, isn't it?"

Fred didn't move a muscle. Didn't let his face betray anything. "Why would I lie?"

Enos snorted a laugh. "You tell me."

Years of friendship urged Fred to confide in Enos, but he couldn't explain—not now, not ever. He'd told his lie, now he'd spend the rest of his life making it true—just as Phoebe had. He shrugged casually and sent Enos his most congenial smile. "Like I said, next time I'll know better."

"Yeah?" Enos wiped his face with his palm, and some of his hostility faded. "Well, so will I."

Fred widened his smile a bit. "Does that mean there *will* be a next time?"

"I haven't decided yet. But I don't need you trying to manipulate me into running for sheriff again."

Fred tried to look outraged. "I wouldn't think of it. You're an adult. If you want to quit, then quit. I'm sure nobody would blame you."

"I never said I was going to quit for sure," Enos reminded him. "I said I was *thinking* about it."

Fred toyed with his silverware, adjusted the menu behind the napkin holder. "Well, if that's what you decide to do, I'm sure we'll be fine in Ivan's capable hands."

Enos hmmphed his response to that and slid a little farther down in his seat.

Fred worked up an innocent expression and topped it with a casual shrug. "Besides, you'd probably be much happier without all the pressure."

"The only pressure I have on this job is dealing with you," Enos snarled.

"Well, then, I'll be out of your hair."

"Yeah. I can just imagine what kind of mess there'd be with you and Ivan at each other's throats."

"We'll be fine."

Enos went on as if he hadn't spoken. "Ivan wouldn't put up with your shenanigans."

"We'll get along fine," Fred said again.

"And Maggie—" Enos shot a wistful glance in Margaret's direction. "It would absolutely destroy her if you ended up in jail."

Fred let his smile fade. "I've learned one thing in the past few days, son. There are very few things that absolutely destroy people."

"You're willing to take the chance?"

"It's not up to me," Fred said with a shrug. He looked over at Dane and smiled again. "Why don't you wait awhile? In another four years I'll have a good defense attorney in the family—if my daughter doesn't kill him first."

Enos let out an exasperated sigh and darted another glance at Margaret's table. "He's not a bad kid," he conceded. "He *did* call me when he realized you'd gone sneaking off on your own. Thank God he knew what you had in mind. And I wasn't going to take any chances this time. That's why I called the police in Glenwood Springs to check on you." He pushed away his cup and let his eyes stray to Margaret's face. They lingered there for a moment, and everything about him softened.

She looked up, scowling at something Sarah said, and met his gaze. The corners of her mouth curved, and for an instant both she and Enos looked like teenagers again. Fred saw the happy girl she'd once been. The eager young man still hidden somewhere inside Enos. It lasted only a moment, but it was enough to let Fred know the feelings were still there, strong as ever.

Dane pulled Margaret's attention away. Enos tried to pretend nothing had happened. "I ought to quit," he muttered, "just to let you see what would happen."

"Maybe. But you've spent your whole life doing what you ought to do. Maybe you should try doing what you *want* for a change."

Enos didn't even look at him.

Fred smiled and went on gently. "On the other hand, I wouldn't have you any other way. It's only because you're such an honorable man that I can entertain my own fantasies about you and Margaret. Because if I thought for one minute—"

Enos glanced up at him, red-faced. "Keep your voice down. Good billy hell, Fred. What's the matter with you?"

Fred laughed. He couldn't help it.

Enos looked away again and studied his hands as if he'd never seen anything more interesting in his life. "*Fantasies.* I can't believe you said that."

"When you get to be my age, you'll find it helps to have something to make life interesting."

"And *that* makes life interesting?"

"It's one of the things."

Enos chuckled. It started low in his chest and worked its way up into his throat. It drew curious glances from Margaret, Sarah, and Dane and worked magic on their scowling faces.

Enos shook his head slowly. "I've got to hand it to you, Fred. There's never a dull moment when you're around."

Fred wished that was true. He had plenty of dull moments. This just didn't happen to be one of them. He glanced toward the window and caught sight of Summer Dey standing outside The Cosmic Tradition across the street. The wind lifted the hem of her heavy black dress and teased her long blond hair away from her shoulders. He lifted one hand in a tentative wave, wondering if she could even see him through the window.

Enos followed the direction of his gaze, made a face, and shot a disbelieving glance at Fred when Summer waved back almost shyly. "*Now* what's going on? I thought she drove you crazy."

"Summer?" Fred scowled at him. "No. She's not a bad sort. Not really. She's just different, that's all."

"You can say that again." Enos's lips curved into a teasing grin. "What's she done? Made a believer out of you?"

Fred shook his head slowly. "A believer? No." He resisted the urge to touch the gemstones he'd slipped into his pocket along with his loose change that morning. He wasn't foolish enough to think her silly rocks had contributed to the contentment he'd been feeling all morning, but they'd reminded him it didn't hurt to believe in *something*.

He let his smile grow and said again, "No. She hasn't made a believer out of me."

Enos tried to look stern, but he couldn't quite pull it off this time. "Honest to Pete, Fred, I don't know what to do with you."

"Just be a friend, son."

"I *am* your friend," Enos assured him. "You know that."

"Yes," Fred said softly. "I do."

"But honestly, Fred. You could try the patience of a saint."

Fred leaned back in his seat and grinned. He couldn't help it. Phoebe had told him the same thing more times than he could count. "You might be right," he admitted, "but since there aren't any saints around, we'll never know for sure, will we?"

Enos shook his head in exasperation, but a smile tugged at the corners of his lips, and Fred knew his anger had spent itself. He caught sight of Lizzie, hovering near the kitchen door with a coffeepot in her hand, and motioned for her to bring it over. He watched Margaret smile slowly at something Dane said and saw some of her wariness melt away. Watched Enos flick almost imperceptible glances in her direction and the subtle shading of red tinge his cheeks.

Fred settled himself more comfortably in his seat and watched it all. And for a moment he gave his imagination free rein. After all, it was moments like these that made life worth the effort. And Fred knew better than to let even one slip through his fingers.